BEATEN

Sheppard & Sons Investigations, Book 2

Eveline Rose

Sword & Rose

Dedication

This book is dedicated to all the women who are stronger than they think are, and the men who love them.

Also by

Sheppard & Sons Investigations:

TAKEN: Jack and Meg's story
BEATEN: Jamie and Emily's story
MISSING: Doug and Beth's story

Join the Resilient Hearts Sisterhood for exclusive behind-the-scenes action of SSI. RHS community members receive early updates, sneak peeks, and the chance to join our beloved characters in their exciting Weatherford adventures. As a gift for joining, you'll receive the SSI Origin story; the one tragic call that changed Jamie's life forever.

WebPage

Eveline Rose

EvelineRose.author@gmail.com

BEATEN
Sheppard & Sons Investigations Book 2
by Eveline Rose

Chapter 1

Jamie

Jack ripped me back to reality by shaking my shoulder. "Jamie, wake up, you're having a nightmare."

I sat up, shoving my brother's hand away as I sucked air into my lungs and looked around, blinking as my mind slowly realized I was in my bedroom. Not in a parking lot, holding my dead wife.

As I wiped the sweat from my brow, I took a few deep breaths to steady my heartbeat. The memories of Isabelle's murder by a stalker still haunted me, and while the nightmares occurred less frequently, they were still vivid. Intense. Especially around the anniversary of her death, which was today. The nightmares always left me feeling heart-broken, angry, empty. *I should have been able to protect her.* But I'd failed, as a cop and a husband.

Jack stood beside me, patiently offering his quiet support.

I rubbed my hands over my face. "Sorry I woke you again." *I probably woke Meg, his fiancé, too.* They were living with me, to save money, until they got married in September and moved into their dream home. It helped me too, since I'd invested most of my savings in Sheppard & Sons Investigations, the family business I started with my father four years ago.

"No need to apologize. You want to talk about it?" Jack asked.

"No." Talking wouldn't help or bring Isabelle back. "Did I wake Meg?"

"Yeah, but she understands. Can I get you anything?"

My soon to be sister-in-law also suffered from occasional nightmares. It wasn't surprising, given her history; she'd been trafficked as a teen, kidnapped last year, and witnessed Jack getting shot when we rescued her.

"Nah man, I'm good. Thanks." I looked at the clock: five-ten. *No point in trying to go back to sleep.* "I think I'll take a run." A hard, fast run might help me clear my mind.

"Okay, I'll brew some coffee." Jack placed his hand on my shoulder and gave me a brotherly squeeze.

I didn't run for long, but I pushed myself until my calves burned and my lungs felt like bursting. The dread of the nightmare was still lingering, so I took an ice-cold shower, hoping it'd shock the painful memories out of my head. It didn't. After dressing in jeans and a polo, I went to the kitchen. The last thing I needed right now was to be alone with my morbid thoughts, even if I didn't feel like talking.

My stomach growled as I inhaled the rich scent of bacon, and fresh coffee.

"Mmm, smells good in here." I forced myself to smile.

"Morning Jamie, Jack made coffee and breakfast is almost done," Meg said as she flipped an omelet. Then she walked over and gave me a tight, sisterly hug.

I hugged her back and whispered, "Thanks. I needed that."

Meg wasn't my sister-in-law yet, but I already considered her family. When she had needed a place to stay after a mob boss, hellbent on revenge, abducted her and turned her place into a crime scene, we told her she could stay with us while she recovered from her injuries and looked for a new apartment. She never moved out. And over the last six months, I'd grown to love Meg like a little sister.

I released her. "You didn't have to get up and make me breakfast."

"I didn't have to. I wanted to." Meg threw over her shoulder as she walked back to the stove.

I grinned at her snark. *How many times have Jack or I said that to her?* I didn't know, but there was no point in arguing because we only said it when we needed to put an end to her protests. And fair was fair. When she first moved in, Meg had a hard time accepting our help and we soon learned it was easier to shut down her protests rather than try to convince her it was okay to accept our help.

"Thanks," I said shaking my head. "I'm starving."

Meg divided the eggs and bacon into three servings, and Jack carried them to the table. "Breakfast is served."

"Thanks, both of you." I looked them each in the eye to make sure they understood it was for more than breakfast.

"You're welcome," they said in unison.

"Let me know if I can do anything," Meg said. "Even if it's just another hug. Okay?"

"Okay." I smiled and nodded. Meg had a heart of gold. *Isabelle would have adored her.* And I'd like to think Meg would've liked her too. But we'll never know, because Isab-.

"Are you visiting the cemetery today?" Jack's question kept me from sinking too deep in my head. I nodded, but didn't answer. After a short pause, he added, "Want us to come with you?"

"Thanks, but I'm meeting Isabelle's parents. I'll be back for dinner tonight." We met at her grave every year on the anniversary of her death. I visited a lot more throughout the year, but usually went alone. We'd started the tradition the second year; we'd mourn her death at the cemetery, then celebrate her life at her favorite lunch spot, a small, family-owned restaurant, The Breakfast Joint. They served breakfast all day, and had weekly specials from around the world.

After lunch, I planned on spending some time alone before having dinner with my family. Because cooking was Ma's love language, she was making some of my favorite foods tonight: her famous lasagna, bacon wrapped jalapeno poppers, homemade garlic bread, and good old-fashioned apple pie. Being surrounded by people wasn't easy when all I wanted to do was scream, or cry. *I'll probably do both at some point.* But it was what I needed. I couldn't have gotten through the last four years without the love and support of my family.

My phone vibrated, interrupted my thoughts.

> Thinking of you. Let me know if there's anything I can do.

> Thanks Madi

> I'll call later

> I'll be at mom's for dinner. Video chat about 7?

> That should work. Tell Jack and Meg I said Hi. Love you, little brother.

> 22 minutes Madi

> Love you too

The normalcy of our long-standing joke made me smile. My twin sister Madeleine, Madi, always referred to herself as my older sister and I always reminded her it was only twenty-two minutes. Madi was serving in the Navy, currently stationed in New Orleans, so she couldn't join us in person for dinner, but thanks to modern technology, we could video chat. At some point today I'd probably hear from my youngest brother, Jaden, though it was harder for him to call because he was currently serving as a Marine Raider in a war zone.

I sipped my coffee. "Madi says hi. You can say hi back when we video chat later."

I sensed Isabelle's parents when they arrived, but they held back, allowing me a few more minutes of privacy as I kneeled and placed a bouquet of pink and purple tulips, her favorite flowers, on her grave.

"I miss you Isabelle," my voice cracked. "So damn much." I wiped away a tear as it rolled down my cheek. Sitting back on my heels, I filled her in on all the things that had happened since my last visit. "We finally moved into the new office, I think you'd like it. Jay's transferring to North Carolina soon, and plans on coming home for a few days. Ma is beside herself with joy, and Meg's excited to finally meet him in person." At first I'd felt awkward talking to her, but after four years I'd gotten used to it. I felt connected to her through our one-sided conversations, and it helped ease my pain. But not my guilt. I still carried that every day.

My anger – at myself, at her murderer, at God – built as I sat there, clenching my fists. The joyful tune of birds chirping in the trees was the only sound disrupting the eerie silence.

You didn't deserve this.

Her mom's small comforting hand on my shoulder snapped me back to the present before my anger and guilt could drown me. I reached up and gently squeezed, silently thanking her, before letting go and standing up. She wrapped me in a warm, comforting hug; her head not quite reaching my chin. "It's not your fault, Jamie."

But it was, I should have protected her.

Before she could gently guide me away from the headstone, I turned back whispered, "I miss you."

I stood back to give Isabelle's parents, some privacy. Regardless of what she'd said, it was my fault they were here instead of at home dreaming about their future grandchildren. *I bet we would've had at least one by now.* The thought brought a fresh wave of pain, and guilt. I blinked a few times to force back my tears. I should've been able to protect her. But I couldn't, and I'd never forgive myself for it.

Later, as we ate breakfast for lunch, we shared our favorite memories of Isabelle. After the server cleared our dishes, her mom reached across the table and took my left hand in hers. She gently touched the thin gold wedding band I still wore.

"Isabelle loved you so much, Jamie. She'd want you to be happy." She held my gaze.

"Isabelle would want you to find love and happiness again, she wouldn't want you to be lonely," her dad agreed.

"I know, but I'm not ready." *Will I ever be?* I'd spent the last four years pouring my heart and soul into building Sheppard & Sons Investigations, keeping myself too busy to even think about dating. *If only it could've kept me too busy to feel.*

Later that evening, I shared memories of my late wife with my family. Our after dinner video call with Madi was short but sweet, and filled with love and support. Before saying goodbye, she asked Ma and Meg to give me hugs for her. I accepted without complaint; I needed all the hugs I could get today.

As we were saying our goodbyes, Ma said, "Jamie, I think Isabelle would want you to find someone to share your life with. For you to be happy."

"Her mother said the same thing," I said to my shoes, so she couldn't see my expression. They all meant well; and I was lonely. *But am I ready?* After a few seconds, I looked up and met her eyes. "I don't know if I'm ready." My voice sounded small, sad.

"Start with something small son, maybe take off your wedding ring." Dad hugged me then added, "Give yourself some time to adjust to how it feels."

I compulsively reached for my ring to make sure it was still there, which, of course, it was. It was a part of me, and I hadn't taken it off since the day we said I do, the day I'd sworn to love, honor, and protect her.

I'd loved her with all my heart, honored her with my every fiber of my being, but I'd failed to protect her. *And now she's gone.*

Chapter 2

Emily

Craig had gone too far this time, so when the police showed up after a neighbor called in a noise complaint, I didn't stop them from arresting him. After giving my statement to the arresting officer, and having what felt like a thousand pictures taken of my cuts and bruises at the police department, I went home and packed my bags. *I can't be here when Craig got home.* He'd be pissed, and I was terrified of what he'd do to me in retaliation.

I'd declined the police escort home, thinking Craig would be in jail long enough for me to pack and get on the road. But as I stood alone in our apartment, I second guessed myself. *What if he posts bail right away? What if he's on his way home right now?*

I had to hurry. With trembling hands, I carefully lifted my blood-stained shirt, wincing as the movement reminded me of my bruised ribs, and pulled it over my head. Looking at my injuries in the bathroom mirror, I couldn't help but feel disgusted with myself. *How could I let him keep doing this to me?*

My ribcage was already a disgusting shade of baby vomit green, and would probably be dark purple before I got to Weatherford. The marks on my wrists and arms, where he'd grabbed me, weren't much better. *But at least I can hide them from my brother and parents.*

I brought a shaky finger to the corner of my mouth, but didn't touch it, no amount of makeup would cover up my split lip or swollen, black eye. I let out a long sigh, then gently washed the dried blood and tear stains from my face before putting on a clean shirt. Not caring about wrinkling them I threw a bunch of clothes, and my jewelry, into two large suitcases. Then packed my laptop and a few personal items that I didn't want Craig destroying when he got home and realized I'd left him.

Do I need anything else? I was running on fear and adrenaline and afraid I'd forget something important.

Toiletries and makeup. I grabbed a bag and started dropping stuff in it with shaking hands. swearing each time I dropped something in the sink.

I don't have time to pack everything, and can't worry about leaving unimportant things behind.

Once I was safely on the highway I called my older brother, Chris.

"Hey Em, what's up?"

"Hey. I, uh, I'm coming home." My voice hitched as I blinked back tears. It didn't matter that he couldn't see me, he'd still be able to hear the fear and pain in my voice. So, I decided it was best to get the why out in the open, and blurted out, "Craig's in jail," with a shaky voice. *I probably should've thought that out, said it better.*

"Jesus. Are you alright? What the fuck happened?" He asked, voice was thick with concern.

I mustered up as much courage as I could, and answered, "He hit me." Better to rip off the bandaid quickly.

Craig swore softly.

"It's not bad, but I needed to leave."

"Not bad!" His harsh tone made me wince. "What the fuck, Emily, it's bad enough that he's in jail, so don't you dare play it down for my benefit." He lowered his voice, though the tone was no less angry, "Has this happened before? Is this why you didn't come home last weekend, because he hit you?"

"Can we talk about it when I get there. Please?" I should've texted instead of calling, and starting this conversation while I was driving. Besides, this was a conversation best had in person.

He conceded. "Yeah, sure." I could tell he wanted answers, and was grateful he'd reluctantly agreed. "What time do you think you'll get here?"

The glowing numbers on the dash read seven-thirty. "Shit, around eleven-thirty. Is that too late? I can-"

"I'll be up. You can crash here tonight."

"Thanks." My shoulders relaxed as relief washed over me. My only other option was my parents house and I wasn't ready to face them yet. They'd freak out if they saw me like this and I didn't have the energy to deal with them right now.

Chris was just as concerned, but at least he'd give me some space. At least for tonight.

"Of course." He paused. "But I'll expect answers tonight."

Or maybe not. I sighed. It was probably better to bite the bullet and get it over with. "I know. I promise I'll tell you everything when I get there."

"You're welcome. Drive safe, and text me when you're close."

"Okay." It wouldn't be easy telling Chris how out of control I'd let things get with Craig. But it had to be done.

Sadly, tonight wasn't the first time Craig had hit me, the most recent had been last weekend.

Tears flowed as I remembered how quickly that situation had gotten out of control. I'd asked a simple question and hadn't realized I'd done anything wrong until the half-empty beer bottle whizzed by my head and shattered against the wall.

"See what you made me do?" he'd screamed before hitting me. Then he'd yanked my hair, forced me to my knees, and made me look at the mess. When he said, "I'm sorry I got mad, but you shouldn't question me." I did my best to hide the disbelief on my face as I looked up at him. Craig might've said the words I'm sorry, but his tone said it was my fault. And I knew from experience he'd expect me to apologize.

With a trembling voice, I said, "I'm sorry. It won't happen again." I'd only asked so I would know what time to make his dinner.

"It better not."

I'd shuddered at the threat in his tone and began picking up the pieces of glass. When I cut myself, I cried out. Then, not wanting to get yelled at or hit again, I quickly wiped my hand on my pants and wrapped it with one of the the rags I was using to clean the mess.

Afterwards, I was in the bathroom, cleaning and bandaging my hand. The skin around my eye was already changing color. *How many times can I convince people I accidentally walked into something?* Wincing as I ran my hand under cold water, I hadn't heard Craig came up behind me. *I should have closed the door.* Not that a closed door would've kept him out.

"Let me help." He picked up the bottle of hydrogen peroxide with one hand and held my cut hand in the other. Before pouring it on my cut, he said, "This may sting a bit." A stranger observing might believe he cared, but there was no compassion or empathy in his voice.

After he'd left me alone, I went to our bedroom and texted my brother.

Something came up. I can't make the SSI ribbon cutting. Please tell them congratulations from me.

Sure thing. Everything okay?

Yeah. Just busy.

After my bruises heal. It wasn't the first visit to Weatherford I'd had to cancel.

I shook my head to clear the memory and wiped my eyes. Hoping to drown out the voices in my head, I cranked up the volume on the radio with a shaking hand.

It wasn't always like this. In the beginning he'd been charming, fun, supportive. I couldn't put my finger on when things had changed, but I vividly remembered the first time he'd punched a hole in the wall—he'd apologized and promised it'd never happen again. I'd believed him. At to be fair, he kept his word. He never hit the wall again.

My knuckles were white and stiff from my death grip on the steering wheel, so I shook them out, one at a time, to get the blood flowing again. I should have left him a long time ago, when he first started slapping me around. But he'd always begged for my forgiveness, often surprising me with flowers. He always sounded sincere, so I always forgave him. By the time he stopped apologizing, and started blaming me for his outbursts, I was too scared and ashamed to leave. *And now I'm paying the price for my fear and weakness.*

Not wanting to wake Vicky or Zoe, I texted Chris after I parked so I wouldn't have to knock. He met me in the driveway, held eye contact for a moment, then hugged me. The kind of tight hug that makes a little sister feel loved and safe, even if it did hurt my bruised body.

I saw anger flash across his face as he inspected my face and arms. Through clenched teeth, he said, "Let's get you inside so you can get cleaned up and convince me I shouldn't go to Houston right now and kick his ass."

I couldn't help but laugh. Chris wasn't small or weak, but he wasn't exactly the macho alpha-male kick someone's ass type either. At least not physically, he'd been working a desk job since joining Dad's insurance company after graduating from college.

He helped me carry my bags to the guest room and told me to take a few minutes to myself. "I'll put some tea on while I wait in the kitchen."

"Okay, I'll be right out." I'd cried most of the five-hour drive home, only stopping during moments of anger, mostly at myself, so I was grateful for a chance to wash off the layers of tear stains. *I was so stupid for staying with him so long.*

Once in the kitchen, Chris handed me my favorite floral mug. The warmth felt good in my hands and the Lemon Ginger scent was soothing as I gathered my courage. *No more covering for Craig.* I'd decided on the ride home I'd tell Chris everything. No more secrets. No more hiding. I'd kept Craig's drinking and abuse from everyone for far too long.

Even though I was determined to tell Chris everything, I still struggled to find the words. I didn't like admitting how weak and pathetic I'd become. If I could have just done better, been better, tried harder; then he wouldn't need to get so angry or teach me a lesson. *At least that's what Craig told me.*

"It wasn't always like this. At first it was insults or him getting irritated anytime I wasn't happy-go-lucky. Then he started yelling and throwing things." I sniffled. "But I didn't think he'd ever hit me." The tea sloshed in my cup as I brought it to my lips with trembling hands, I could taste the salt from my tears as I licked my lips before taking a sip. It took another hour of me stopping and starting before I got it all out. Chris was patient, as expected, and tried his hardest to control his anger. Surprisingly, he didn't ask me why I didn't leave sooner, though it was a valid question.

One I'd been asking myself all night but still couldn't answer. I was a smart girl, and knew better than to expect him to change, but somewhere along the way I'd forgotten that. And how to stand up for myself.

We stayed up late; me pouring out my guts, sharing my fear, shame, and guilt, and him reassuring me I didn't deserve the abuse, and that none of this was my fault.

I wiped my eyes for the millionth time, then blew my nose, adding the tissue to the growing pile on the table. "I've kept you up. I'm sorry."

He reached across the table and held my hand. "No need to apologize. I called off work tomorrow so I can stay up all night if you need me to."

I didn't ask what excuse he gave, trusting he wouldn't have told Dad the real reason. "Thank you." I open my mouth to say something else but was so overcome with gratitude I started crying again before I could get the words out.

Chris came around the table, put an arm around me and gave me half a hug as he handed me a tissue. "That's what big brothers are for."

When I was ready for bed, I gathered up my used tissues and threw them away before collecting our mugs and putting them in the sink. "Thanks again for letting me stay tonight."

"You can stay as long as you need to." Then added, "But you can't hide this from Mom and Dad, you'll have to tell them."

He knew me too well; the thought had crossed my mind. I nodded and whispered, "I know."

"You don't have to give them details, but they love you and they'll want to help."

"I'll talk to them tomorrow, after I've rested and calmed down. It'll be hard enough for them to hear it as it is without me acting like a blubbering fool."

"Hate to say it, sis, but I think they'll react the same way whether you're calm or a blubbering mess." I half laughed at his honesty. "They'll be worried. And pissed. Dad will probably want to drive to Houston and crack Craig's skull open."

Sweat broke out on my brow as panic flooded my system. "He can't." Craig wouldn't hesitate to beat my father senseless. Dad talked tough but he wasn't in fighting shape; he'd settled into a happily married lifestyle with a good cook, and it showed. My lip quivered as I asked, "Will you go with me tomorrow? Help me keep him from doing something stupid?"

And provide emotional support. Not wanting to sound too pathetic, I kept that last part to myself.

"Of course, but I doubt he'll follow through with any threats he makes, and I think you know it too. He's not the vigilante type, but he'll do everything in his power to protect you if Craig shows up, we both will."

"I know." But I couldn't let either of them get hurt because of me. I'd go back with Craig, give him whatever he wanted, before I'd let that happen.

"You're exhausted. Go to bed and try to rest. We'll figure out the best way to tell Mom and Dad in the morning."

"Alright. Is it okay if I take a quick shower?" A hot shower sounded good.

Having all day to think about how I'd explain my appearance, and the abuse, to my parents didn't make it any easier. Luckily, I spent a lot of that time with my six-month-old niece, Zoe. She didn't care about the bruises, or my past; she was just happy to be held. Chris must have told Vicky what had happened before I got up, because my appearance didn't surprise her. She didn't say anything, but her actions were sympathetic and supportive.

When I offered to watch Zoe so they could have a few hours to themselves, they rushed off to bed, hand in hand. And napped.

Before lunch, I called my mom and asked if we could come over for dinner, and of course she agreed. I did my best to sound casual, a giggling Zoe in the background helped. I'm sure she thought it was weird I was in Weatherford in the middle of the week, especially since I'd cancelled my last few trips with lame excuses. I told her I broke up with Craig, and said I'd fill in the details at dinner.

The evening went exactly as expected. Mom's expression switched from a big welcoming smile to somewhere between anger and sadness in the span of a heartbeat when she saw my face. Not wanting to hide the truth from them anymore, I hadn't put on any makeup.

Dad's anger rolled off him in waves, but he was gentle as he held me in a papa bear hug and asked what he could do to help. I had a feeling Chris had given them a head's up about what to expect because their emotions were more subdued than I'd anticipated: mom didn't cry or freak out, and dad didn't threaten to go to Houston and kick Craig's ass. *That, or they suspected the truth so it's not a surprise.* Not that I was complaining, I didn't want or need them freaking out.

"You can stay with us as long as you need to," my mom said as we set the table.

"Thanks mom." Chris and Vicky had offered too, but it'd be too hard for them with the new baby. "That'd be helpful."

"Will you have to quit your job?"

"No, I work from home most of the time, so it doesn't matter where I live." I designed and managed websites for businesses. It was the perfect job; I set my own hours, had no commute, and it paid well.

"That's a blessing."

I agreed. Having to look for a new job with a bruised face and my self esteem at an all-time low would've sucked.

"Can you tell everyone dinner's ready?"

"Sure thing." My stomach growled; I'd been too worked up to eat, and the smell of mom's fried chicken had my mouth watering.

As I walked into the living room, I overheard Dad ask Chris, "Have you talked to Jamie? I'm sure he could help."

"Not yet, but I'm meeting him for drinks tomorrow and can talk to him then."

Of course he'd talk to Jamie—his best friend since forever, who also happened to own a private investigation and personal security company. The same company who's ribbon cutting ceremony I had to miss.

"When were you going to tell me?" I wasn't mad he wanted to talk to Jamie, though I wasn't thrilled about it either, but I was upset he hadn't talked to me about it first. My plan was to hide until my cuts and bruises had healed enough that makeup could cover them before going out in public. The last thing I wanted was to see an old family friend while looking like I'd been used as a punching bag.

"Sorry, Em. I was going to talk to you about it after dinner." He had the good sense to look ashamed. "We made plans to grab a beer and catch up at the ribbon cutting ceremony, before any of this happened."

"Do you really need to tell him?" I wanted to hide until my bruises faded away, then start over with no one in

Weatherford knowing what I'd let happen to me. Besides, we'd filed a restraining order, so he couldn't come near me.

"Not everything, but I want to ask his advice on how best to protect you."

Dad nodded. "He's right, Jamie's a good guy and he'll know what to do."

He was, but I wasn't okay with him knowing my shameful secret. *But maybe he can help me.* Damn it. My emotions were all over the place; I was grateful for the support, embarrassed by my circumstances, and afraid Craig would come here and try to drag me back home. No, not home. The apartment we'd shared wasn't my home anymore. Tears welled in my eyes as my emotions got the best of me.

"Emily, you know Jamie won't judge you," Chris said, addressing one of my unspoken fears.

But I didn't believe him. How could anyone look at me and not judge me for being so weak?

"Okay." I didn't think I had a choice, besides he was right, Jamie was a trained professional. I'd known him for as long as I could remember. Craig hadn't killed me, but my embarrassment might—I had a major crush on Jamie back in junior high and high school.

"Anyway, dinner's ready."

Chapter 3

Jamie

The bar stool felt harder than I remembered as I waited for Chris. We used to be regulars here, and we'd chosen it out of nostalgia rather than any real desire to hang out in a loud sports bar. Looking forward to the evening, I'd arrived early. A night out with my best friend was exactly what I needed to get out of the funk I'd been in for the last week.

It'd been great seeing Chris at the ribbon cutting ceremony but there hadn't been much time to talk, so I was happy he could get away for a few hours tonight. It'd been too long since we'd last seen each other, and it'd be nice to catch up. I was busy with SSI; and my god-daughter, Zoe, had him and Vicky burning the candle at both ends. I made a mental note to plan a day we could all get together. I could use a day with them—Zoe's laughter was the best anti-depressant. Thinking of Chris's family reminded me I wanted to ask him about Emily, he'd seemed off when Jack asked about her at the opening.

When I saw Chris walk in, I waved him over. We shook hands and hugged, clapping each other on the back, the way men do. "It's good to see you, man. How's dad-life treating you?"

"Good, other than the sleepless nights and non-stop dirty diapers." Chris's laugh made it obvious he was loving every minute of it. "How about you? How's the new place working out for SSI?"

We started SSI in a spare room at my parents house until we could afford to rent an office, then we saved until we could build our own dream office and training facility. Sheppard & Sons Investigations, SSI, the family business. After Isabelle's death, I turned in my badge and started Sheppard & Sons Investigations, a personal protection and investigation company, with my dad and brother, Jack. It hadn't been easy for Dad and I to leave the police force, we were third generation cops, but it was the right decision for both of us. We were still serving our community, but we didn't have to wait for the 9-1-1 call to help. We could offer protection before the crime was committed, and didn't have to deal with the bureaucracy or red tape of law enforcement.

"It's great. We've grown a lot in the last year and we'll be hiring another full-time person sooner rather than later." I waved the bartender over. "Let me buy you a beer."

"Thanks. Is it cool if we grab a high top instead of sitting at the bar?"

The change in Chris's tone caught my attention. "Yeah, no problem."

After we sat down, I asked Chris what was going on. He made a joke that I never missed anything, saying, "Must be a cop thing." But his laugh sounded forced.

"It is." It was also a best friend thing. "Spill it."

"You remember my sister, Emily?"

I raised an eyebrow. Of course I did. She was the awkward teenager in braces who wanted to tag along everywhere we went. She and Jack were were about the same age and were sophomores when Chris and I were seniors. I'd only seen her a few times since graduating. The last time had been at Isabelle's funeral, but I'd been so consumed with grief I barely remembered talking to her.

"She's in trouble, and I could use your expertise."

My back stiffened. It had to be bad if he needed my kind of expertise. "What kind of trouble?"

Chris sucked in a deep breath and exhaled slowly before answering, "Her ex hit her."

"Fuck." The thought of any man hitting a woman pissed me off. The thought of someone hitting Emily made my blood boil. I'd do whatever it took to help Chris, and Emily. But first things first. "Is she somewhere safe right now?"

"Yeah, she's staying with our parents."

I nodded. Glad she was nearby. And easier to protect.

He continued, "She left him two days ago, while he was in jail, but she's worried he may come after her."

Without thinking, I switched to professional mode. If the asshole got arrested, it was bad. "Tell me everything you know." I took out my phone and typed notes as Chris filled me in.

Chris didn't know if Craig was still in jail, so I made a note to check if he'd made bail. "Has he made contact?"

"Not that I know of, but I can ask." He took a swig of beer. "She said it wasn't the first time he-"

"Not the first time?" *How long has this been going on?* My expression must have looked accusational because his tone was angry when he replied.

"Don't look at me like that Jamie. Christ, if I'd known, I would've dragged her out of there."

"I know." Unfortunately, families rarely knew when a loved one was being abused. I softened my tone, and my expression. "What else can you tell me?"

"This was the first time she pressed charges. After giving the police her statement, she packed a few things and drove straight to my place." Chris told me he'd never liked Craig but hadn't expected abuse. "Emily said he's a violent drunk, and he'd been drinking more lately."

"Damn." Abusive was bad, but drunk and abusive was worse, it made him less predictable.

"God, I feel so stupid. I should have seen the signs, known something was up." He ran his hands through his short brown hair.

"It's not your fault. Abusers are good at fooling people, and the abused are usually too afraid to speak up." I offered what little comfort I could, knowing full well it wouldn't help. I was all too familiar with the weight of guilt after failing to protect a loved one.

"We encouraged her to file a restraining order, and thankfully she agreed. We're hoping it'll discourage him from contacting her."

"It might, but it's just a piece of paper and difficult to enforce." I didn't tell him some people got more violent, and vengeful, after being served with a restraining order. I wanted to learn more about Craig first.

Chris sighed. "I was afraid you'd say that. Can you look into him? Find out if he has a history of doing shit like this."

"Yeah, of course. I'll do it first thing in the morning. I just need his full name and address." I knew myself well enough to know I wouldn't wait until morning, but I didn't want Chris to expect an answer tonight. Gathering background information was never as quick and easy as it was on TV.

"I'll text you the info." Some of the tension left Chris's shoulders.

"Thanks." I also wanted to talk to Emily because she might tell me things she hadn't told Chris, and I needed as much information as I could get before coming up with a game plan. "Any chance you can bring Emily by the office tomorrow? I'd like to ask her a few questions."

"I'll ask her tonight. And Jamie, since this is more than a quick favor, I'll pay you for your time."

Not willing to wound his pride, I agreed to bill him. But he didn't know our rates, so he'd never know he was getting the friends and family discount.

With that out of the way, we ordered nachos and talked about more pleasant things. I loved how happy he looked as he told me stories about Zoe, but it made me feel sad, too.

It reminded me of the future I'd lost. If Isabelle hadn't been killed, I'd probably be a dad by now and we'd be swapping parenting stories about our children.

And I wouldn't be feeling like a hollow shell.

I wondered if our baby would've had thick black hair like Isabelle, or thin brown hair like me. I came back to the present when I heard Chris ask if I was okay.

"Yeah, just thinking. Sorry, I'm not being a good friend at the moment."

"It's okay, I know this time of year is hard for you." He finished the last of his beer.

"Thanks." I contemplated asking if he wanted another beer but I was eager to go home and start researching the asshole who'd hit Emily. Chris's revelation was a shock and had taken the night in an unexpected direction, but it gave me something to focus on. And keeping busy always helped lessen the pain.

Chris stood up after we settled the bill. "I should get home. I'll let you know what Emily says."

"Any time after eleven works, just shoot me a text so I know when to expect you." I threw a ten on the table before walking out with Chris.

He shook my hand and gave me a quick hug. "Thanks again, Jamie."

I patted him on the back before releasing him. "Anytime. Give the girls a kiss for me?"

"Of course. I'm sure Vicky will send one back, but you'll have to use your imagination for that."

As soon as I got home, I looked up Craig David Hopper, twenty-eight, of Houston, Texas. To say I didn't like what I found was an understatement.

Houston PD released him on bail the morning after Emily left and his court date was set for mid-July. That was a long time for someone to sit around stewing in anger.

Records showed this wasn't Craig's first arrest, nor was it the first time someone had filed a restraining order against him. It was, however, the first time the person he'd hit had pressed charges. *He'll be pissed.* But would he be pissed off enough to come after her?

Not wanting to worry Chris any more than he already was, I hadn't told him the restraining order might make things worse, but given Craig's history, we had to prepare for it. *I'll warn them tomorrow.* It wouldn't be right to keep them in the dark, because in this case ignorance wasn't bliss.

As a cop, I'd answered far too many calls, and called too many coroners, after abusers violated their restraining orders. A cold chill spread across my body, making the hairs on my arms stand up.

Wanting to make sure I wasn't reading too much into the reports, or over-reacting because it was personal, I asked Jack to take a look.

"Yeah, I'll be right there." Jack got up and gave Meg a quick kiss on the top of her head before joining me at the kitchen table.

I miss that. Will I ever have it again? I shook my head to clear it, there was no point in thinking about it. I had to focus on helping Emily.

I summed up the situation, but didn't tell him it was for Chris. Jack and Emily had hung out in the same circles and had graduated together, it'd be just as hard for him to be impartial as it was for me.

I leaned back and turned my laptop so Jack could read the files on my screen. "So, what do you think? This guy likely to be a problem?"

After scanning the files, he answered, "Yeah, he fits the profile." Then he stood back, crossed his arms, and looked at me with one eyebrow raised. "Want to tell me why you need me to confirm something you already know? What's going on?"

He sounded both annoyed and intrigued. He knew I'd only be asking if I doubted my objectivity, which I rarely did. This was why working with family could be a blessing or a curse. We always had each other's backs, a sentiment that included our team members, but we also called each other out on our bullshit.

"You remember Emily Taylor?"

"Chris's sister? Yeah, or course, we went on a couple of dates but didn't click."

I'd forgotten about that. I hadn't thought it was a big deal, but Chris had, and threw a fit. It hadn't mattered that he'd known Jack forever and knew he was a good kid—no one was good enough for Emily in Chris's eyes. Thinking back, I'd felt the same way about Madi. No one was good enough to date her, and I wasn't shy about saying it, nor did I care that it irritated her to no end.

"We lost touch after graduation." Jack shrugged. I saw his jaw clench when he put it together. "Tell me this asshole didn't hit Emily?" he asked through gritted teeth.

I nodded. "Chris and I had drinks earlier, and he asked for my help. He's worried about her."

"Did she press charges? File a restraining order? Where is she now?" Jack threw a handful of questions at me without giving me a chance to answer. He may not have stayed in touch with Emily, but that wouldn't stop him from stepping up and helping her. I filled him in on what little I knew, and said I was expecting her to stop by the office tomorrow around eleven-thirty. Jack said he'd have Meg add them to our schedule.

Not mine, ours.

"Thanks."

Meg was our administrative assistant. Dad had poached her from Ma earlier this year and happily suffered the endless teasing, saying it was worth it. Meg was an asset we hadn't known we needed. She was great at putting our clients at ease with her warmth and compassion, which was exactly what they needed. Not that the rest of us lacked compassion, but we were the strong silent types, whereas Meg was the friendly, outgoing type and she put people at ease just by being herself.

Jack's a lucky guy. Meg was the love of his life, and the perfect partner for him. Jealousy washed over me. I missed having someone to share my life with. *Maybe it's time for me to think about taking my ring off.* I shrugged off the thought. I wasn't ready to date again, or even think about it.

"Earth to Jamie." Jack snapped his fingers in front of my face. "You okay?"

"Yeah, I was just thinking it'll be helpful to have Meg there to greet Emily, help put her at ease. I'm sure she's still pretty shaken up." I was still fiddling with my wedding band, a fact that hadn't gone unnoticed by Jack.

"Sure." He nodded towards my hands. "When you're ready to talk about what was really going on in that head of yours, let me know."

Asshole. I hated it when he called me out. Though I supposed I deserved it, I'd done the same to him more than once. "Thanks."

Jack probably knew me better than anyone, despite having grown apart after high school. I'd been a rookie on the police force, eager to prove myself, and Jack was overseas serving in the Army. But we'd grown closer than ever since he moved in with me a couple of years ago. I'd made the offer under the pretense of saving him money while he worked off his partnership, but in reality I was lonely in the home I'd built with Isabelle and I wanted the company. Not that I'd ever tell him that. *Not that I need to.*

Chapter 4

Emily

I was sitting in my brother's car, twisting my thumb ring, as he drove us to the SSI office. He thought I'd be less nervous telling someone outside the family about what happened, but I was actually more so. Jamie might not be family, but I'd known him most of my life and he'd been like a second brother growing up, much to my disappointment. Because of the whole I had a crush on him issue. Knowing Chris had filled him in last night, didn't make it any easier, but it did make me question why I had to embarrass myself by talking to him. When I asked, Chris said there were questions he couldn't answer, plus Jamie had some information for us.

Will Jamie think I'm weak and stupid for staying with Craig for so long? Not that I could blame him, I thought it too. I never should have moved in with Craig, but I thought it'd make him happy, less jealous, if I did. *I was wrong.* So very wrong. He got worse. Not only did he act more jealous after

I moved in, but he became controlling and eventually ended up hitting me. I should have known better, it's not like there aren't thousands of stories out there about this exact situation. All the signs were there, but I thought it'd be different for me. *How could I be so blind, so stupid?*

Overcome with nerves, I blurted out, "We should go home."

Chris turned towards me for a moment, then back to the road, but didn't say anything.

"I'm sure we'll just be wasting his time. I mean, you told him everything last night and I got the restraining order so Craig can't come within fifty feet of me so it's not like I need protection." I was wound up and rushed the words out. There was a pit in the bottom of my stomach, and I wanted to go anywhere except the SSI office.

"Emily, you know Jamie wouldn't have asked us to come to the office if he thought it was a waste of his time."

Instead of answering, I stared at the houses as we drove by, wondering if anyone inside was suffering behind the closed doors, like I had.

When I didn't respond, he continued, "Look Em, I know your embarrassed, but you shouldn't be. None of this is your fault."

"I just, I feel so stupid. I should have seen the signs." My voice sounded distant, weak.

"You're not stupid for wanting to see the good in people, or for placing your trust in the wrong man."

I wished I could believe him.

We drove the last few minutes in silence. I wasn't any less nervous by the time we parked; my heart was racing as I wiped my sweaty palms on my jeans. I was dreading this meeting with Jamie. It'd been hard finding the courage to tell my brother and parents, and ask them for help, and I didn't think I had enough left over to talk to Jamie.

Chris put the car in park and turned to me. "I know you're a little freaked out." He put his hands over mine to comfort me. "But Jamie's a good guy, and he wants to help. He just needs to ask you a few questions so he can help me help you. I'll be with you the entire time, unless you don't want me to be. Okay?"

"Okay," I answered automatically. This situation was anything but okay.

Chris opened the glass door to the Sheppard & Sons Investigations office and ushered me in ahead of him. I think he was worried I might run away if he went in first. I'm not going to lie; the thought had crossed my mind.

My mouth hung open as I looked around, my embarrassment temporarily forgotten. I didn't know what I'd expected exactly, maybe a dark dingy office with stacks of paper everywhere, but the SSI office was nothing like that. The reception area was open and brightly lit, the walls were a warm cream color with navy blue accents. Throw rugs decorated the hardwood floor, and a plush leather couch and chairs filled the waiting area. There was a second story above half the office, and the reception area had a vaulted ceiling with skylights. The space was littered with plants of all shapes and sizes, I couldn't tell if they were fake or real, but it didn't matter, they gave the space a warm, welcoming atmosphere.

Chris urged me towards the receptionist, a woman about my age who was talking to the man leaning against her desk. I couldn't see his face, but something about him felt familiar.

Then he turned around.

Jack. I quickly inspected my shoes hoping to hide my bruised face.

Chris squeezed my hand and whispered, "You're going to be fine." He knew Jack and I had gone on a few dates in high school, and probably guessed that my anxiety had just shot through the roof. I knew Jack worked at SSI, so I wasn't sure why I was surprised to see him, but I was. And I was mortified he'd see me like this. I'd tried to hide the last of my fading bruises but was sure I'd wiped away my makeup along with my tears on the drive here.

I lifted my head when I heard the woman's chair slide back as she stood up. "Hi, you must be Emily and Chris. I'm Meg, you know Jack."

Jack stood to his full height as he stepped around the desk to greet us. *Damn, was he always that tall?* Or maybe he seemed taller because Meg was at least half a foot shorter.

"Hey Chris." He reached forward and shook Chris's hand, then turned to me. "Hi Emily." He stepped closer and asked, "Permission to give an old friend a hug?"

He glanced at my wrists. *I should have worn a long sleeve.* But it was June, and it had seemed pointless to hide them, since I was coming here to talk about Craig hitting me. The regret I felt for making a bad decision was nothing new. *At least they aren't dark angry purple anymore.*

I nodded and blinked back the tears that were threatening to overflow. Again.

"It's good to see you again," Jack said so only I heard it. "Though I wish it was under better circumstances."

"Thanks," I whispered after he released me.

"I'll let Jamie know you're here."

"Thanks, Jack." Chris answered for us. I was still reeling from seeing Jack but had to give him credit for not reacting to my bruises. He'd clearly noticed them, I saw his jaw clench and his eyes narrow briefly, but otherwise there was no outward sign. Which I appreciated, that and he hadn't asked me how I was doing, because clearly, I wasn't doing very well.

Meg, on the other hand, hadn't hid her reaction as well, but at least it was empathy and not pity I saw reflected in her eyes. *I can handle empathy.* At least I hoped I could.

"Can I get you a coffee or a water while you wait?" Meg asked as she stepped around the desk and walked towards a counter with a coffee maker on top and a cooler with water and soda below.

"A water'd be great, thanks," Chris answered. Good lord, I wouldn't have thought I'd ever be happy to have my big brother speak for me, but today I was beyond grateful as I seemed to have lost my ability to speak for myself. I'd have to remember to thank him for being the best big brother a girl could ask for. *I should probably apologize for being a total pain in the ass little sister when we were kids while I'm at it.* The thought made me smile. I couldn't help it, I loved my big brother. Always had, always will.

I looked up briefly when Meg handed me a bottle of cold water and said, "Thank you." I'd finally found my voice, as shaky as it was. *She probably thinks I'm an idiot.* I put my water down on the counter so I could wipe my eyes.

She gave me a soft smile and told me to let her know if I needed anything else, then added so only I could hear, "It's never easy coming here to ask for help, but you're in good hands. I know because they helped me."

That caught me off guard, she looked so strong, so collected. *I wonder what made her come to SSI for help.*

I didn't have time to think about it, or even sit down, because Jamie came out of his office, talking quietly with Jack as they walked towards us. Jamie's hazel eyes radiated concern as he held my gaze. He didn't look much different than the last time I'd seen him. At least not physically. The last time I'd seen him was Isabelle's funeral, when he'd had lost, haunted look in his eyes.

"Chris, glad you could make it." Jamie greeted Chris with a handshake and a quick man-hug. "Emily, it's good to see you too, though I wish the circumstances were different."

"Me too," I whispered.

"Would you like a tour of the new office?" Jamie asked me, since he'd given Chris a tour during the grand opening.

I nodded and squeaked out, "Yeah, sure."

Jamie named the offices we could already see, creating a semi-circle around the reception area, then took us down the hall, where there was a small, but full, kitchen and two bathrooms.

"It's a lot bigger than our old place. And while I didn't hate sharing an office with my dad, I love having my own. Jack likes his too, though sometimes I think he misses AJ." Jamie laughed, then added, "They shared an office in the old building, but now that Jack is a fully vested partner, and we have the space, he has his own. AJ spends more time in there than the office he shares with Doug, our only other full-time investigator."

He pointed out two other offices, available for future new hires, and one that the part-time security personnel shared. Jamie explained that the FBI rewarded SSI with a hefty sum of money for taking down Sullivan, a Boston mob boss on their most wanted list, which helped them fund the new building. He told us they'd be adding a training building in the future, complete with indoor and outdoor shooting ranges.

I looked around in awe at the open space while we walked up the open stairway. There were two small meeting rooms, a large conference room, and an open classroom for training on the second floor. When I said, "It looks great," I meant it, their office was truly impressive.

"Thanks, Meg and Ma helped us design the space, so it's functional and welcoming."

"It shows." Chris laughed. "There's just a hint of feminine without being obvious."

"Yeah, I doubt any of us would have thought to have plants or a comfy couch in the reception area," Jamie added as we walked back downstairs.

"Let's head to my office." He held out his arm to point the way. Jack smiled softly and nodded his support when I made eye contact with him on the way to Jamie's office.

Once in his office, Jamie sat in one of the guest chairs near us rather than behind his desk, making it feel less like an interview and more like old friends catching up. And at first that's what it was. He asked me about my job, my hobbies, and what I did for fun. Then he told me a little about starting SSI with his dad and brother, and how great it was working with his family. I assumed he did it to help me feel less nervous, and it worked.

Right up until he asked, "Do you think you're ready to talk about Craig and what happened?" And my heart started beating a little faster as I averted my eyes and twisted my thumb ring.

"It's okay if you're not ready yet, we can just chat some more." His tone stayed calm, conversational. *He's really good at this.*

I paused for a second before nodding. "I think I'm ready." And much to my surprise, I meant it. I didn't know if it was because of his calm voice, how relaxed he seemed, or him taking time to talk to me before he started asking his questions. *It's probably a combination of all three.* But it didn't matter, I felt a little less nervous answering his questions about the embarrassing circumstances that landed me back in Weatherford, and in his office.

"Will it be okay if I take a few notes while you talk?" When I nodded, he got up and walked to his desk. "Would you like for one of our guys to check your phone for a location tracker while you're here?" he asked as he grabbed his laptop.

I stared at him with wide-eyes and my mouth hanging open. *He thinks Craig put a tracker on my phone.* I shook my head and started to say no, and tell him Craig wouldn't have done that, but Chris cut me off.

"Em, I think it'd be a good idea. It's the kind of thing a guy like Craig would do."

I didn't want to believe it but figured it couldn't hurt to check. I grabbed my phone from my purse and handed it to Jamie.

"This won't take long." He took my phone and walked to the door. I heard him call Meg over before he stepped out and pulled the door mostly closed. I could only assume he was asking Meg to have one of the other guys check it. *Oh man, I hope it's not Jack, this is embarrassing enough as it is without Jack getting a glimpse at how sad and pathetic my life has become.*

"Doug will have your phone back in no time, he won't even have to unlock it." I sighed in relief.

I waited for him to sit back down before asking, "So what do you need to know? I mean, Chris already told you what happened." Damn, that sounded a lot ruder than I'd intended. I was frustrated and nervous, but none of that was Jamie's fault. And while I thought it seemed unnecessary to tell him what Chris had already told him, it wasn't an excuse to be rude, so I apologized.

"Accepted. Chris gave me the short version of what happened the night you left but I need to know the full story of what transpired that night, and any other time he hit or threatened you. It may seem like overkill, but no incident is too small. The details will help me evaluate what kind of threat he is-could be." Jamie quickly corrected himself.

But I'd heard it. *He thinks Craig is a threat.* Tears welled up in my eyes.

"Where should I start?" I hated that my voice was still shaking and my mouth was dry. I wanted a drink but realized I'd left my water in the lobby.

"Let's start with what happened the night you left."

I felt my pulse ratchet up as I recalled that night. "Craig came home from work drunk and got mad at me because I didn't have dinner waiting for him." I paused, then added, "I'd gotten caught up in a work project. I usually work from home and sometimes I lose track of time." I knew that made me sound irresponsible, at least that's what Craig always said, so I was surprised when Jamie chuckled.

"I do that a lot when I work from home. Sometimes, I forget to eat."

"Craig hated that I could work from home. He called me lazy because I didn't have a typical nine-to-five office job." I hadn't meant to say that out loud and immediately regretted it when I saw the look on Jamie and Chris's faces. Craig was a used car salesman. He didn't work nine-to-five either but he did have to go into the office every day.

"Did he say shit like that a lot?" It was Chris who asked, but Jamie was clearly waiting for my answer.

"He always said he was just joking and would tell me I was over-reacting if I got upset." I felt the tears welling up in my eyes as I thought back to all the times Craig had made me cry, then called me stupid for crying. *I really should have seen the red flags sooner, maybe I'm as dumb as he says I am.*

Chris reached over and took my hand. "Emily, none of this is your fault."

"I feel so stupid."

"You're not stupid Emily. Guys like Craig are master manipulators who know how to prey on women's insecurities. We see it far more often than I care to admit." Jamie got up and grabbed a box of tissues and a bottle of water off his desk. He put the tissues on the glass table beside me, then opened the bottle of water before setting it next to them. I couldn't help but notice how casually he provided support, acting like he wasn't doing anything special.

But he was.

"Thanks." I took a tissue and dabbed under my eyes a little too roughly, causing me to wince. My bruises had faded but were still sensitive if I touched or rubbed them too hard. At least the cut on my lip had healed enough that it no longer attracted attention.

"What happened after he got home?"

I told Jamie I'd stopped working to make him dinner while he sat on the couch and drank beer. He'd started mumbling, loud enough for me to hear, about how I should manage my time better, that dinner should be waiting for him when he got home, and about how useless I was. I'd apologized, and focused on making dinner but he lost it when I said I didn't have time to make meatballs. That was the straw that broke the camel's back.

The absurdity of it caused me to choked out a laugh as I said, "I got beat up over meatballs."

Neither of them laughed. It wasn't funny, not in the least, but it sounded so damned pathetic.

I tried to keep my voice from shaking while I told them the rest of the ugly details. But it wasn't easy. My body shook as I remembered how scared I felt knowing he'd probably end up hitting me. And how terrified I was he wouldn't stop once he'd started. It wasn't helping that I could see the anger in Chris's tense body and hear his occasional muffled exclamation.

I didn't even look at Jamie, I couldn't.

"I kept apologizing and promised I'd make him his favorite meal the next night. He huffed and said whatever, before grabbing another beer and going back to the living room. He put on his favorite show and left me alone. I was grateful he wasn't yelling at me anymore, and hoped he'd calm down while I finished making dinner."

Chapter 5

Jamie

It was taking every ounce of effort I could muster to keep my face neutral while I listened to Emily tell us what happened that night. Luckily she kept her head down most of the time, focusing on the thumb ring she kept twisting, so she didn't see me struggling to maintain control. Chris and I made eye contact occasionally, and I could see the anger rolling off him in waves. Not that I blamed him, that asshole had abused his baby sister, and he hadn't known about it.

He wasn't trained to hide his emotions while taking witness statements, but I was. It sounded cold and impersonal, but as a retired cop I knew it wouldn't help her if I showed too much emotion. So, I did my best to hide my anger. Focusing on her words and body language gave me something to think about besides finding, and beating, Craig. She probably didn't realize it, but she was telling me two stories, her words indicated some level of acceptance and indifference to his abuse, while her body screamed just how terrified she was of him.

She tried to maintain her composure, but told her story in stops and starts. Pausing occasionally to wipe her face and blow her nose. I couldn't help but admire her strength, she might be struggling to get through this, but she was determined not to give up. She reminded me a little of Meg when she'd finally decided to open up to us and ask for help. I had a feeling Emily would turn out to be a fighter too, she just needed someone to remind her that she had it in her.

Recognizing this interview was going to take longer than I'd originally anticipated, and not wanting to interrupt Emily, I quickly emailed Meg and asked her to clear the rest of my afternoon and to order us lunch. I didn't expect Jack to clear his schedule too, but Meg reminded he was here if I needed a second set of eyes.

I wanted to give Emily as much time as she needed, not cut her short because I had another appointment. It didn't take long before Meg replied to let me know Dad would handle my only other appointment and she'd ordered a variety of sandwiches and a large salad, because she wanted to make sure there'd be something Emily would like.

This is what makes Meg so invaluable. I probably would've just ordered a pizza.

It was difficult to ignore my instinct to comfort Emily. Hell, I might've reached out to hold her hand, my need to comfort her was that strong, if it had been appropriate. *But it's not.* Instead, I grabbed a box of tissues and a bottle of water and set them on the table beside her. It wasn't much as far as comforting gestures went, but at least it was something.

I lost my composure when she told us Craig bitched non-stop while they ate then threw his plate against the wall, breaking it and making a huge mess. She told us he slapped her when she didn't get up to clean it fast enough, then grabbed her by the hair and punched her a couple of times before shoving her to the ground. He'd kicked her as he yelled insults at her, then threw his beer bottle, adding to the mess on the floor when it shattered. She said a neighbor must have heard him yelling because someone called the police.

"I was still on my hands and knees, bruised and bleeding, when they knocked on the door. Craig told them to go away, but they insisted on coming in." Emily paused to wipe the tears off her cheek. "They threatened to kick-in the door, so he finally opened it, but only a crack."

I knew the tactic; I'd used it when I was still a local cop and didn't have time to wait for a warrant. Once we'd knocked, the abuser would often get more violent, so time was of the essence. The responding officers would have known this wasn't the first call for a domestic at the address, so they wouldn't leave without checking on everyone inside. *And every experienced cop knows that someone not opening the door all the way after yelling go away, is hiding something.* Threatening to kick in a door, with the implied 'with guns blazing' threat attached to it, was often enough to get the offender to open the door. A crack was all we needed to gain entry.

Emily said she'd looked up when she heard Craig yell, and saw the door get ripped out of Craig's hand as the officers forced their way inside.

"When they saw me, one of them grabbed Craig, pushed him against the wall, and cuffed him. Craig tried to fight back but was too drunk. The other officer helped me off the floor and made sure I was okay-"

"Okay? You weren't okay!" Chris interrupted, outraged.

I explained that in this situation okay meant she wasn't in need of immediate or emergency medical attention, otherwise they would have dispatched an ambulance. Emily added that she'd asked them not to call an ambulance, claiming she wasn't hurt enough to go to the ER.

Chris still wasn't happy but sat back when I encouraged Emily to continue. I didn't miss the look he shot my way; he wasn't happy I wasn't taking his side. But I had a lot of experience he didn't, so he'd have to trust me on things like this.

"There isn't much left to tell. Craig kicked and screamed as the officers forced him out of the apartment and into the police car. More cops came and one of them followed me to the station so I could give my statement. That's when I told them I wanted to press charges—I was too afraid to say it in front of Craig. Then a social worker came and took pictures, and gave me a bunch of pamphlets with resources for help and support. When they were done, I went home and packed."

She took a long sip of water.

"And I left." She gave a sad laugh. "He's going to kill me for not cleaning up the mess before I left." Her voice wavered at the end, stirring my protective instincts.

"That's not funny Emily." Chris looked scared, and rightfully so. Emily had just admitted, however unintentionally, that she believed Craig was capable of murder.

Before Chris could hijack the conversation, or scare her any more than she already was, I said, "I'm not going to let that happen." I stood up and moved to kneel in front of her. Against my better judgement, I blurred the professional line when I reached out and gently held her hands. "He'll never hurt you again, I promise."

Fuck. I know better than to make a promise I might not be able to keep. But I couldn't stop myself.

Emily looked at me, then at Chris, and then back at me. I looked over to see Chris staring at me. Apparently I'd shocked them both with the intensity of my promise.

That makes three of us.

"I asked Meg to order lunch, so let's eat, then you can tell me about the other times, and I'll fill you in on what I found out. Then we'll decide how to move forward."

Chapter 6

Emily

After lunch I told them he hadn't always been like that. In the beginning, Craig was sweet and kind. But then he slowly changed, getting more jealous and controlling and eventually progressing to verbal, then physical abuse.

I wasn't surprised when Jamie told us this wasn't the first time Craig had been arrested on domestic violence charges. Apparently, Craig had been arrested twice before but both women dropped the charges. *I wish I'd known that before we started dating, or at least before I moved in with him.*

I thought coming to Weatherford and getting a restraining order would be enough, but Jamie shattered my sense of safety when he said the restraining order couldn't prevent Craig from driving to Weatherford and seeking retribution.

"A restraining order is just a piece of paper, and unless someone sees him violating it, there's nothing that can be done." He explained a man like Craig wouldn't see himself as the guilty party, and he'd probably blame me for his arrest. Then he asked me where I was staying.

"With my parents." I quickly added, "For now." I didn't know why I was embarrassed about staying with my parents. It was the least embarrassing thing in my life right now.

He nodded. "Does Craig have their address?"

My heart skipped a beat. *Of course he knows where my parents live.* We hadn't visited them often, Craig always made up some excuse why we couldn't but really, he just didn't want to. But we had visited a few times over the last few years, so he'd have their address in his phone.

I asked Jamie if my family was in danger. His pause before saying he didn't think so wasn't comforting. Or convincing. Chris felt the same way, and called Jamie out on it.

"Guys like Craig tend to focus their anger on one person." Jamie looked at me. "He may get nasty and be verbally abusive but he's not likely to physically attack them, unless they get in his way." I must not have looked convinced because he added, "Most bullies are cowards. Based on his history, he won't risk coming for you while you're with other people unless he goes completely off the deep end."

I sat there trying to take it all in. How had my life come to this? *I feel so stupid.* It wasn't bad enough that I'd stayed with Craig and let him hit me, but now he might hurt my parents. I didn't believe Jamie when he said Craig wasn't likely to hurt them, I knew he would if they got in his way. I snapped back to the conversation when I heard Jamie say he'd assign someone to shadow me.

"What? I don't need a bodyguard." Nor could I afford one. I could work from anywhere so I still had my job, but I had to save money for a new apartment and furniture.

But Jamie and Chris were adamant that I have protection. Jamie explained I wouldn't have a bodyguard, but someone who would follow me around, discretely, and keep an eye on me. *That sounds a lot like a bodyguard.* I argued that Craig was only violent when he was drunk, and that I had a restraining order against him, so it would be overkill for someone to follow me around all day.

"Besides, I work from home so it's really not necessary."

Chris argued, repeating what Jamie had said earlier, "A restraining order is just a piece of paper, it can't stop him from hurting you. And you said yourself that he's been drinking a lot more lately."

I tried to convince them I didn't need protection, but they were united and refused to budge.

Jamie said, "No tracker." Then gave me my phone back. He had me add his cell number, and the SSI office number, to my contacts and asked for mine. He said he'd be shadowing me tonight, because it was short notice, but he'd email us a list of who'd be on duty for the next few days. "Let your parents know there may be someone sitting outside the house whenever you're there. That way they don't think it's Craig."

"Thank you, Jamie," Chris said as they shook hands. "Bill everything to me."

"Chris you–"

He cut me off. "I'm doing this Emily. Please just accept it."

"I can't let–"

"You can. We'll talk about it later. Jamie doesn't need to hear us argue." I almost laughed, Jamie had heard us argue thousands of times when we were younger.

Jamie raised on eyebrow and grinned as shook his head. "I've heard it before." He nodded towards the door. "Hell, Jack and Meg have a similar argument on a regular basis."

Meg met us in the lobby as Jamie walked us out. She had some paperwork for us, so we sat in the spacious lobby while Chris filled it out.

Meg asked, "Was lunch okay? I wasn't sure what you'd like so I ordered a little of everything."

"It was, thank you. Though you didn't have to order so much, I would have eaten anything. I'd hate for all that food to go to waste."

Meg laughed. "You haven't seen these guys eat. Trust me, food never goes to waste here."

Her laugh was infectious, so I laughed with her. *God, it feels good to laugh.*

Chris stopped writing, glanced up at me, and smiled. The only other time I'd laughed, or sounded relaxed, since coming home was when I was playing with Zoe.

While Chris did the paperwork, I took the opportunity to really look at Meg. She was about my age and pretty, with long strawberry blond hair. The roots were darker, like she was growing out a color she'd gotten tired of. And she had the most amazing emerald green eyes I'd ever seen.

"Your eyes are so pretty." I blushed; I hadn't meant to blurt it out like that.

"Thank you." She smiled and looked at the engagement ring she was playing with.

"Are you engaged?"

She practically glowed as she answered, "Jack proposed on New Year's Eve."

Jack? I was surprised Chris hadn't mentioned it. Not that I was jealous, we only went on a few dates before realizing we were better friends.

She lifted her left hand and showed me her ring. It was a beautiful, a round diamond with two smaller heart shaped emeralds, one on either side.

"He designed it himself, isn't it pretty?" Her eyes sparkled as she watched the ring twinkle in the light. She was clearly head over heels in love with Jack. He was a lucky guy. I was about to tell her so when I saw him come out of his office.

"I see Meg's showing off her ring." He put his hand on her shoulder. I could tell from his expression that he was just as head over heels in love with her as she was with him.

Good for them. We may not have worked out, but it wasn't because Jack wasn't a good guy. He was, and he deserved to be happy. *I wonder if I'll ever find someone like him.*

"It's gorgeous. You're a lucky guy, Jack."

Meg blushed and said, "Oh stop, I'm the lucky one."

At the same time Jack said, "Don't I know it."

Chris made a gagging sound. "Oh please." He dragged out the 'e' sound and rolled his eyes.

"Oh come on, you forget I've heard you gushing over Vicky, and Zoe." Jack laughed as he gave my brother shit.

It felt good to laugh with them. Jack and I had been friends in high school and while I didn't love the circumstances, it was nice to see him again. I'd lost touch with most of my old friends, especially the males ones, after I started dating Craig. He'd get jealous any time I talked to another man, even co-workers, accusing me of flirting, and asking if I wanted to sleep with them. Eventually I stopped talking to everyone because it was easier. Safer.

God, I was so blind. All the red flags were there. But he would tell me he loved me and ask me to forgive him. And I always did, right up until the last time.

Chapter 7

Jamie

I assigned one of our part-time employees to shadow Emily until I could get there, then called Jack into my office so we could set up a schedule. I wanted to have at least the next seventy-two hours on the books. Knowing it wasn't a matter of if, but how many, I asked Jack what shifts he wanted. I told him I planned on taking a few shifts too.

Who am I kidding I'll be taking as many as I can.

One of the perks of owning my own company was being able to make my own schedule. *It almost balanced out all the extra paperwork.* I could save Chris money by volunteering to work off-the-clock for the evening shifts I covered. It meant fewer nights off, but I didn't mind, it's not like I had a full social calendar. Besides, I liked staying busy, especially this time of year.

Jack and I sat down and made a schedule for the rest of the week. We agreed to cover most evenings, the highest risk time, and split the over-night hours among our part time staff, made up mostly of active duty and retired police officers. AJ and Doug would split most of the day shifts. I wasn't surprised when Jack said he'd volunteer his time, he'd always been the type of guy who'd do anything for a friend. And it didn't hurt the company because we were only volunteering for hours we weren't scheduled to work at SSI.

"Does Emily have to pick anything up from the apartment? If so, we should go sooner rather than later so Craig doesn't destroy everything she left behind."

"Damn, I didn't think to ask. She said she took anything of value which means she most likely left some stuff behind. I'll ask when I send her the schedule. Thanks for thinking of it."

Jack laughed and asked, "What would you do without me?"

"Probably have fewer headaches." I tried to sound annoyed but couldn't pull it off, and we both ended up laughing. "Can you have Meg schedule a meeting before the end of the day, have her include Dad, he'll want to be kept in the loop."

"Can do." Jack saluted as he stood up to leave.

I shook my head and rolled my eyes. Jack had always been a bit of a smart ass, a fact that had gotten him in trouble in high school and to a lesser degree in the Army. Because I'm a by-the-book kind of guy, I'd expected us to butt heads a lot more than we did. Not that we didn't, but it didn't happen nearly as often, or in the ways, I'd expected. Jack had been an investor from the beginning, but we hadn't assumed he'd be a good working partner just because he was family. Lucky for us, he'd been an asset to SSI from day one.

Now I can't imagine SSI without him.

Funny how relationships evolve over time. Jack and I were brothers and teammates in school, had grown apart in early adulthood, and now, we were not only brothers and business partners, we were the best of friends.

Doug and I were talking while we waited on Dad, Jack and AJ in the conference room. When Jack and AJ finally walked in they were arguing over which actor was the best Batman.

Jack asked, "Who do you two think was the better Batman: Keaton or Kilmer?" I knew Jack thought Keaton was the best Batman, so I assumed AJ was arguing for Kilmer.

"West," Dad said from behind them. Both Jack and AJ turned around to stare at him, then plopped themselves into chairs like unhappy six-year-olds. Dad had a way of making it clear that a conversation was over with nothing more than his tone of voice. A skill John Sheppard had learned in the Marines, then perfected as a cop and the father of three rowdy boys. A skill I'd hated as a kid but admired as an adult. A skill I'd tried to mimic as a cop, and hoped to use someday as a father. *If I'm lucky enough to find love again.*

"Jamie, update us in on the Taylor detail." Dad took a seat and opened his small notebook to a blank page. I shook my head; some habits died hard. AJ and Jack had printed out the email, and Doug had his laptop.

I filled everyone in, adding in the new development that wasn't in the email: Jack and I would be escorting Emily, and Chris, to Houston to pick up her remaining things and turn her keys in to the landlord. Because of the restraining order, we could easily get Emily removed from the lease. Meg would give Craig advance notice so he could leave the apartment. Then I took full ownership of my personal connection to the case, letting everyone know that Chris and I had been friends most of our lives.

"Keeping Emily safe is important to me on a professional and personal level." I didn't mention that Jack and Emily had dated, thinking it wasn't relevant.

But apparently Dad did because he asked Jack, "Didn't you two date?"

"A couple of times but we never clicked."

"Ooh, does Meg know?" AJ decided to tease Jack even though we all knew Jack didn't keep secrets from Meg. After the issues they'd had last year, when keeping secrets almost ruined their relationship, there was no way he wouldn't have told her.

"Nah, I thought I'd let her find out when some jackass decided to ask me about it." Jack shot AJ a death stare, clearly pissed off at his best friend for bringing it up. "Of course she knows and before you ask, no, she's not worried about it."

Why is this conversation pissing me off? Jack had been open about dating Emily, and had made it clear they hadn't slept together, which shouldn't have mattered to me one way or the other. *But it does.*

Jack waved off their knowing glances. "Seriously guys, it's not worth wasting time on. So, drop it."

"I think he doth–" AJ started but I cut him off.

"That's enough. Let's show Ms. Taylor the respect she deserves." Based on their faces, I'd say I'd finally mastered my father's skill.

We discussed the protection plan, and finalized the schedule for the next two weeks. The four of us taking most of the waking hour shifts.

More than one eyebrow lifted when Dad offered to take a few shifts.

"What? I haven't been out of the field so long that I've forgotten how to do my job. Besides, the Taylors are family friends and we protect our own."

I shouldn't have been surprised, he and ma had been friends with Mr. and Mrs. Taylor for as long as I could remember, and like he said, we protect our own.

Chapter 8

Emily

A few days after our meeting with Jamie, we drove to Houston to get the rest of my things. I rode with Jamie in his SUV, a big black intimidating vehicle, especially when compared to Chris's white mini-van. Jack rode with Chris. I felt a little awkward riding alone with Jamie, but they all said it was necessary, so I didn't argue.

When Jamie said he wanted to call Craig and remind him we were coming, so he wouldn't forget and "accidentally" violate the restraining order, I asked why Chris or I couldn't do it. He said if I called, I'd be violating the terms of the restraining order. "And no offense to Chris, but I know how to handle the situation if Craig gets belligerent." He glanced over at me and grinned. "I'm a trained professional, after all."

Despite the seriousness of the situation, and the rocks in my stomach, I couldn't help but smile back. He was right, Chris wouldn't know what to say any better than I would.

I got out my phone to pull up Craig's number for Jamie when he reminded me he already had it. I expected him to put his phone on speaker so I could hear, but he used his headset so I only heard his side.

"Mr. Hopper, this is James Sheppard of Sheppard & Sons Investigations," Jamie said politely before pausing. Knowing Craig, I could only assume he was demanding to know why Jamie was calling.

"Mr. Hopper, I am calling on behalf of Emily Taylor." His tone was less polite this time. I saw the muscles in his neck strain as he clenched his teeth. "I'm calling to remind you that Ms. Taylor will be collecting her personal property from your shared residence between one and five today." Jamie's voice had taken on a harsh quality, whatever Craig was saying, it was pissing him off.

He's probably swearing and yelling. Judging from the vice grip Jamie currently had on the steering wheel I was probably right.

"Mr. Hopper, Ms. Taylor is listed as a resident on the lease so I assure you she has every legal right to enter. If you've changed the locks the landlord will let us in." Jamie's voice radiated ice cold authority.

I felt a flutter in my stomach, but this time the butterflies weren't because of nerves; Jamie's protective, controlled, confident manner was kind of hot. Not that I was attracted to him, because I wasn't, but he was the exact opposite of Craig in every way, and it was a turn on. *Jesus, cut the shit. He's your brother's best friend.* I'd been so caught up in my thoughts that I'd missed the rest of the conversation.

"Emily?" Jamie called my name, judging by his tone it wasn't the first time. I felt the heat rise in my cheeks. "Are you okay?"

"Yeah, I, um, do you think he'll show up?"

"I doubt it, but we're not taking any chances. I made sure he knows he'll be in violation of the restraining order, and get arrested, if he does. Hopefully that's enough to keep him away."

I was glad Jamie was on my side. Actually, I was grateful for everyone who was on my side. I couldn't remember the last time I'd felt safe going to my old apartment, but for the first time in a long time, I did, because I trusted Chris, Jack, and Jamie to keep me safe. Not only were they bigger and stronger than Craig, but they were trained professionals, and I was pretty sure they had guns. *Well, at least Jamie and Jack are.* Even though Chris wasn't a trained professional, I was grateful he'd taken the day off to come with us. There was a lot to be said for a big brother's moral support.

The closer we got to my apartment, the more I fidgeted with my thumb ring. I couldn't let go of my fear that Craig might show up and cause trouble. *What if someone gets hurt?* It occurred to me as we parked in front of the apartment, that Craig might have changed the locks.

I said as much to Jamie, "I hope I haven't wasted everyone's time." *God only knows how much this is costing Chris.* He'd be paying Jamie and Jack for a fourteen-hour day. I made a mental note to find out so I could start budgeting to pay him back.

"What do you mean?"

"What if he changed the locks?" I asked.

"He said he didn't, and even if he did the landlord will have to let you in."

That's right, he said that to Craig. *My nerves are making me stupid.*

"Oh, right, good." I got out of the car wondering how I was going to get through the rest of the day without having a complete meltdown.

Chris and Jack had already grabbed a bunch of boxes and were waiting for us. Jack said, "Let's get moving, we have four hours to pack up and get out of dodge."

"I don't think it'll take that long. None of the furniture is mine, so the hardest thing to move will be my books."

"That's fine, I wanted to give us extra time so he wouldn't accidentally come home early and intercept us." Jamie made air quotes around the word accidentally.

I reached out to unlock the apartment door but Jamie stopped me and held out his hands for the keys. "I'll go in first and verify he's not here. Jack and Chris will stay out here with you until I give the all clear."

"Oh, um, okay." I really didn't think Craig would risk getting arrested again, but apparently they weren't taking any chances.

After Jamie stepped into the apartment, gun drawn, Jack pulled the door as if to close it but didn't let the latch catch.

"Does he really need a gun?" I asked Jack, though I figured I already knew the answer.

"Better safe than sorry." Jack looked relaxed as he watched the door, but I had a feeling he could spring into action in a heartbeat if he needed to. He'd set the boxes down and his hands were hanging at his sides as he scanned up and down the hallway.

This is so surreal; I feel like character in a cop show.

Jamie said, "All clear," near the front door just before opening it. I walked in and cringed as the smell of rotten food assaulted my nose. I'd always kept the apartment clean, and I liked scented candles, so it had always smelled nice in here. Now it smelled like a dumpster. Chris and Jack followed behind me carrying the boxes. No one mentioned the smell, though there was no way on God's green Earth they hadn't noticed it.

We needed fresh air while we packed, at least I did, so I opened the balcony door. I inhaled deeply before turning back to the mess.

It didn't surprise me that Craig had taken out his anger on some of the things I'd left behind. Several books were torn and scattered around the living room. He'd smashed frames and torn pictures of us. And there were pieces of broken ceramic and glass knickknacks on the floor.

"I'm guessing these are your things," Chris said looking around at the carnage.

"Yeah. We can leave most of it." I was sad so many things had been destroyed, but at least none of it had sentimental value. "No point in packing broken shit. I have some clothes in the bedroom, and a few things in the kitchen."

"Why don't you tell Chris what's yours in the kitchen, he can pack in there while you grab your clothes. Tell me which books are yours, so I can pack them. I'll make a list of the ruined ones so you know what you need to replace."

I noticed he hadn't assigned anything to Jack, apparently he wasn't there to help pack.

We worked quickly while Jack stood near the door. In no time, we had several boxes packed and ready to be carried out so Jamie and Chris carried them down to Chris's car.

While taking a water break in the kitchen, my breath caught in my throat and my whole body tensed when I heard the door open.

What if it's Craig?

It only took a second, then I laughed at how pathetic I sounded. *Jack is standing in the doorway.* I shook out my fear and got back to work.

I had music playing on my phone as I finished packing in my closet, *not mine, not after today,* when I thought I heard the bedroom door close. I was shaking off the flash of fear, assuming it was one of the guys, when I heard him.

"You fucking bitch!" Craig's angry growl was low enough that no one else would've heard him.

Out of habit, I bit back my scream as I turned around and faced him, my heart beating out of my chest. From my position in the closet doorway I could see the open balcony door. The second door I'd opened to let in the fresh air. It hadn't occurred to me he might climb up the tree outside and come in through a second-story balcony door.

No one knows he's here. My hands started shaking as I broke out in a cold sweat.

"I saw your brother and your friends. Did you really think I'd be afraid of them?" Craig was closing the distance as he taunted me. "I'll be gone before they even realize I'm here."

He paused when Chris called out from the hall, "Em? You alright in there?"

Craig practically hissed, "Don't say a fucking word." Before turning towards the door.

Taking advantage of the distraction, I moved to the other side of the bed, creating a barrier between us. Then prayed Chris would realize something was wrong when I didn't answer.

"Em, you decent? Can I come in?" Chris asked through the door.

I opened my mouth to call for help, but Craig growled, "Tell him no."

"No." My voice cracked. I knew Jamie and Jack wouldn't hesitate to run in and save me if I screamed, but I was too terrified to try.

"Okay, let me know when it's okay."

"Say okay." Craig pointed at me, a scowl on his face. He looked like shit; his hair was greasy, he hadn't shaved in a while, and eyes were bloodshot.

"Okay." My voice squeaked with fear. *Please God, let him hear the fear in my voice.*

Craig glared at me; head cocked towards the door as he waited for Chris to say something else. After a few seconds with no response, he started circling the bed.

"You fucking bitch. You're gonna pay for getting me arrested."

I tried to back away but bumped into the bedside table. My surprised yelp was barely above a whisper. Or maybe it was louder, it was hard to hear above the sound of my heart pounding in my ears. Craig would reach me in a matter of seconds. *Please God, don't let this happen.* After what felt like an eternity, but was in reality only a few seconds, the door crashed open.

Craig spun around as Jamie and Jack rushed in, guns drawn and pointed at him.

"On your knees!" Jamie ordered as he and Jack surrounded Craig. "Put your hands where I can see them!"

I cried out as my knees buckled underneath me. I wasn't sure if it was from fear or relief.

Probably both. I hugged my knees to my chest and tried not to think about how close I'd come to getting beaten again.

Looking over the bed, I watched as Jack shoved Craig roughly to his knees, grabbed his hands and yanked them behind his back, then zip-tied his wrists. Craig swore the entire time.

Jack stood, gun pointed at Craig, and said, "I got him. Check on Emily."

Chapter 9

Jamie

I walked around the bed, intending to offer Emily a hand up, but she was shaking so badly that I holstered my gun and kneeled in front of her instead. After gently prying her hands away from her legs, I helped her to stand. At no point had I intended to hug her, but it felt like the right thing to do. So I did. She didn't resist when I pulled her towards me and turned her face away from Jack, who was yanking Craig to his feet, then wrapped my arms around her, one hand holding her head to my chest.

"Shhhh…" I ignored the strong sense of possession I felt take over as she wrapped her arms around me and buried her face against my chest and cried. Words wouldn't help her feel any better or calmer, so I simply held her. Using my body to tell her she was safe, since my words wouldn't help.

"Jack, get him out of here and call Houston PD."

"No!" Emily cried out as she jerked back.

What the Fuck? Why would she want to let him get away with this, after everything he'd put her through?

Jack held Craig, and waited for instructions.

I cupped her face and forced her to make eye contact. My anger evaporated at the stark terror I saw in her eyes. "Emily, he violated his restraining order -"

"Jamie, please," she begged as tears flowed down her cheeks. I had to resist the urge to wipe them away. "It'll be worse if I have him arrested again. I have everything I need. Can't we just leave? Please?"

My heart broke hearing the desperation in her voice. And worse, she was probably right. If we had Craig arrested again, they wouldn't hold him long and he'd be even more determined to get revenge. I was torn, for the first time in my life I was considering ignoring the rules to help Emily.

I looked at Jack, wanting to know what he thought. He raised one eyebrow and nodded. I should have guessed he'd side with Emily.

Damn it. It went against my by-the-book instincts, but I conceded. I didn't want to make things worse for Emily, and I'd feel better the sooner we got her back to Weatherford.

I called Chris in and asked him to stay with Emily while Jack and I escorted Craig out of the room. "It's your lucky day," I said through gritted teeth as we forced him out into the hallway.

Jack turned Craig so he was facing the wall, his hand on his pistol sending a clear message to Craig—don't move.

Then, I got in Craig's face. "If you try to fight or argue, we'll call 9-1-1 and have your ass thrown back in jail. Understood?"

When Craig asked, "who the fuck do you think you are?" Jack pushed him into the wall, not hard enough to hurt him but hard enough to make it clear he could, and would. I'd told him who I was when I called earlier, so I didn't waste my time answering him.

"Consider that your only warning," Jack said as he held Craig's face against the wall, then said to me, "I've got him."

He'd hold him there while we removed all the boxes, then wait with Craig in the apartment until I came back.

Craig tried to turn his head like he wanted to say something, but changed his mind when Jack applied more pressure.

I went back inside and checked on Emily. She was shaken up and begging to leave so we grabbed the last few boxes and carried them to my SUV. When we were done, Emily asked if we could stop for food on our way home, saying she was worried about upsetting her parents and wanted some time to settle down before going home.

Her heart is so big. Despite what she'd just gone through, her biggest concern was for her parents.

Chris said it was typical of her to be more worried about them than about herself. "She's too kind for her own good."

I couldn't disagree, knowing Craig had taken advantage of her kind heart and it had cost her.

Emily suggested a restaurant just outside Houston, saying it was her favorite place to stop when she drove back home.

I asked Emily to text me the address after we made plans to meet there.

"Thanks Jamie, I don't know what I would've done without you and Jack there to help."

"Let's not think about it." I waited until Chris pulled away before going back inside.

Jack was standing in the doorway, his right hand resting on the grip of his gun, watching Craig who was now standing in front of the couch, his hands still zip-tied behind his back.

Craig took what he probably thought was a menacing step forward when I came in and asked, "Who the hell do you think you are?"

"I wouldn't do that if I were you." Jack sounded calm, but out of the corner of my eye I saw his hand tighten on his gun. Craig saw it too and stepped back.

"Whatever." He shrugged his shoulders.

"We're the guys you'll have to deal with if you so much as think about violating your restraining order ever again."

He opened his mouth to reply, but thought better of it when I glared at him. Then he turned his shoulders and lifted his wrists. "You gonna untie me?"

I looked at Jack, silently telling him to cover me. He nodded.

"Turn around and face the kitchen." I made sure Jack had a clear shot if Craig got violent, then cut the ties with my pocket knife and stepped back out of reach.

"Hands where I can see them," Jack commanded.

Craig put his hands out in front of him in the classic surrender position and sat down.

"Whatever." He put his hands on his thighs and leaned back in an attempt to look relaxed. But the vein popping in his forehead, told a different story. Jack and I waited for ten, long tense minutes.

"We're leaving. Sit your ass right there and don't move. If you follow-"

"Yeah yeah, you'll call the cops. You sound like a broken record." He pointed at the door. "Get out of my fucking house."

"Gladly. Just so you know, we're returning Ms. Taylor's keys to the landlord, and giving him a court order to remove her from the lease."

"Whatever."

Jack covered me as I walked out, then shut the door behind us. A few seconds later we heard a thump against the door.

"That guy is a piece of fucking work," Jack said after we got in my SUV.

"Christ." I ran my hand through my hair. "I'm glad that's over and she never has to see him again." Except maybe for the court date. But I'd be there with her, keeping her safe.

"Yeah, me too. Let's get out of here. I'm starving, and I'm sure Emily could use some extra support."

Chapter 10

Emily

Chris ordered an appetizer sampler while we waited for Jamie and Jack so there'd be food on the table when they got here. I played with my glass of water and worried about facing Jamie. *I can't believe I hugged him.* I didn't think about it, didn't plan it, it just happened. Sure, he hugged me first, but he was just being nice. Then I'd held on to him like a drowning person clinging to a life preserver and slobbered all over his shirt as I cried my eyes out. *I'm sure he's mad at me for telling him not to call the cops, but I didn't want to give Craig another reason to come after me.*

I felt stupid, weak, and pathetic for still being afraid of him after Jamie and Jack tied his hands, but I couldn't help it. *If I'm lucky, I'll never have to see him again.*

I don't know what I would have done without Jamie, and Jack. *Who am I kidding? I wouldn't have gone back. I would've let Craig keep everything.*

I mumbled hi, when Jamie and Jack sat down, too embarrassed to say anything else or look them in the eyes. *All I want to do is go home, drink a bottle of wine, and eat a tub of caramel brownie ice cream.*

"How are you holding up?" Jamie asked softly after he and Jack settled in.

"I'm doing better now that we're out of there." Damn it, my squeaky voice didn't sound like I was doing better. I stared at the appetizer plate in front of me to avoid looking at him. "Do you think he followed you?" *Stupid question.* We wouldn't be sitting here if they thought Craig had followed them.

"No." Jamie and Jack answered together. Their confidence helped put me at ease.

"We watched for him." Jamie reassured me.

"We tail people professionally, so we know exactly what to look for to make sure we aren't being followed. Craig isn't smart enough to get the drop on us twice." Jack sounded a little too confident and if I hadn't seen him in action earlier I might have thought he was arrogant.

Chris looked at me then to Jack. "It's rather arrogant to assume he's not smart enough to surprise you, don't you think?" Clearly he was still freaked out by what happened. And he had a point, Craig had surprised us all by climbing up the tree to the bedroom balcony. Though, if I hadn't opened the door he wouldn't have gotten in unnoticed.

"Not arrogant, confident. Trust me Chris, we're taking this very seriously." Jack said, as he and Jamie exchanged a tense look. "And we won't make the same mistake twice."

"So, he's not a threat?" I asked. *Please tell me he isn't a threat anymore.* Somehow I knew they wouldn't.

"That's not what I said, and I'm sorry if I implied it." Jack sounded apologetic. "We know he didn't follow us here. But he was pissed off when we left, and there's every possibility he'll make more bad decisions."

"We'll be watching for him, and won't let him get to you." Jamie added before asking, "Does he know about this place?"

"Maybe, but he's never been here with me. I love this place and would ask him if we could stop but he never wanted to. Ashley and I used to come here all the time when we drove back and forth from college."

Damn, I hadn't talked to Ashley in what felt like forever and made a mental note to call her. We were best friends in high school and went to college in Houston together. We stopped hanging out after I moved in with Craig because he didn't like her. He thought she was a bad influence. I'd admit she was a bit of a party girl, but she was hardly a bad influence on me. I did my fair share of partying without her influence, especially that first year away from home. I'd never been a wild child, but I wasn't innocent either. *She'll be thrilled I finally left him.* Ashley thought he was too controlling, and she was right. Unfortunately, I didn't see it until it was too late.

"Good. Let's eat, then we'll take you home." Jamie said as he grabbed a mozzarella stick.

I didn't realize my hands were still shaking until Jamie reached over and placed his hand on top of mine. His touch was gentle and comforting. I could feel the callouses on his warm palm. Jamie was a man who used his hands a lot. Craig had soft hands; *I don't think he ever lifted anything heavier than a pen.*

"It'll be okay Emily. I can't promise he won't, as Jack said, make more bad decisions, but I can promise we won't let him hurt you again."

I shivered, not from the cold but from the conviction in his voice. *I wonder if he talks to all his clients like this?*

"Thank you." I raised my head and looked him in the eye, tired of hiding, of feeling scared and embarrassed. "For everything."

His hazel eyes held mine and I couldn't help but notice they were more green than blue. They were gorgeous, and I was staring.

Chris cleared his throat. "Do you know what you want, Em?"

Color crept up my neck and face, I was so preoccupied thinking about Jamie's eyes I hadn't heard our waitress approach. I pulled my hand away from the table, and Jamie's touch, and placed it in my lap. Chris managed to look curious and annoyed at the same time, but I ignored it. I glanced at Jack, wondering if he'd noticed anything. Judging by the way he was smirking at his brother, he had.

Oh God, I hope he doesn't think I like Jamie. It's not like that. I'm just overwhelmed and it was nice to have a man be nice to me. A nice, protective, good looking man with gorgeous eyes.

"What'll you have sweetie?" the waitress asked.

At least I didn't have to look at the menu, I always ordered the same thing, a grilled ham and cheese with a side of homemade tomato bisque. The sandwich was generously buttered and grilled to golden brown perfection, and they sprinkled fresh shaved parmesan on the soup, I always asked for extra. It was one of their house specials, and my favorite dish.

My brother ordered a tuna salad sandwich with a side salad. Jack and Jamie both ordered burgers with bacon and cheese, and french fries. They were clearly not watching what they ate. *Not that they have to.*

The three of them had played football together in high school and spent a lot of time practicing and working out so they could eat whatever they wanted to back then. But now Chris had a desk job and was developing a dad bod. It wasn't a judgement, fatherhood suited him. But Jack and Jamie had physically demanding jobs and looked like they still spent a lot of time working out, so they could still eat whatever they wanted. *I wonder if Chris is as jealous as I am?*

By the time our food arrived, I'd finally calmed down enough to enjoy our late lunch. It was the first time we had a chance to talk like old friends since I'd come home. Jack asked me if I planned on staying in Weatherford, and if I'd be able to keep my job if I did. I didn't actually know what my plans were, so I told them I planned on staying with my parents for a few more weeks while I figured things out, and since I worked remotely, I could keep my job no matter where I lived. Luckily, my boss had been supportive when I called to ask for a few days off. I didn't want anyone in the office to get hurt, so I told him Craig had been arrested and they shouldn't let him in. They didn't need to know the details, but I felt like

I needed to warn them, just in case. The chances were slim he'd show up, since he knew I only went in once or twice a month, but slim wasn't none.

When I asked Jack why he changed his mind about going to the police academy, he said it was a no brainer to invest in SSI, instead of joining the police force, after leaving the Army.

I remembered Meg saying she'd needed SSI's help at one point and asked Jack if that was how they met. When he said he met her at Grannie's I was surprised. Mary had a strict rule about her kids not dating her employees, disappointing a few of my friends who'd worked there. Jack and Jamie had always been good looking, and they were nice guys, so of course all the girls wanted to go out with them. Isabelle won the jackpot when she and Jamie started dating. She also crushed my childhood fantasy because I was that girl; the one who had a silly school girl crush on her big brother's best friend.

"She was a barista at Grannie's, and it was love at first sip."

Jamie groaned and Chris rolled his eyes.

Jack flipped them off before continuing, "I think you'd like her."

"She seemed nice when I met her at the office."

"I'm sure she'd love to meet you for a coffee. You can have a girl's day out at Grannie's."

"Jesus Jack, a *girl's day out* really?" Jamie teased him.

Jack gave Jamie both fingers. "You're just mad you didn't think of it first."

I interrupted their brotherly banter. "I'm sure she's too busy."

"Nah," he said, brushing off my concern. "She hasn't been in Weatherford very long so most of her friends work at Grannie's or SSI. I'm sure she'd love to talk to someone her own age."

"Not to mention female. Right now, she's surrounded by us all day," Jamie added with a laugh.

"You should do it Em, you said yourself she seems nice. I know Jack is probably biased, but you can trust that she's good people if Mary and John trust her." Chris knew I'd lost touch with most of my friends from high school and college. I could probably reach out to a few of them, but I only had one friend in the area I really wanted to reconnect with and that was Ashley. She lived in Dallas so it wouldn't be too hard to get together.

"Alright, I'm sure it'll be fun and I haven't been to Grannie's since I've been back. I always think about how much I miss Grannie's any time I'm at a chain coffee shop. They're never as good." I wasn't sure about going out and meeting new people yet, but this wouldn't be too bad. *Meg is Jack's fiancé, we're meeting at Grannie's, and someone from SSI will probably be there too.*

"Ma'll be happy to hear that, she loves her shop." Jamie laughed. "She was none too happy when we stole Meg from her."

"She'd probably still be giving us shit if I hadn't saved the day by asking Meg to marry me." Jack preened like a peacock.

"Whatever little brother."

"Have you set a date yet?" I asked just as Jack opened his mouth to reply to Jamie.

"September, about a year from the day we met."

I said, "That's so sweet." As Jamie made more gagging sounds and Chris rolled his eyes again. It'd been a long time since I'd been around them, and I'd forgotten how close they were.

"Meg picked the date," Jack said before shoving a couple of fries in his mouth while giving his brother the stink eye.

"And what Meg wants, she gets." Jamie wasn't done giving his brother shit.

"Damn straight I spoil her as often as she'll let me. She deserves it."

Jamie added, "That she does, if for no other reason than putting up with you."

Jack threw a balled up napkin at his brother, who caught it easily and set it on the table. He turned to me and whispered loud enough for everyone to hear, "She's been good for him. Keeps his sorry ass in line."

I laughed, not a polite chuckle but a good hearty belly laugh. *God it feels good to laugh.*

Jamie tried to pick up the bill, but Chris grabbed it and insisted on paying, saying it was the least he could do. I thought about saying something about the fact that he was paying them to be there but decided it wasn't a good idea to stir that particular pot. I didn't want to upset any of them.

I asked to ride back with Chris, so I'd feel less awkward. After everything that had happened, and still remembering the hug, I didn't want to spend the next couple of hours alone with Jamie. With Jack's encouragement, Jamie reluctantly agreed, then told Chris they'd follow us to my parents house.

When we finally got there I suggested unloading Jamie's SUV first, so they didn't have to stay, but they insisted on helping unload everything. I thought about arguing but gave up instead—it'd been a long stressful day and I was exhausted. It'd go a lot faster with the extra help, and the sooner we finished the sooner I could take a hot bath, then settle down with a good book, a tub of ice cream, and a bottle of wine.

As we lugged in boxes, I thought about how badly I'd fucked up my life. Never in a million years would I have guessed I'd be in as much danger after leaving an abusive ex as I was when I lived with him.

Chapter 11

Jamie

Jack and I helped Chris, Emily, and their dad unload the boxes, then stuck around for a bit to put her parents at ease. They had a lot of questions, which was to be expected. We did our best to answer them without violating our confidentiality contract, leaving it to Chris and/or Emily to tell them the rest. It felt a little awkward having to address Christopher and Annette Taylor in a professional capacity, they were friends with our parents and we'd known them most of our lives.

Afterwards, they thanked us repeatedly for being there to help Emily, and her dad offered to help cover our expenses. Her mom, who we'd both been addressing as Mrs. Taylor, said, "Please boys, I think you're adult enough to call me Anne."

"Thank you Mrs. Taylor but Ma'd kill us if she ever heard us doing that," Jack said with a grin. He might be exaggerating, but not by much.

She hugged us both and thanked us again as she handed us a tin of homemade cookies. *What is it with women thanking us in cookies?* Meg loved to thank us with baked goods too. We'd get fat if the trend continued. Of course, that didn't stop us from accepting the tin. I thanked her, knowing there were plenty of people in the office to share them with. Jack took the tin, opened it, then thanked Mrs. Taylor around a mouthful of cookie. Before leaving, I made sure AJ was in place across the street.

We stopped for a beer after leaving the Taylor's.

"If people keep thanking us with cookies, we're going to get fat," Jack said around a bite of chocolate chip cookie.

"And yet that's your third one," I said as I reached for my second cookie. When Jack raised his eyebrow at me, I shrugged and said, "What? They're good."

When I thanked him for offering Emily the chance to hang out with Meg, he said, "I think they'll get along, and Meg really does need more female friends." Her only real female friends were Beth and Ma, and she was quite a bit younger then either of them. And while she and Beth were close, they didn't hang out, not only was Beth fifteen years older but she had a five-year-old son, so she didn't have a lot of free time. She was more like a close aunt to Meg than a friend.

"You're acting like my helping Emily is a personal favor to you." He studied me over the rim of his tipped beer. "Care to explain that big brother?"

"It kind of is. Chris is my best friend, he was the best man at my wedding; a favor to him, is a favor to me." I didn't want to admit that I was taking this case more personally than I should be. When I saw Craig in Emily's room, I had to fight the urge to shoot him on sight. I'd also had a hard time respecting her wishes when she asked us not to call the police, I wanted that asshole behind bars where he couldn't hurt her ever again. *Or six feet under.*

"I think she'll be happy to get out, she said she hasn't done anything besides work and hang out at home since she came back." Though I was sure part of the reason was because she didn't want anyone seeing her bruises. Weatherford was a small town and it was unlikely she could go out and not run into someone she knew.

"Makes sense, she's been through a lot and needs some time to adjust. I wasn't lying when I said I think they'll get along." Jack finished his beer and laughed. "If for no other reason than they both love to read."

"Yeah, I had flashbacks of helping Meg move as Emily pointed out which books were hers." Not wanting to add to her stress, neither of us had said anything to her, but good lord she had a lot of books. A lot more than Meg. We had thought Meg would have a lot more than she did, since she always had a book with her, but she couldn't afford to support her habit so she borrowed a lot of them from the local library.

"I felt bad that asshole ruined so many of them, but at least we didn't have to carry them," Jack said.

"We? If I recall, you were holding up a wall while Chris and I did all the heavy lifting." I teased him. His job had been far more important than carrying a few boxes, but he'd refused to take the bait.

He shrugged. "Somebody had to do it."

Before going to bed, I checked in with AJ. I didn't doubt his ability to do his job, but I couldn't ignore the impulse to make sure everything was quiet.

Andrew Janerek, AJ, came with a glowing recommendation from Jack. They'd met while serving together in the Army and had been best friends ever since. He joined SSI as a bodyguard after his enlisted ended, and would soon have his private investigators license. And the pay raise that came with it. I often wondered if it bothered him that Doug started with us a PI, but knew there was nothing I could do about it. Doug had the college degree and field experience required for his PI license when he applied, AJ hadn't.

AJ would do his job, and do it well, and I told him as much when he asked why I was checking up on him when he'd updated me less than two hours ago. I exaggerated the truth and said I was still antsy after the situation with Craig earlier. That was part of it, but not all. I wanted to be there, making sure everything was secure at the Taylor house. *Fuck. I'm taking Emily's safety far too personally.*

I couldn't help thinking about how scared she'd looked when Craig had her cornered. Knowing how violent he'd been in the past I'd almost called 9-1-1 after she and Chris had left, but she'd made me promise I wouldn't, and I couldn't go back on my word. Even if the bastard deserved to go back to jail. Hell, he deserved to have his ass kicked and I'd be happy to be the one to do it. Guys like that thought they were tough when they were beating on a woman, but could rarely hold their own if challenged by a man.

Which was what happened when Jack and I confronted him. He tried to talk a tough game, protect his tough guy image, but he hadn't tried to physically challenge us.

I looked down at my hands, I'd been twisting my wedding band off and on while I paced across my bedroom floor. *What the fuck is wrong with me?* I rarely ever played with my wedding band.

I stopped pacing and stared down at my hand, thinking back to what my parents, and Isabelle's, had suggested. Was it time to take my ring off? Was I ready to move forward and find happiness? I knew Isabelle wouldn't want me to be lonely, but it was so damn hard trying to imagine being with anyone else.

I took my ring off and placed it on the dresser in front of our wedding picture. *God, she was so beautiful.* She'd worn her long, thick, black hair down that day, instead of the traditional wedding up-do. She did it for me, because I always told her how much I loved it when she wore it down. Her naturally dark skin glowed against the white of her dress making her look like a Mexican Goddess. I'd worshipped her, and our wedding day was the happiest of my life.

I looked in the mirror. *I look old.* I'd always considered myself to be a decent looking guy, but grief had aged me.

Isabelle wouldn't want this for me. She'd want me to live my life to the fullest, and to find someone to share it with.

I looked back at our wedding picture. "I miss you."

For the first time since I'd said I do, I left my ring on the dresser. Then changed into my running clothes. I needed to clear my head, and nothing worked like a good long run.

Meg was in the hallway when I came out of my room, she looked me up and down, a concerned look on her face. "You okay?"

"Yeah, I just need to clear my head."

"Alright. Be careful."

"I will." *Isabelle would have loved her.*

Chapter 12

Jamie

I came back in after my run and stopped short when I overheard Meg ask Jack, "Is Jamie okay?"

"I think so, but he took the whole situation today a little too personally."

I bit back a laugh when I heard Meg's reply. "You'd never do something like that." I could imagine her rolling her eyes at him.

"Who me? Never."

Jack had most definitely taken Meg's unofficial case too personally.

"Do you think it's because he likes her?"

Did she notice I wasn't wearing my wedding ring?

"I don't know, maybe." Jack paused. "He claims it's because Emily's a family friend, but I think there might be more to it."

"Did he say or do anything to make you think so?"

"No, nothing specific. But he's called AJ twice tonight to make sure everything is okay." Jack said it like he assumed Meg would know that wasn't normal behavior.

I should have known AJ would rat me out.

"It'd be nice for him to find someone. He's too good a guy to be so lonely," Meg said.

Not wanting to hear any more, I retreated to my bedroom.

The next morning I stood in front of my dresser debating whether or not I should put my ring back on. The sunlight caught the scuff marks in the gold as I picked it up; this ring and I had seen a lot of action. I felt naked without it, but decided not to put it back on, yet. *I can always put it back on later.*

The sweet scent of sausage filled my nose before I reached the kitchen. Jack was scheduled to relieve AJ at seven so he'd gotten up early, and unsurprisingly Meg got with him so they could have breakfast together. *It's what Isabelle would have done.*

"Morning Jamie. We made plenty of eggs and sausage so help yourself," she picked up her mug, "and of course, lots of coffee." Not that she needed to remind me, there was always plenty of coffee in this house. Not only had Jack and I grown up in our mom's coffee shop, developing a deep love of good coffee, but we worked crazy schedules and often relied on the caffeine boost.

It was nice to see Meg settling in and relishing the role of housewife, despite not being married. She said it was because she hadn't had a real home since her grandmother died, when she was fourteen, and she loved taking care of us. She always added that we took care of her too. I'd thought it might be weird when Meg first moved in with us, but it'd actually been nice having her around. *I'll miss them when they get their own place.*

I poured myself a cup of coffee and sat down. Feeling self conscious about not wearing my band, I was absentmindedly playing with my bare finger. Of course Jack noticed. I would have if our situations were reversed.

Jack nodded at my hand; his question unspoken.

Meg noticed and followed his gaze. She was far more observant than the average person, a survival skill she'd learned living in an abusive household. It didn't hurt that she now lived and worked with private investigators.

She smiled, opened her mouth to say something, closed it, opened it again, bit her bottom lip, opened her mouth, then closed it and looked at Jack.

He shook his head and laughed. "Just ask him before your head explodes."

I feigned offense. "I'm right here."

"Sorry. I'm just surprised to see you without your wedding band and wanted to say something but it seems rude to ask and–"

I cut her off. "It's okay Meg." If I hadn't, she'd ramble on, and embarrass herself. Something she did frequently when she got nervous. "I think Mom and Dad might be right, so I'm trying it."

"Does this have anything to do with the blond I'm about to go shadow?" Jack asked.

I gave him a dirty look. "No. I talked to them about it before Chris hired us to protect Emily." *Damn it. That didn't sound convincing.* If I couldn't convince myself, I'd never convince Jack. Or Meg.

Emily was off limits for a lot of reasons, including the fact that her brother was my best friend.

"Uh huh." Jack grinned. He wasn't convinced but I wouldn't give him the satisfaction of arguing.

Meg ran around the table and gave me a big hug. "I don't care why you're doing it Jamie, I'm just glad you are. I know it's hard to let go, to move on, but Isabelle would want you to be happy."

"Thanks." I was as grateful she'd prevented Jack from giving me shit as I was for her support. Knowing Meg, it was probably her intention.

From the stupid grin on his face, Jack was about to try again. But Meg interrupted him. "You'll be late if you don't get moving." She looked at me and winked, a trait she claims she picked up from 'The Sheppard Men' as she liked to call us. It was probably true, since we all tended to wink. She used to make fun of Jack for it even though she seemed to like it. I remember the first time she saw dad wink; she was in the hospital and his wink had made her laugh. That was when Meg started to feel comfortable around him. Before that she thought he didn't like her. *Now they're thick as thieves.*

I offered to help clean up, but Meg insisted on doing it herself, informing me I could clean up after dinner, which I'd be cooking.

"You should let him help you, he's assigned himself to Emily duty tonight. And most nights this week. So he won't be around to help later." Jack raised an eyebrow at me before walking up behind Meg and hugging her. "I'll happily make dinner for you tonight Princess. I'll even clean up afterwards."

It wasn't much of an offer since he cooked everything on the grill, but Meg didn't care. "So, I should thaw some steaks."

"Yup." Jack kissed her. "Gotta run. Love you."

"Love you too."

Jack nodded as he left. "Later bro." Half way down the hall he yelled back over his shoulder, "You need me to check in with you every fifteen minutes, or do you trust me to do my job?"

I didn't answer, at least not verbally, I let my middle finger and scowl do the talking for me. I trusted him to do his job and he knew it. *Sometimes working with family is a real pain in the ass.*

I stood up and started helping Meg. "He's right, I'll be gone every night this week so I'll make breakfast, and clean up my mess, for the rest of the week. Deal?"

"Deal. Ooooh, can we have banana chocolate chip pancakes tomorrow?" Meg asked excitedly.

I laughed. "Of course." Jack and I rarely ate a carb heavy breakfast, usually opting for eggs and bacon or sausage. Meg never complained, but she'd request pancakes any time we asked what she wanted.

"Thanks Jamie. You're the best big brother ever." Which wasn't saying much because Meg was an only child. She leaned against the counter and crossed her arms, trying to look serious. "So, now that Jack's gone, you can tell me, do you like her?"

"Who?" I played dumb to buy myself some time because I wasn't sure how to answer. I felt protective of Emily, but wasn't sure if I was attracted to her. *I mean, she's pretty, and it felt good holding her in my arms, but I'm sure it felt good because I was comforting her during a difficult situation, not because I like her.*

Meg's look said it all, so she didn't need to say anything. But she did anyway. "Don't play dumb, you know I mean Emily."

I laughed. *So this is what it feels like having a pain in the ass little sister.* Madi had been a pain in the ass, but she never let me forget that she was twenty-two minutes older, so technically she was a pain in the ass big sister.

"What's so funny?"

"I was just thinking, I now know how Chris felt growing up with a pain in the ass little sister."

"Aw, you're so sweet." Sarcasm dripped from her voice thicker than molasses. She lowered her voice a few octaves. "Stop trying to avoid the question." Meg was a pro at changing the subject, so it was easy for her to notice when I did it. "Now, answer me or I'll get your mom involved."

Damn! She went straight to playing the mom card. I sighed, not because of her threat, she'd never really go through with it, but because I didn't know the answer. "I don't know. Jack's right, her case feels personal, but I don't know if it's because she's a family friend who I've known most of my life or if it's because I'm attracted to her."

Did I just admit that I'm attracted to her? Shit. I took a deep breath and ran my hand through my hair. "It doesn't matter. I shouldn't even be thinking about it. Chris is my best friend, he was my best man, and I'm a godfather to his daughter. I can't think about his little sister like that."

"I'm sure Chris wouldn't mind. He might be shocked at first, but I'm sure he'd be good with it after he gave you the obligatory protective big brother speech. You're a great guy Jamie, you deserve to be happy. So does Emily."

"Cart in front of horse, Meg. Besides, I'm not ready to think about it yet." I said it to end the conversation, but realized it was the truth. I didn't want to think about what feelings I might or might not have for Emily, let alone talk about them.

"Okay. I'm here if you want to talk. So is Jack. He's just not as nice as me." She winked at me before stepping in and giving me a quick hug. "Now you finish cleaning the kitchen while I get ready for work. You know how cranky my bosses get if I'm late."

I shook my head and laughed. I was one of her bosses, and was never cranky. "Only because the whole operation would crash and burn without you."

"Aw, thanks."

It might not crash and burn, but life at SSI was a hell of a lot easier with Meg there.

After washing the dishes, I finished getting ready for work. My ring caught my attention as I walked by. I picked it up and rolled it between my fingers for a few seconds, contemplating whether I should put it back on. *Am I ready to signal to the world that I'm ready to move on?*

I put the band down and glanced at my wedding picture. "I'm trying."

Meg knocked on my office door mid-afternoon to let me know Emily had emailed to inform us she was going to Dallas tonight to have dinner with a friend.

I was glad she let us know in advance, even if it was only a few hours. She was doing her best to follow the protocols we'd put in place, even if she didn't understand the need for them. Clients didn't always understand that coverage, specifically shift changes, was trickier when they went out of town, which was why we needed to know in advance where they going, and for how long.

We weren't providing a driver with Emily's current protection detail, so I made a mental note to ask her if she wanted me to drive her there and back.

"Did she say who?"

"Ashley York. Want me to run a background check?"

"That won't be necessary. Did she say what time she's leaving?" Ashley was Emily's best friend in high school, and she'd mentioned wanting to visit her in Dallas.

"Four-thirty. She said they're hanging out at Ashley's and will probably order delivery for dinner."

"She didn't happen to say when she planned on coming home did she?"

"She didn't, but I can ask."

"I'll take care of it. Can you let Jack know I'll relieve him at four? There's no sense in both of us having to drive to Dallas." I was scheduled to relieve him at six but could go early since I didn't have any appointments.

"Can do boss man." She saluted me from the doorway before asking, "Want me to pack you some food?"

"That'd be great. Thanks, Meg."

I texted Emily and asked if she had a minute to talk. I wanted to get more details about her plans with Ashley, and offer to drive her there and back, and it'd be easier over the phone.

There was no point in taking two cars, plus there was a pretty good chance they'd be drinking, and I didn't want Emily to worry about the ninety-minute drive home, late at night, after drinking. It'd also give me the opportunity to spend some time alone with her. I wanted to get to know Emily better. And if I was lucky, make her smile, because she had a beautiful smile. *Stop it!*

When I asked, she declined so quickly I'd barely finished asking. I was disappointed, but knew it was probably for the best. I thought about trying to convince her but reminded myself that this was a job, even if it felt more personal to me, and I had to respect her wishes.

I'm her bodyguard, not her friend, at least while I'm on the clock. After she gave me Ashley's address and phone number, I reminded her to drive conservatively so I wouldn't lose her on the highway.

She laughed. "I've never been a speed demon."

"Good to know. I'll be at your place by four, we can leave as soon as I relieve Jack."

"Okay." She paused. "Thanks for not forcing me to take the ride."

"You're welcome." I hadn't considered how aggressive I might have sounded if I tried to force the issue. *Now I'm glad I didn't.* The last thing I wanted to do was remind her of her abusive ex.

Chapter 13

Emily

Soon after emailing Meg about my trip to Dallas to visit Ashley, I got a text from Jamie asking me if I had a minute to talk. He asked for a few more details, then offered to drive me there and back, saying it made sense to take one car instead of two.

It made perfect sense, but I didn't think I could sit in a car alone with him for ninety minutes.

Thankfully, Jamie didn't push back when I said I wanted to drive. Though I felt bad because he'd follow me there, wait alone outside, then follow me home. *Should I tell Ashley I can't stay late so Jamie doesn't have to sit in the parking lot too long?* No, I shouldn't, it was part of the job.

The other reason I didn't want a ride was a matter of independence. Craig would offer to drive me places, sometimes insisting, then he'd sit outside fuming that I was wasting his time. No matter how quickly I returned, he'd complain that I took too long. So, the idea of Jamie driving me and waiting outside, was more than I wanted to deal with right now.

I knew it wasn't the same, but that didn't mean I could stop myself from thinking about it. Chris was paying Jamie to keep me safe; it was literally his job to sit outside and wait. Safe from the very man the situation was reminding me of. *It's not fair to compare them. He's nothing like Craig.*

When I asked Jamie if he remembered Ashley, he said yes. And I knew she'd remember him, she'd always thought Jamie was 'super-hot' and had no problem saying so. It might have been an issue for us having the hots for the same guy, but Jamie was so in love with Isabelle that we didn't stand a snowball's chance in Texas of ever going out with him, and we knew it.

I fought the urge to wave to Jamie as I walked to my car. It was weird ignoring him, but I didn't want to get in trouble, so I did as I was told.

Jamie called me a few minutes before we got to Ashley's and asked me to stay in my car after I parked until he gave me the all clear. It seemed like overkill to me; there was no way Craig could know about my plans, so there was no reason to think he'd be waiting for me.

I tapped my hands on the steering wheel while I waited for him to finish. A few seconds after Jamie parked in the guest spot next to me, my phone lit up with a text alert.

> Have fun tonight. I'll be right here if you need anything.

Thanks.

As I waited for Ashley to buzz me in, I started to feel bad about Jamie having to wait for me. But that triggered more memories of Craig, and I didn't want to think about him.

Anytime I went somewhere without him he'd accuse me of cheating on him or keeping secrets if I left out one tiny unimportant detail during his interrogation. I couldn't even go on a run without him telling me I looked like a slut, whatever that meant. He was the reason I hadn't seen Ashley in so long.

Well, fuck him. I'm having guilt- free fun tonight.

Choosing to forget about Craig, and Jamie, my anger turned to excitement as I saw Ashley get off the elevator. It had been far too long since I'd seen her. *Fucking Craig.* I'd let him control too much of my life. I squared my shoulders.

Not anymore! Wanting, needing, to vent with a friend, I couldn't wait to get this night started. Ashley would make me laugh as we thought of creative ways to curse Craig.

Ashley opened the door and immediately pulled me into a tight hug as she said, "I'm so glad you're here. I've missed you so much!"

"I missed you too." Dammit, I said I wouldn't get all weepy, but here I was tearing up before we even finished saying hi. I blinked away the tears before they could fall free from my eyes. Tonight was for reconnecting with my best friend, cursing asshole exes, and having fun. I'd brought two bottles of wine to make sure that happened. I didn't think we'd drink them both, since I'm not usually a big drinker, but I figured I'd leave whatever we didn't finish here.

"You look great," I said after we broke the hug. Her dark brown hair was in a ponytail, and she didn't have any makeup on. She didn't need it, she was naturally beautiful. And judging by how fit she looked, she clearly still worked out. We used to run together in high school and college, but that was pre-Craig. I had to stop running because of Craig, so I did yoga and body weight exercises at home instead. I had to do something, he'd complain if I gained any weight, even though he wouldn't let me run or go to the gym.

Then it dawned on me. "I can run again."

"What?"

I hadn't meant to say it out loud, but apparently, in my excitement, I had. "Nothing, just thinking out loud."

Ashley's two-bedroom third-floor apartment was spacious. The living space and small galley kitchen had gorgeous hardwood floors. Unusual for an apartment. I told her my apartment in Houston hadn't been half this nice, but at least I had a decent sized kitchen. Though I wouldn't mind having a small kitchen in my next place, because it'd be all mine.

"Oh, I don't care about the kitchen, I eat out more than I cook so it's fine."

"Some things never change." We laughed as I put the bottles of wine on the counter. She grabbed two stemless wine glasses.

"I'm glad you finally left Craig. It's no secret I never liked that asshat, too fucking controlling."

"Thanks. It feels good to be free." I'd told Ashley on the phone I'd left him, but hadn't filled her in on all the ugly details. That wasn't a conversation I wanted to have over the phone.

"How bad did it get?" she asked.

"Bad. Let's open one of these bottles, order some food, and catch up on the good stuff before we go there."

"Sounds good." She gave me a quick side hug, expressing her understanding and sympathy without words. "You want Chinese or pizza?"

"Chinese."

Ashley ordered us enough food to feed a small army. When I asked why she ordered so much, she said she always ordered extra so she had leftovers. I couldn't argue with that, leftovers had been a staple in college. Sometimes eaten cold.

Craig hated leftovers, said I was just being lazy if I served them. *Forget about him!*

We opened the red blend first and put the white in the fridge to chill. Ashley poured two very generous glasses before we plopped down on the couch and started talking.

Ashley shared a few of her dating adventures. She was currently a serial dater, claiming she wasn't ready to settle down. I envied her strength and carefree lifestyle. *Ashley would never let a man hit her.* I didn't think I could be quite as carefree, or be as adventurous, as Ashley. *But it might be fun to try.*

Ashley suggested we got to a nightclub to celebrate my new freedom and maybe hook up with some hot guys. When I told her I wasn't quite ready yet, she chuckled and said she'd make it her life's mission to take me out.

"Maybe we start with something a little less crazy in a few weeks." I wanted to wait until things with Craig had settled down a bit and I no longer needed protection. *I still haven't told Ashley.*

After our food arrived, we sat on the floor and ate at the coffee table. White cardboard containers full of tasty Chinese food covered half the surface. I thought the Egg Rolls and Crab Rangoon were average, and the General Tso Chicken was too spicy, but the Cashew Chicken and Pork Fried Rice were perfect. Fried rice was a staple any time I ordered Chinese. At least it was when I wasn't with Craig, he always reminded that rice would make me fat.

Stop thinking about him.

Before long, we'd finished the red wine and opened the white. Ashely and I agreed it went really well with the fortune cookies. But that might've been the wine speaking since we didn't actually know anything about pairing wine with food.

After we cleaned up and put the leftovers in the fridge, we refilled our wine glasses and sat back down on the couch.

"Okay Em, spill it. What made you finally leave Craig?" Ashley sat on the far end of the couch, and turned so she was facing me, her legs criss-crossed.

I studied my wine to buy myself a second before lifting my head and looking into her chocolate brown eyes. "He hit me." My voice was barely above a whisper.

"Oh Em." She reached out for my free hand and squeezed it. "I'm so sorry. Are you okay?"

"I am. He got arrested; a neighbor called the police." I pulled my hand away and cradled my wine in both hands, hoping to find some courage in my glass. "It wasn't the first time the neighbors called the police, or the first time he hit me. But it was the first time I pressed charges."

"I'm so sorry, I knew he was controlling, but I didn't think he'd hit you. Is he still in jail?"

"No, he made bail. Chris is worried he might come after me for revenge."

"Fuck. Is there somewhere safe you can go?"

"I'm staying with my mom and dad until I figure out if I want to stay in Weatherford." I gulped my wine. *How is this my life?* I figured now was as good a time as any to bring up my shadow. "Do you remember Jamie Sheppard?"

"Oh yeah." She nodded, a grin on her face. "He was so hot! What about him? You got a thing for him?" Ashley had a wicked gleam in her eyes like she was waiting on some juicy tidbit of gossip.

"What? No. Nothing like that. He and his father started a personal protection and investigation company shortly after Isabelle was killed."

"That's right. Didn't he see it happen?"

"No, but he was the first officer on the scene. It almost destroyed him." I took a deep breath and got back on topic. "Chris hired his company, and Jamie is one of the guys watching out for me in case Craig comes after me."

"Oh really? Is he still hot? God, we had the biggest crush on him, remember that? Is he still single? Any chance you can set me up with him?"

I laughed at her rapid-fire questions. *I knew she'd ask if he was single.*

"You're blushing."

Am I?

She sounded like a teenager again, reminding me of junior high when we would tease each other for thinking boys were cute. "You like him!"

"It's not like that. It's just, I'm grateful he's helping me, that's all."

She squinted her eyes at me. "You didn't answer my question, is he still hot?"

I rolled my eyes at her persistence. "Yes, he's still hot, more ruggedly handsome than he was in school. And he's definitely stayed in good shape." I thought about how strong he felt when he'd wrapped his arms around me to steady me at the apartment.

"Hmmm, sounds to me like maybe you're more than just grateful." She wiggled her eyebrows at me. She was only half-serious, and trying to lighten the mood, but I rushed to defend myself anyway.

"Don't be stupid, I just got out of a nasty relationship." I tried to brush her off. "I don't have it in me to have feelings for anyone."

"You have that look on your face." I'd forgotten how well Ashley could read me.

"I don't. Besides, he's Chris's best friend, so I couldn't even if I wanted to. That, and I'm just the pesky little sister from high school, and a client, to him. He'd never go for someone like me."

Shit, I hadn't meant to say that out loud. I knew she'd twist my words and think I wanted him to like me, but it would never happen. Besides, I didn't really like him in that way. I'd never deny that he was easy on the eyes, or that he was caring and sweet. *But I don't like him like that.* I think of him more as the protective, big brotherly type, not the boyfriend type, right? *So why am I working so hard to convince myself?*

"I repeat: Hmmm." Ashley took a sip of wine and wiggled her eyebrows above the rim. I couldn't help but laugh at her.

"Is there someone outside now?" she asked as she got up and went to the window.

"Yes, Jamie, but you can't see him from here."

"Bummer. I was going to check out just how in shape he still is." She sat back down. "Seriously though, are you doing okay with all of this? You seem calm, but I'm worried about you. What if asshat comes looking for you?"

"The guys from SSI." She raised her eyebrows in question and I realized I hadn't told her the name of their company. "Sheppard & Sons Investigations will stop him. Besides, I have a restraining order against him. He knows if he comes within fifty feet of me, he'll go back to jail."

"A restraining order is just a piece of paper, Em. People violate them all the time. A co-worker's ex-girlfriend violated the one he placed against her—she hit him with a hammer."

My hand flew to my mouth as I gasped.

"He's okay. But my point is, it can't stop him." Ashley put one concern to rest.

"Jamie said the same thing." I paused to collect my thoughts before continuing. "Craig actually showed up at the apartment while we were packing the rest of my things. Jack and Jamie stopped him from hurting me."

"Jesus. What a stupid ass."

"Agreed." I held my glass up, and we clinked. "I just wish I'd seen it sooner."

"None of this is your fault, Em. Please don't blame yourself for seeing only the good in people."

"Thanks." *Chris said the same thing.*

"Do you have someone with you twenty-four-seven?"

"Yeah, but they're not with me so much as shadowing me. Jamie said their goal is to see, and stop, Craig before he gets to me."

"Hey, didn't you date Jamie's brother, Jack?"

I laughed and nodded. "Yeah. We went on a few dates, but we didn't click."

"He was hot too." I could see Ashley's thoughts. "Do you know if he's still single?"

"He's not. He works at SSI, so does his fiancé. Well, technically, he's part owner."

"Wow. That's cool." She stood up and held out her hand for my wineglass. "I'll pour us some more wine, then we'll gossip about everyone from high school."

"I'd rather hear about your adventures!" I yelled at her as she walked to the kitchen.

I checked my phone out of habit. Craig would get pissed if I didn't reply to his texts fast enough. Then shook my head to clear it. *He won't text me.*

My heart just about stopped when I saw a text alert pop up. He wouldn't be dumb enough to text me. *Would he?*

I breathed a sigh of relief when I saw the text was from Jamie. He wanted to check that everything was going okay, and ask if I knew what time I'd be leaving.

I texted back that I could leave now if he wanted to go home. *Dammit, Craig had trained me too well.* Then I got mad at myself for being so spineless. Jamie was getting paid to be here, so I could stay as long as I wanted.

Shame replaced my anger when I read his almost instant reply. "Nah, stay as long as you like. I was just curious. Have fun. Text me when you're ready to leave."

I'd totally over-reacted. Of course, Jamie was nothing like Craig. I sent a quick text to say thanks, hoping to put my phone away before Ashley saw it.

"What's that look for? Who are you texting?" She handed me my wineglass.

"Nothing. No one. Jamie was just checking in."

Ashley and I opened, and finished, a third bottle of wine as we gossiped. It felt so good to relax without having to worry about getting yelled at when I got home. Though I should text my parents and let them know I was still here and everything was fine, so they didn't worry. I sent my mom a quick text, knowing she'd tell my dad.

She replied a few minutes later: we know.

What the fuck? I'd expected her to say thanks or, I don't know, something, but not: we know. How'd she know?

I typed as fast as I could, wanting to be done with this conversation before Ashley came back from the bathroom.

When I asked, how? Mom responded with, Chris told us.

I should have known Chris would call Jamie and check up on me. He should have called me, not Jamie, if he was worried. I was probably over-reacting, but I was sick and tired of guys not trusting me and checking up on me and telling me what to do.

Maybe it was the wine going to my head. Or maybe it was because I was more sensitive lately, crying over the littlest things, getting angry over the stupidest things, then crying about the fact that I was mad for no real reason. *God, I'm a mess.*

I was thinking about what I wanted to say to Chris to convey my irritation when Ashley interrupted my thoughts.

"Who pissed in your boots?" Ashley asked a second before I felt the couch move as she plopped down beside me. I was so focused on being mad at Chris I didn't hear her come back in.

"Fucking Chris. He called Jamie and checked up on me." I hadn't intended to sound so angry, but couldn't help it. "Can you believe this shit?" It'd been a long time since I'd had this much to drink and I could hear my words slurring.

"Okay, calm down. This is Chris you're talking about, he probably wanted to check in without interrupting you."

"Maybe, but I'm still pissed."

"How'd you even find out? Did Jamie rat on him?" She was giggling.

"No, I didn't want my mom and dad to worry, so I texted them to let them know I was still here. But they already knew because Chris had told them."

"Em, it's sweet how much he cares, and it was actually kind of nice of him to make sure your parents weren't worried."

"Maybe." She had a point, but I still wanted to be angry. I'd never been an angry person, sure I'd get mad occasionally but I never stayed angry just for the sake of being angry. But right now, angry felt good.

Must be all the pent up frustration from living with Craig and never being allowed to argue or have anything other than happy feelings around him.

Ashley refilled my glass as soon as it was empty. I'd passed tipsy a few glasses ago and probably should've said no. I usually stopped drinking at the first signs of being tipsy, knowing I'd get screamed at if I came home drunk. *But Craig isn't here and he can't ever yell at me again. So I'm going to drink as much as I want.* My inner voice sounded like a bratty twelve-year-old, and I suddenly had the urge to stick my tongue out at the voices in my head, which caused me to bust out laughing.

"What's so funny?"

I tried to tell her but couldn't without the image of me sticking my tongue out, thumbs in my ears and fingers wiggling, every time I tried. *I've finally lost it.*

"Come on Em, I want to laugh with you." Ashley sounded as much like a twelve-year-old as I felt, which only made me laugh harder.

I finally caught my breath enough to answer. "Nothing, I was just thinking about how long it's been since I could drink without getting yelled at for being drunk. And then-"

I started laughing again, I held up my hand to signal she should wait, "Then I saw myself sticking my tongue out at the world because he can never yell at me again."

"Not sure the first part is funny, but I'm down with the rest of it." She raised her glass. "To getting drunk-I-mean-having-fun without getting yelled at and giving the world the middle finger."

We clinked glasses and lost control, laughing until tears streamed down our faces. Every time we stopped laughing one of us would do or say something that'd set us off again. Then I started snorting, which made us laugh even harder. It was a vicious cycle. When we finally stopped, Ashley drained her glass, stood up and put her hands on her hips, looking very determined.

Oh shit, what's she doing?

"Let's go say hi to this sexy bodyguard of yours."

"He's not, I don't think, it's not-" I was too drunk to form a full sentence. I wasn't supposed to acknowledge or draw attention to him unless I needed help. Which I most definitely did not.

I also didn't want him to see me drunk.

"Oh, come on, it's not like I'm a stranger. We'll just say hi and ask him if he wants some Chinese food or maybe some wine."

I hesitated, but she reached down and pulled me up. I gave up arguing as my drunk mind overruled what little logic I still possessed. We walked, or more accurately, stumbled, out the door, down the hall and into the elevator. We stumbled off the elevator, arm in arm, laughing. Jamie was halfway to the lobby door by the time we got there.

"Is everything okay?"

Shit, he sounded worried. "How'd he know we were coming out?"

I didn't realize I'd asked out loud until he answered me. "I saw you get off the elevator and stumble towards the door. Are you okay?"

Fear had a sobering effect. I looked down at my feet, too embarrassed, too worried, to answer. *He's going to be mad at me.*

"We're good. Very, very good." Ashley was practically drooling as she gave Jamie the once over. I looked up to see Jamie staring at me and blushed, knowing I must look like the drunken fool I was.

"We, um, Ashley-" *I'm so embarrassed.* He's going to be mad, and he'd probably tell my brother. *I'm in so much trouble.*

"What's she's trying to say is, would you like to come up and have some Chinese food and wine?"

"Thanks, but I'm good. I'll walk you back to your apartment, then come back down." Jamie answered Ashley without taking his eyes off of me. "You shouldn't be walking around in your condition."

"Why? We've got you to protect us." When Ashley put her hand on Jamie's arm, he gently removed it. She wasn't slurring, or tripping over her words as much as I was, but she was definitely acting drunk. Ashley was a flirt in general, but she was a much bigger flirt when drunk.

This was a bad idea; we shouldn't have come down. *Jamie will be so angry with me.* I wasn't supposed to draw attention to the person shadowing me and here we were talking about it in the lobby.

"Aw come on, don't be a party-pooper," Ashley whined.

Jamie never took his eyes off me. Instead of answering Ashely, he asked, "How much have you had to drink, Emily?"

"I um, I'm not sure." I couldn't tell if he was upset or disappointed. Expecting to get yelled at, I mentally braced myself.

"A lot!" Ashley answered eagerly. "She's finally free from Asshat Craig so let her have some fun."

"Alright, let's get you two upstairs." I wasn't sure, but I thought I detected humor in his voice. "Ashley, Emily is in no condition to drive, can she stay here tonight?"

"Hell yeah, BFF Sleepover." Ashley raised her hands in the air like a cheerleader leading her squad.

I wanted to share in Ashley's girlish joy at the thought of a sleepover, but I couldn't let go of my worry that I'd be in trouble when Jamie told Chris. *Jamie's just being nice, and not yelling, because Ashley's here.* I'd hear about it tomorrow. From Jamie, and Chris. *I just know he'll tell Chris all about this.*

"Emily, it's okay that you're having fun. We all," he paused and grinned before continuing, "have fun from time to time. But you can't drive like this. Do you want me to text Chris so he and your parents don't worry?"

Wait, what? Did he just ask me what I want? Was I wrong when I assumed he'd report me back to Chris? Would he tell them I'm staying without mentioning that I got drunk?

I needed to answer him.

"I'll tell them." Then I added as an afterthought, "Thanks."

When we reached Ashley's door, she asked, "You sure you don't want to come in?" She batted her eyelashes as she spoke.

"If it's okay, I'll just use the bathroom, then leave you two to your sleepover."

The minute Jamie was out of sight, I slapped at Ashley's arm. "What the fuck Ash, you practically threw yourself at him."

"Sorry." She raised her eyebrows at me. "You said you didn't like him, but you sound… a bit jealous. Tsk Tsk." She wagged her finger at me like a scolding school marm.

"Shhhh." I put my hand over her mouth and looked over her shoulder. Jamie was coming back.

"Alright, I'm going to leave you two to your fun." He grinned. "I recommend drinking some water and maybe taking some aspirin before going to bed."

God, he has a sexy grin. I bet he's a good kisser.

Must be the alcohol talking, or Ashley's influence. If I said it enough, I'd believe it. *I mean, I can think a guy has a sexy grin without liking him. Right?*

"You sure you don't want to stay?"

"I can't, I'm working."

What the fuck, is he into Ashley? Why did it sound like he would've said yes if it weren't for me? And why does it bother me?

"It was good seeing you again, Ash."

"No one calls me Ash anymore."

"Sorry, Ashley. Emily, call me if you need anything, okay? I'll be right outside."

"Are you really going to sleep in your SUV all night?" My voice sounded small and shaky, guilty.

My emotions were all over the place, and being drunk wasn't helping me sort through them.

"I won't be sleeping. But yeah, as long as you're here, I'm here."

I opened my mouth to apologize, but he cut me off. He must have known I was about to apologize because he took one of my hands.

"No apologies. It's part of the job. Now go have fun with Ashley. You deserve a worry free night out."

Whoa. I wasn't expecting that. I'd expected him to be mad, tell me to be more responsible, tattle on me to Chris, but he didn't do any of those things. *He said have fun.*

Ashley didn't wait for him to get out the door before saying, a bit too loudly, "He's hot and sweet. I'd totally hit that."

I saw Jamie shake his head and was glad I couldn't see his expression. I was sure he'd lose his patience soon if she didn't stop acting like a gushing school girl. At the elevator he turned around and waved, I could see him chuckling; relief flooded my system as most of the worry drained from my body.

"Remember to lock the door. Goodnight ladies."

"Goodnight Jamie," Ashley and I said in unison. We looked at each other and started laughing. I was laughing because I was so embarrassed at how we'd acted, and relieved that Jamie wasn't mad, that I couldn't do anything else. I didn't know why Ashley was laughing so hard.

She locked the door and secured the door chain, then turned to look at me. "Let's get into pjs and watch a chick flick while we eat cold Chinese and drink more wine."

"Ew, cold Chinese does not sound good to me right now."

We scrounged up some snacks instead, poured more wine, and plopped down on the couch to watch a rom com. A movie we both loved and pretty much knew by heart. We talked throughout the movie, quoting our favorite lines along the way.

We giggled, a lot, and I cried a little. We finished our fourth bottle.

Despite taking Jamie's advice and drinking water, we'd probably still have nasty hangovers in the morning.

Before going to bed, I called Jamie and put him on speakerphone. I was drunk enough to not care about the rules anymore.

Of course, his first question was, are you okay? I told him we were fine, to which Ashley and I both giggled. Ashley told Jamie she insisted he come up and sleep on the couch instead of in his truck.

"I won't be sleeping."

"You could if you'd stop being stubborn and just come up here."

"Ashley, I can't sleep because I'm working."

We rolled our eyes at him.

"You can be Broody McBroodypants Bodyguard from the comfort of my apartment."

I hiccupped. She giggled. We really shouldn't have called him. I apologized and Ashley threatened to keep calling him until he gave in.

Jamie said he recognized a losing battle when he saw one and said, "You win. I give up, I'll come up when you're ready to go to bed."

"We're ready now, so come on up," she said sounding like a game show host.

Chapter 14

Jamie

Ashley had always been a force to be reckoned with, and it appeared time hadn't mellowed her one bit. She'd convinced Emily to call me, then insisted I sleep on her couch. I'd never admit it to them, but a sleepless night on Ashley's couch sounded way better than a sleepless night in my SUV. It was going to be a long night and my bladder already felt like it held my body weight in coffee, so it'd be nice to have a bathroom nearby.

I'd probably help myself to some of the left Chinese food they'd offered earlier. Meg had packed a sandwich and some snacks, but it wasn't enough to get me through an overnight shift. In her defense, she would have packed more if she'd known I'd be staying. I'd been up since six that morning and knew I'd need more food and coffee to stay awake. *I'm not as young as I used to be.* Overnight stakeouts after a full day in the office weren't as easy as they used to be.

I rang the bell so Ashley could buzz me in. She was waiting at the door when I got off the elevator, waving like a maniac. I held back my laugh as I waved back. I ushered her inside, then closed and locked the door behind us before saying, "Thanks."

Ashley pushed me towards the couch. "Your bed for the evening thir."

I didn't bother hiding my amusement. I was pretty sure she was trying to sound like a butler and failing miserably. Partly because she was slurring her words, partly because she was wobbly on her feet, and partly because she couldn't stop giggling. Neither of them could. They reminded of Madi's slumber parties when we were kids.

"Thanks Ash." Then I remembered and corrected myself, "Ashley." I gave her a quick half bow, which set off another giggling fit. My God, they're like a couple of teenagers tonight. Then I smiled; Emily needed a night like this. No worries, no fear, just fun.

I tried not to notice how cute Emily looked in Ashley's pajamas. At least I assumed they were Ashley's since Emily hadn't planned on staying the night. The bright pink shorts and matching tank top had cute little designs all over them. The shorts showed off Emily's lean legs. Muscular, but not too bulky. *Sexy.* Shit, I shouldn't be thinking about her legs. *It's better than thinking about her small, firm breasts pushing against the thin fabric.* I shifted my stance to hide the uncomfortable evidence of my reaction.

Get your head in the game, Sheppard!
Emily blushed. *Shit.* She'd noticed me staring.

Ashley broke the silence, which couldn't have been more than a few seconds, but felt like a lifetime. "Come on, Em, let's give your hot bodyguard some privacy." She grabbed Emily's arm and turned her down the hall towards the bedrooms. They skipped arm in arm, or tried to—they bumped into the walls a lot. I heard Ashley's loud whisper, "If we're lucky, he sleeps naked."

"You suck at whispering Ash." I laughed as I used her old nickname, just to be a wiseass.

"I wasn't trying to whisper, James," she called back over her shoulder.

Touché. She obviously remembered that I didn't liked being called James—it always felt too formal.

I set my phone alarm to go off every sixty minutes, it wasn't my intention to fall asleep, but I was only human. After setting the alarm on vibrate so it wouldn't accidentally wake the girls, I turned the TV on, lowed the volume, and watched old sitcoms to pass the time. I'd dozed off a few times throughout the night and was grateful I'd set my alarm. I wasn't worried about taking cat-naps, knowing I was between the door and Emily and would wake up at the slightest sound, but after his stunt at her apartment, I didn't want to risk sleeping too long or too soundly.

Around six-thirty, I started a fresh pot of coffee. By that point, I'd been up for over twenty-four hours and was in desperate need of a cup. While it brewed, I searched the fridge for something to make for breakfast. Emily and Ashley would need something greasy when they got up. Unless they were still drunk, which they might be. They had a lot to drink last night. Unfortunately, Ashley's kitchen was pretty bare bones. *Apparently, she doesn't like to cook.*

There were a few eggs and some cheese in the fridge and I lucked out when I found a pound of bacon in the freezer. *Perfect hangover food.* I put the bacon in the sink to thaw, then poured myself a coffee and checked my emails. I'd emailed Meg at the office after texting Jack last night, wanting there to be an official record of the overnight stay at Ashley's. It didn't affect billing since we were providing round-the-clock coverage, and I was volunteering my time, but I'd always been detailed oriented and was a stickler for keeping accurate records.

I checked the clock: seven-thirty. I didn't expect the girls to wake up for a while, but I was hungry, so I started frying the bacon. The thick, rich smell quickly filled the tiny kitchen. I ate a slice while I cooked the second batch. While the last pan of bacon was sizzling, I scrambled some eggs, then cooked them in the bacon grease, sprinkling on some grated parmesan cheese. I'd offer to replace the food I cooked this morning, though I didn't think Ashley would mind since I'd feed them, too.

I'd just sat down to eat at the bar separating the kitchen from the living room when I heard groaning coming from the hallway. I stood up and checked to see who it was. "Morning Ashley. How're you feeling?"

She lifted her head and grunted at me. Her hair was a rat's nest, and her eye makeup was smudged, giving her a raccoon mask.

"I made coff-."

She perked up as she cut me off, "Do I smell bacon?" Her voice was deep and scratchy.

"You do. I can cook you some eggs too, if you want."

"Marry me," she said as she walked by me, rubbing her temples.

I followed her to the kitchen and watched her pour herself a huge mug of hot coffee. Her large yellow mug had a smiley face on it, in complete contrast to the grumpy expression she currently wore. She inhaled deeply, her nose almost touching the dark liquid. "Mmm, thanks."

"You're welcome." I grabbed the eggs from the refrigerator and turned around to find Ashley sitting in my chair, eating my breakfast. I chuckled; apparently, she couldn't wait.

She looked up sheepishly. "Oops." She circled the fork over the plate. "Was this yours?"

I couldn't help but notice she'd used the past tense. If I wanted my breakfast back, I'd have to fight her for it. Not that I would, it was her food. "Eat up. I'll make more." I grabbed a bottle of water from the fridge and put it down in front of her. "Drink this."

She shoved another bite into her mouth, then thanked me around a mouthful of eggs.

I cooked more eggs and topped off my coffee. We ate in silence, except for the occasional happy moan Ashley made every couple of bites.

"I almost feel human again." Ashley leaned back and finished her bottle of water. "Aspirin should fix the rest."

"I'm surprised you're up this early. I expected the two of you to sleep in for a few more hours."

"Em might, she's a lightweight, but not me, I do this all the time." She glanced up at me and backtracked. I wasn't judging, but she felt the need to explain, anyway. "Not get crazy drunk, but I drink often enough that I've built up a tolerance over the years. Don't judge."

"No judgment." I raised my hands in surrender. "I'm just glad it was here and not at a club where it'd be harder to keep an eye on her."

"Is she really in danger? I mean, I know you're all afraid Asshat Craig might come after her, but how realistic is that?"

I grinned, loving the nickname they'd given Emily's ex. "It's hard to say, but based on his history of drunken violence, we're assuming it's likely." I couldn't tell her anymore than that without violating our client confidentiality agreement. Besides, it was Emily's place to tell her, not mine. Though it was safe to assume Emily had already told her some of what had happened.

"So you probably wouldn't approve of me dragging her out to go dancing one night." Something about her posture made me think this was a test.

"It's my job to keep her safe, not to tell her what to do" I sipped my coffee and thought about how much I'd hate it if she went out dancing. *I don't think I can handle watching guys hit on her.* "It might make our job a little more difficult, but we can handle it."

"So it wouldn't bother you if I took her out and tried to hook her up with some hot guy in tight jeans for the night?"

I almost spit out my coffee. "Jesus Ash. No, it wouldn't bother me."

So why did I feel like I was lying? The thought of Emily going out and meeting people, men, shouldn't bother me. She's an intelligent, beautiful woman, and she deserves to have fun. Just not with hot guys. *No, that's none of my business. She can do whatever she wants.* And she should. She should totally go out and have some fun. I could feel my shoulders tightening as I thought about some guy grinding up against her.

"Riiiiight," she drew it out while nodding her head slowly. "You're not a very good liar, Jamie."

"Just thinking about the logistics of providing protection in a loud and noisy nightclub, that's all." I lied, again, as I got up and cleared our dishes, hoping she'd drop the subject. I didn't want to think about how I'd reacted. And I sure as hell didn't want to think about how strongly I felt about breaking the arms off any random guy who touched her.

"Lucky for you, she's not interested in going out." She paused for dramatic effect. "At least not yet."

I didn't give her the satisfaction of getting a rise out of me. Instead, I grabbed the coffeepot and refilled my mug, then held it up in her general direction. "Refill?"

"Yes please. Anyone ever tell you you'd make a great housewife?"

I almost choked on my spit when I laughed. "No, they haven't. Though Isabelle used to tell me I was a great husband."

"I bet you were." Her tone turned more serious. "I'm sorry about Isabelle, Jamie. I didn't mean to remind you of your loss."

"Thanks. It's getting a little easier to talk about her as time passes." I hadn't meant to drag the conversation down with my confession.

"Hot and sensitive, you'll be a great catch for some lucky woman." She grinned before taking a sip of her coffee. "When you're ready."

"Thanks." I laughed. I was about to ask her how things were going with her when my phone buzzed. It was Chris, wanting to know how Emily was doing. I sent a quick reply, assuring him she was still sleeping, safe and sound, and said I'd check in when we got back to Weatherford. Then I called Jack and asked him to rearrange the schedule. The morning shift was due to start soon, but I'd be covering until Emily got home.

When I asked him for an update, he said, "Doug's reviewing the surveillance footage around Emily's office to see if Craig has shown up. So far nothing."

"Good. Let me know if he sees anything."

"Yes, sir." I could almost see his salute. "How's Emily this morning?"

"Still sleeping it off."

"Tell your hottie baby brother I said Hi." Ashley was waving her arm back and forth like a maniac.

"Ashley says hi."

She rolled her eyes at me when I refused to finish her message.

"Tell her your hottie baby brother says hi back." I heard him laughing as I relayed an abbreviated version of his message—edited for my sanity.

Then I remembered I was supposed to make breakfast for Meg. "Shit, tell Meg I'm sorry about breakfast. I'll make it up to her."

"Oh, she knows and be prepared, because you'll be making banana chocolate chip pancakes for the foreseeable future." My predicament clearly amused him.

"Do I need to go shopping on my way home or do we have everything I'll need?"

"Nope. Meg stocked up on pancake supplies last night. She didn't want you to have any more excuses."

"Surely keeping a client safe is an acceptable excuse." I chuckled.

"She's more than a client, and you know it."

"I didn't mean Emily." Damn it, I gave myself away. Trying to cover my tracks, I added, "It was a general statement about the only acceptable reason to skip out on making breakfast for Meg." I heard someone talking to Jack in the background.

"Dad says to take the rest of the day off and get some rest before your shift tonight. Just let us know what needs to get done today."

"Thanks, man. I'll do what I can while I'm here and let you know."

"No problem. Later Bro," Jack said before hanging up.

Well, that didn't go as expected. Jack was too perceptive for his own good. And while it made Jack a brilliant investigator, our best in fact, it annoyed the hell out of me when I was on the receiving end. He was smart, quick-witted, and perceptive. Qualities he chose to mostly ignore while in high school, but not only embraced but honed to a sharp edge while he was in the Army. If I was being honest with myself, I was a little jealous of his ability to think outside the box. I wasn't stupid or unobservant, but I generally thought inside the box.

I turned around when I heard Emily shuffling down the hallway. She looked miserable. Then again, who wouldn't?

"Good morning Emily." I watched as she lifted her hand to wave but didn't follow through, letting it fall instead. "I made coffee, eggs, and bacon if you want-"

She put her hand on her stomach and moaned. "Maybe just coffee and water for now." She sat down next to Ashley. "Why'd I let you talk me into drinking so much?"

Ashley got up and poured her a cup of coffee. "Do you still take cream and sugar? And don't blame me, you brought two bottles."

"Cream only. Thanks."

Now that I knew Emily was okay, I could go back to my SUV. I needed to get some work done, and I was supposed to be watching from a distance, not hovering over her shoulder. "Excuse me ladies, I'm going back downstairs. Call if you need anything."

"Aren't you going to make Emily breakfast?"

"She said she didn't want any," I answered Ashley, then turned my attention to Emily and offered again. "I can cook you some eggs if you want."

"That's okay. I'm not ready to eat yet." Her voice sounded shaky.

"Alright. Let me know when you're ready to leave."

"Thanks."

"You're welcome." I turned to Ashley. "Can you lock the door behind me." It wasn't a suggestion.

"Yes, sir." She stood up and saluted.

Why does everyone feel the need to salute me? When we got to the door, I handed her my card. "Emily isn't looking so good. Call me if she gets worse or if she needs anything."

"I'm sure she'll be fine after she eats and takes some aspirin. She won't be doing cartwheels or anything, but she'll be functional."

"I hope so." It crossed my mind that I might need to drive her home and come back later to get her car. I opened the door and turned to remind Ashley to lock the door, but she beat me to it.

"I know. I know. Lock the door." Her eye roll was less than subtle.

Emily didn't feel any better two hours later, when I went upstairs to use the bathroom, but kept insisting she was okay to drive. I took one look at her and couldn't, in good conscience, let her. After several minutes of arguing, I put my foot down and made my intentions clear.

"Your options are to stay here a while longer, or let me drive you home."

She crossed her arms over her chest and kept arguing, "This is stupid. How will I get my car home?"

"One of the guys will help me. You don't need to worry, just let me take care of the logistics. You're not looking so good."

Emily glared at me with blood-shot eyes. That hadn't earned me any brownie points.

"Please Emily, I'm worried about you driving."

Recognizing she needed me to ask, not demand; I changed tactics. "Let me help you. Please?"

"But…"

Not wanting to argue anymore, I asked, "Would you feel better if I billed you for the extra travel expenses?" I wouldn't, but I needed her to quit arguing so I could get her home safely. And so I could go home and get some much needed sleep.

I could see her contemplating her options as she stared at me. "I guess so. But it still seems stupid to me. I'm perfect–"

"Then it's agreed. I'll drive you home and come back later to get your car."

"What if I need my keys?" She stood up too quickly and wobbled on her feet. She tried to pretend it hadn't happened, but I raised my eyebrow to let her know I saw it.

"Do you have a spare set at your parent's house?" When she nodded, I said, "I'll have Doug pick up your spare set. Can you let your parents know it's okay to give them to him?" I could pick up the keys myself when I dropped her off, but I didn't want to get delayed by her parents.

"Sure." She sounded like an annoyed teenager, but at least she'd stopped arguing.

"Thank you." I thought about reminding her this was for the best, but kept my mouth shut. I didn't think she wanted to hear it. We said goodbye to Ashley, who had been shockingly quiet while Emily and I sorted out the ride home situation. Which was good, I didn't need her riling Emily up.

We didn't talk for the first thirty minutes of the ride. I had the radio on but turned down low so it wouldn't add to her headache. Not liking the silence, I'd attempted to start a casual conversation, only to have her grumble in response. I told myself it wasn't personal, but it still sucked. I'd thought she'd fallen asleep, with her head resting against the window, until I heard her sniffle.

"Emily, are you okay?" It was a stupid question, but I didn't know what else to ask.

"I'm fine." Her clipped reply made it obvious she was not fine.

"Look, I know you're upset with me because I didn't want you driving home in your condition."

"My condition?" She whipped her head around too fast and closed her eyes while she steadied herself. "I'm hungover, not dying." Her voice was barely above a whisper.

I only want to help. Why was she being so stubborn? "Yes, hungover. So much so that you made yourself dizzy just by turning to look at me. That could go bad fast on the road." I tried to reason with her.

"You're treating me like a child." I saw her wipe her cheeks from the corner of my eye. "Reporting my every move to Chris, and my parents, not letting me drive, telling me what to do."

"What? What are you talking about?" I'd checked in with Chris once, to tell him Emily was staying at Ashley's for the night, but hadn't said anything else.

"Did you tell Chris I was too drunk to drive home last night?"

"All I told Chris was that you were having such a great time that you thought it'd be easier to stay at Ashley's rather than come home late. I didn't mention the drinking."

Her beautiful, blue, bloodshot eyes opened wide as she realized her mistake. "Oh. I, um, I'm sorry." She looked out the window.

"It's okay." It wasn't. I didn't like the idea of her thinking I was like her ex. Not even a little.

I broke the silence after a few minutes; it was still bothering me she thought I was treating her like a child. I remembered Meg complaining about the same thing whenever Jack got too protective or 'all bossy' as she liked to call it. He thought he was doing the right thing and being helpful; she thought he was being overbearing and pushy. I didn't want Emily to feel that way.

"Emily." I waited for her to look at me. "I'm sorry if I seemed pushy about driving you home. Maybe I'm being selfish, but I don't think I could handle watching you get in a car wreck knowing I could have prevented it." There I said it. It was as much about me, and my fears, as it was about her.

Her eyes opened wide as she realized the depth of my fear. "I'm sorry Jamie. I didn't think about that." She sighed. "I guess I'm just tired of someone telling me what to do all the time."

"I can understand that." There was so much more I wanted to say, but I couldn't sort through it all. "I'll try to be less bossy in the future." I looked back over at her. "Forgive me?"

She smiled. "Yeah, I forgive you." She reached over and patted my hand. The warmth of her touch lingered after she pulled it away. "Thanks."

"You're welcome."

Chapter 15

Emily

This had to be the worst hangover I'd ever had, but that wasn't the reason I was being a grumpy bitch. That was because I was sick and tired of everyone telling me what to do.

Jamie took one look at me when I said I was ready to leave and insisted I wasn't safe to drive home. He was probably right; my head was throbbing, and I got dizzy if I moved it too fast. But I argued anyway because I didn't want him telling me what to do, even if I was kind of grateful he'd offered to drive me home.

I finally gave in, but made it clear I wasn't happy about it. Then I yelled at him on the way home. *God why am I being such a bitch? After everything he's done for me?*

When he mentioned his fear about seeing me in get in a car accident, I felt like a total asshole.

Reaching over to touch his hand when I apologized felt like the right thing to do. But I lingered longer than I'd intended before pulling my hand away. *I'm sure he didn't notice.*

We sat in silence for a few more minutes. I wanted to talk to him about going to the county fair for the Fourth of July festivities with Ashley, but wasn't sure how to bring it up after being so bratty. I didn't need his permission. *But I'm supposed to notify SSI of my plans.*

Ashley and I used to go every year when we were kids. First with our families when we were young, then with friends when we were old enough to go without our parents. It was a tradition we'd kept until I started dating Craig. He'd thought it was stupid, so I couldn't go.

Ashley said she'd come home for the weekend so we could go together and act like silly teen-age girls again. But I was afraid to ask Jamie because I was being so bitchy. Then I reminded myself that I didn't have to ask. I could make my own decisions. All I needed to do was tell him.

But what came out was a question.

"Ashley and I want to go to the county fair for the Fourth of July. Do you think it'll be okay?" Damn it, I sounded weak and whiny. *He'll say no.*

"Yeah, of course. We'll have to assign two bodyguards for the day, but it's totally doable." He looked over and smiled.

My jaw hit the floor. Well, not literally, but it might as well have. *That was too easy.* I'd expected him to say it would be too dangerous or something like that. *I should probably ask Chris since he'll get billed for the extra person.*

"Actually, Jack's taking Meg since she's never been and really wants to go. I was going to go with them. Would you have any objection to going with us? I think AJ's going too, so you'd have plenty of protection without feeling like you had an escort."

I hadn't thought he could shock me anymore, but I was wrong. Never in a million years would I have expected him to invite us to hang out with them.

I smiled. "That sounds perfect." *Shit, was that too eager?*

"Good." He smiled at me. "It's a date."

A date? Did he mean a date-date, or just a bunch of friends getting together date? I thought it'd be fun to go out with Jamie and the others. *But a date?* I was probably over-reacting, there was no way he just asked me out on a date. *It's just a figure of speech.* Crap, I hadn't even thought about Ashley, though I was sure she'd be okay with it. She'd joked about hooking up with Jamie, but she was just trying to force me to admit I liked him. *And now we're going on a date? Well, a group outing, but he said date.* I wasn't sure how I should feel. I mean, I was grinning like an idiot, despite my killer hangover. But I shouldn't get my hopes up or make this a bigger deal than it was. *I wonder what Chris will say?*

"Emily?" I turned at the sound of my name. "Everything okay?"

I had a feeling he'd called my name more than once. "Yeah, just thinking. I need to ask Ashley if she wants to go with the group."

"Let me know what she says, and we'll work it out."

It wouldn't be a date. Hell, it wouldn't even be a group outing. Because he'd be working. I was a fool for reading too much into it.

"I'm sure she won't pass up the opportunity to hang out with the hot Sheppard brothers."

Did I really just say that out loud? I was quoting Ashley, but Jamie wouldn't know that. I felt the heat rise in my cheeks and glanced out the window.

He chuckled. "She hasn't changed much, has she?"

"Not much, no." Then I felt the need to defend her, so I added, "There's a good person hiding beneath her party girl exterior."

He nodded, but I wasn't sure he believed me. Then again, he probably did. He'd known her a long time, and I was sure he knew she was more into having adventures and trying new things than partying just for the sake of it.

We filled the rest of the ride back talking about high school and college. I told him about my job as a web page designer slash social media manager and how much I loved it, especially since I could set my own hours and work on projects all over the world, all while working from home.

Jamie told me about his time on the police force, and then starting Sheppard & Sons Investigations with his father and Jack, who was a silent partner while he finished his tour in the Army. It surprised me when he said it was just him and his dad working out of John's house in the beginning.

I asked about his twin sister, Madi. We weren't really friends and only did things together because of our families, but I knew she and Jamie were close. Jamie beamed as he bragged about how great Madi was doing in the Navy. She was earning her nursing degree and was thinking of resigning her commission and looking for a job in the private sector. Madi had been quiet in school, at least compared to Jamie and Jack. Well, mostly Jack. Jamie was social, but wasn't as outgoing as Jack, and he didn't take risks. He hadn't wanted to ruin his chances of getting into the police academy.

I thought it was weird that Jamie was the only Sheppard who hadn't serve in the Military, even his dad served in the Marines before joining the Parker County PD. Not that I judged him for it. He'd gone to college on a full scholarship, graduated early, and went straight into the police academy. Being a cop was all he'd ever wanted. Jack wanted that too, but hadn't earned a free ride, so he joined the Army and took advantage of the GI Bill to pay for college.

When we came to a natural pause in the conversation, the soft music and steady hum of the tires on the pavement lulled me to sleep. I woke when I felt Jamie gently squeezing my shoulder.

I blinked a few times to get my bearings. Home. When I noticed Doug parked outside the house, I asked, "I thought Doug was going to get my car?"

"Change of plans. AJ and Jack had some business to take care of in the area, so they're doing it."

"When did you find out?" I asked, a little snappier than I should have.

"Meg sent a text while you were napping. I was going to tell you when you woke up, but you noticed Doug before I could."

"Sorry. I-"

"Please don't apologize."

I nodded; if I opened my mouth, I'd probably apologize again.

"They should be back in a couple of hours. I'll let you know if it changes." He smiled. "Call if you need anything. Now, go get some rest."

"Thanks, Jamie. You too." God, I sounded like an idiot. "I meant get some rest, I'm sure you won't need me." I laughed nervously.

"Thanks." He smiled. "Bye Emily."

"Bye." I got out and walked to the front door. My mom must have been watching for me because she opened it before I could put my key in the lock. I turned and waved to Jamie, who was waiting to make sure I got inside. Even though Doug was parked across the street.

We have a date. Not a real date, but it'd still be fun. I just need to ask Ashley if she wants to go with the group.

After a long nap, a hot shower, and some delicious homemade pot roast, I felt almost human again. I texted Ashley to tell her it wouldn't be a problem for us to go to the fair. Then I typed, erased, and retyped at least four attempts at mentioning that Jamie asked if I, *we*, wanted to join him, Jack and Meg. I didn't want to imply that he'd asked me out on a date, because he hadn't. *It's just a phrase.* Just a group of friends getting together, that's all.

I settled on phrasing it like it would be easier for them to do their jobs if we all went together.

> Jamie asked if we want to go to the fair with him, Jack, Meg, and AJ. I think it'd be more fun to go as a group instead of them following us around. What do you think?

I didn't tell her I'd gushed like a schoolgirl in a teen rom com when I told Jamie we could all go together.

> Sounds fun. Is AJ as hot as Jamie?

> *eye roll emoji* Is that all you can think about?

> No. Well, maybe. It'll be more fun if we each have our own hot guy to hang out with.

> I don't even know if he's single.

I might like the idea of having a hot, protective guy to hang out with, but knew I'd actually be alone. I was too tired to argue with her about her insinuation that Jamie and I would be hanging out as a couple, so I didn't. It was enough that I knew we wouldn't be.

> I'm still down. It'll be fun. Is Jack's fiancé nice?

> I only met her once, at the office, but she seemed nice enough.

Cool.

So, how are you feeling?

> Better. Sleep, lots of water, and some of mom's pot roast were just what the doctor ordered. You?

All good. I took a nap and am ready to hit the town tonight.

> Have fun. We'll plan for the 4th soon.

I planned on lounging around in comfy clothes and reading. *God, my life is so boring.*

After making myself some tea, I curled up with the fourth book in the Outlander series. I was totally hooked on the historical romance story of a modern English woman who falls back in time to seventeen-forty-three and meets the second love of her life, a gorgeous, strong Scottish highlander. Holding the book up to my nose, I inhaled. The smell of a new book was one of my favorite scents. I had to buy a new one to replace the copy Craig had destroyed. He'd destroyed all the books I had in this series, plus a few others. So far, this was the only one I'd replaced, because I was in the middle of reading it when I left him.

Sunday was a quiet day. I did some laundry and helped my mom make dinner. I decided to read before bed, but before long fell asleep with the book in my hand. When my alarm went off, I rolled over, dropping my book on the floor with a thud. Luckily, I pre-set my alarm to go off Monday through Friday or I might have overslept. *I must have been more tired than I thought.* I almost never fell asleep while reading.

During lunch, I called Chris to talk to him about going to the county fair. He thought it was a bad idea because it'd be harder for Jamie and SSI to protect me if Craig showed up.

It would have been a smarter choice to wait a few days before talking to him because he was still mad at me for getting drunk at Ashley's and spending the night without prior planning. I could have told him Jamie was okay with me going, and that Jack and AJ were going too. I also could have dropped it, and talked to him about it at a better time.

But I started a fight instead.

I was so tired of everyone around me treating me like a fragile child. I reminded him, loudly and with no shortage of snark, that Ashley and I had stayed in her apartment, safe and sound, with Jamie there the whole time. Then I yelled at him for spying on me during my night out. He tried to calm me down by saying he only checked on me because he was worried. *Whatever.*

I yelled back, "I don't need you to worry about me, I'm a big girl."

Then he had the gall to say, "I'm the one paying SSI so not only does it make sense for me to be kept in the loop, but I have every right to check on things, especially if your actions require extra services at the last second."

Not caring that I'd been worried about the extra costs, I screamed at him, "I have twenty-four-hour coverage, so it didn't cost you anything extra. And I didn't ask to have someone following me everywhere I go." My voice squeaked as tears welled up in my eyes.

I didn't asked for any of this.

Then I remembered I told Jamie to bill us for the extra time because Jack and AJ picked up my car. I should have apologized, but I was too angry, so I doubled down instead. "Jamie said it's not a problem." I spat out the words. *God, why am I acting like a brat?*

I paused, then apologized, and finally admitted that Jamie had said Ashley and I could go with him, Jack, and AJ since they were going anyway.

"If Jamie thinks it's safe for me to go, why don't you?" I asked, this time without the attitude.

"Maybe he's not as worried about you as I am," Chris sounded exasperated.

I don't know why it pissed me off, but it did. A lot. Did he really think Jamie didn't care about me? Or that he didn't care about doing his job well?

"Are you fucking serious, Chris? He refused to let me drive home because I was too hungover. He's almost as over-protective as you! And you can't tell me what I can and can't do. Jamie said I should invite you and Vicky to join us, so consider yourself invited." When Jamie first mentioned inviting Chris to join us, I'd thought it was a great idea. Now I was hurling the invite at him like a weapon.

"Come or don't come, whatever, but I'm going."

"Emily-"

"I have to get back to work." I hung up on him.

Not my finest moment.

I buried my face in my hands and cried.

One perk of working from home, no one can see me crying.

I didn't understand why I was being such a bitch to Chris. He didn't deserve it. He was worried about me, and I should be happy, grateful he cared. But I'd been lashing out any time he, or anyone, tried to tell me what to do over the last few days, which wasn't like me. I didn't get angry, and I certainly didn't yell at people.

I owe Chris an apology. I loved my big brother, and didn't want this lingering between us, so after washing my face, I called him back.

"Emi-"

I didn't give him time to finish before blurting out, "Chris, I'm so sorry. You didn't deserve that."

"Apology accepted." After a short pause, he added, "Em, I want you to know that I'm not trying to tell you what to do. I'm just worried, that's all." He sounded sad.

"I'm sorry. It's just, I've been extra sensitive to people trying to control me lately." I could feel the tears welling up in my eyes again. Anger wasn't the only emotion I was overly sensitive to lately.

"I guess I can understand that. Just remember I'm on your side, okay?"

"Okay."

"If I seem over-protective, it's because I never want to see you hurt like that again."

More tears. "Thanks Chris, you're the best big brother."

"Damn right I am." I could imagine him patting himself on the back. "And Em, if Jamie says it'll be okay, then I'll defer to his professional opinion. I'll talk to Vicky tonight; I'm sure she'd love to go."

Chapter 16

Jamie

I'd just relieved Dean, one of our part time security guys, on Tuesday evening when I saw Emily come out the front door in running gear. Jumping out of my truck and covering the distance to her front porch in a few long strides, I said, "Emily, you can't go for a run-"

Emily cut me off, anger oozing out with every word. "What do you mean, I can't go for a run? I'm so sick and fucking tired of everyone telling me what I can and can't do. You're supposed to be my shadow, not my boss."

I ran my hand through my hair. When she stopped to take a breath, I said, "Jesus Emily, will you let me finish? You can't go alone."

"Then shadow me," she spat back. Something, or someone, had pissed her right the fuck off, and I was getting the brunt of her anger.

"Emily." I tried again, this time choosing my words more carefully. "If you'll please give me a few minutes to change, I'd be happy to run with you." I could have followed her in the car, but I liked the idea of running with her instead.

She stared at me with her mouth hanging open. I'd taken the steam out of her fury. *Thank God.*

"You'd do that, run with me?"

"Yes. I have a gym bag in my truck. Would it be okay if I changed inside?" She nodded, so I asked, "Will you please wait inside for me to change?"

She stared down at her shoes, but I'd seen the hint of shame in her eyes before she did. "Yes."

I lifted my head towards the door. "Will you please wait inside while I go get my stuff?" I don't think I'd ever tried so hard to be overly polite.

She laughed. "Yeah, and Jamie?" She made eye contact. "I'm sorry I yelled at you. I've been extra grumpy lately, which is why I want to run. It clears my head."

I knew the feeling and had already forgiven her. "No worries, you've got a lot going on. I'll be back in a second."

It took me less than five minutes to grab my bag and change into my running shorts and shoes, and a t-shirt. I wondered if Emily was a hard runner or more of a jogger. *I'll find out soon enough.* After securing my gun in my running belt, I put my clothes in my bag.

It only took me a few minutes to grab my bag and change in the bathroom. As I walked back towards the front door, I took a second to appreciate Emily's outfit. Emily Taylor had grown into a beautiful woman, all traces of the awkward teenager I'd known growing up were gone. Her black leggings showed off every curve of her hips and ass, and her tight blue tank top matched the blue in her eyes. There were no traces of the bruises left on her perfect, pale skin. If I pulled her head back by her long blond ponytail, I could easily kiss the hollow at the base of her neck. *Shit! Where did that come from?* I couldn't even think about kissing Emily. Not only was it unprofessional, but her brother was my best friend. Emily was off-limits twice over.

I cleared my throat to break the silence. "Would you like for me to run with you, or follow behind?" I could easily do my job either way, so I figured I'd ask. Emily needed some opportunities to take back her power. *Not to mention she just bit my head off when she thought I was telling her what to do.*

"It's fine if you run with me. It'll be nice to have company, even if we don't talk."

"You got it. I'll let you set the pace and adjust to it, so don't worry about me. Okay?"

"What if I run a lot faster than you?"

My heart fluttered when I noticed the sparkle in her eyes. *She's teasing me.*

She'd done a one-eighty in the attitude department since I first confronted her on the steps; not that I was complaining.

"If you're going too fast, I'll swallow my pride and beg you to slow down for me."

She laughed and agreed. I didn't think I'd have to, but hell, if it made her laugh, I could pretend to be winded.

I took a second on the porch to give her some quick self-defense advice, finishing with, "Keep your eyes up and your head on a swivel."

Emily tilted her head back and looked up at the sky, then turned her head back and forth so fast she almost lost her balance.

I held back my laugh as I said, "Sorry, it means looking left and right, not staring at your feet, or phone. It also helps to keep the volume low, or only use one earbud, if you listen to music."

She blushed. "Oh, that makes a lot more sense."

Chapter 17

Emily

Damn. Jamie looked good in his running shorts. And his well-loved Parker County Police Academy t-shirt, which fit snug, showing off his flat stomach and thick biceps. *He's in great shape.* I had to force myself to look away as he walked towards me. My mother's ficus tree suddenly needed my undivided attention.

He gave me some safety tips, then we stretched. *I can't believe I teased him about running too fast for him to keep up.* I hadn't run in almost a year because of Asshat Craig.

After jogging for a few blocks to warm up, I picked up speed and ran at what I thought was a fast pace. Jamie ran beside me, always between me and the road, and matched me stride for stride. I felt a little awkward at first, but eventually I found my stride and settled into a rhythm.

I snuck a peek at Jamie when we stopped to wait for traffic at a four-way intersection. He was sweating, we both were, it was summer in Texas, but he didn't look winded. Not even a little. Unlike me, I wasn't gasping for air or anything, but I was grateful for the mini-break while we waited for the pedestrian light to change to the walk signal.

When we started running again I set a quicker pace, wanting to see if I could outrun him. He kept up without effort, so I pushed myself harder, speeding up again when we reached the running track at the park. He didn't bat an eye as he adjusted his stride to mine. It wasn't long before I was gassed and had to rest. *What was I thinking?* I spotted a water fountain and used taking a drink as an excuse to catch my breath. I doubted I was fooling Jamie with my I need for water act, but he didn't say anything other than: thanks, I needed a water break.

"Do you run a lot?" I asked as he wiped away water that had splashed on his upper lip.

"Not as much as I did when I was on the force, but often enough." His grin told me what I'd already guessed—I wouldn't be outrunning him. At least he was nice enough to not say it out loud. "How about you?"

"I haven't run in about a year." I didn't mention Asshat Craig. "And it probably shows." My laugh sounded nervous.

"You're keeping a good pace for taking a year off," he said it casually but I felt heat rise in my cheeks at the small compliment.

"Thanks. Ready?"

"Whenever you are." He winked as the left side of his mouth lifted in a lop-sided grin.

Is he flirting? Because he legit just winked at me.

I set a slow, steady pace for the run back. We both knew I couldn't out run him, so there was no point in running myself stupid trying.

When we got back to the house, I invited him in. "You can take a shower if you want." I didn't think he'd relish the idea of sitting in his car in sweaty gym clothes or putting on his street clothes without showering.

"That'd be great. Thanks," Jamie said before grabbing his bag and heading towards the full guest bath on the first floor.

I thought about running upstairs and showering, but decided it'd be better to wait until he was done. Most men I knew showered much faster than I did, mostly because of my long hair, and I wanted to see him again before he went back to shadowing me.

When Jamie was getting ready to leave, my mom invited him to stay for dinner.

"Thanks for the invite Mrs. Taylor, but I'm on the clock so I can't."

"But you'd be here with us, surely you could protect us from the inside as well as from the outside."

I had to constantly remind my mother that not only did she not need to feed the guys from SSI during their shifts, but she wasn't supposed to interact with them at all.

"Not quite as well. The idea is to see, and stop, him before he gets too close." Jamie showed off his diplomacy skills by adding, "But I wouldn't object to having some leftovers delivered curb side." He smiled at my mom, causing her whole face to light up. He'd made her day by letting her break his rules.

"I'll send Emily out with a plate."

"Thank you Mrs. Taylor."

"Please, call me Anne."

He nodded but didn't respond, instead he asked me, "Walk me to the door?"

My mom went to the kitchen while I walked with Jamie. I had a feeling he wanted to say something, so I waited for him to speak first.

"Does your mom try to feed everyone?" He didn't sound mad, just curious.

"She wants to, but I don't let her. She knows she's not supposed to talk to them but pretends to forget."

I shook my head and rolled my eyes. "Thanks for that. I know she means well but it's for everyone's safety that we ask you to ignore us while we're here." Jamie's hazel eyes looked distant, like he was thinking about something else. Not sad, per se, just thoughtful.

"You okay?"

Jamie blinked twice in rapid succession. "Yeah, I just wish things were different."

So do I, but I doubted he meant it the same way I did.

"Do me a favor, text me before you bring out my dinner. I want to make sure there aren't a lot of people milling around."

I nodded as I answered, "Sure, I can do that."

"Thanks Em. I'm right outside if you need me."

He called me Em. I smiled as I sprinted upstairs to my bedroom.

After dinner I got a text from Jamie, asking me if he could give Meg my number so we could arrange a time to get together. At first I thought it was weird, since Meg had my phone number but then it occurred to me that she had access to my number in a professional capacity but we hadn't exchanged numbers personally.

I texted back and said it was okay, and made sure to thank him. It meant a lot that he was asking instead of assuming. *He did that on our run too.*

A few minutes later I got a call from Meg. She said she couldn't wait to get to know me, claiming the Sheppards had lots of nice things to say about me. My small smile soon turned to a much bigger one when she asked if I wanted to meet at Grannie's the next day for lunch. I loved Grannie's and hadn't been there since I'd come home, so I readily agreed. We agreed to meet at one o'clock.

"Do I need to tell Jamie?" I corrected myself, "Or someone from SSI, that I'm going out for lunch tomorrow?"

Meg's soft laugh held no judgement when she said, "You just did. I'll take care of everything. See you tomorrow Emily."

Right. "Thanks. See you tomorrow."

We didn't talk for long, but I got the feeling I was going to like Meg.

The next day, Doug offered to drive me to Grannie's, saying it'd be easier, but I still didn't like the idea of being driven around so I politely declined.

He simply nodded and said, "Let me know when you're ready to go."

There was a brief moment, while I crossed the street to Grannie's, that I regretted my choice. If Doug had driven, he would have been walking beside, not a few feet behind, me. Not that it would have stopped me from having a minor panic attack when I thought I saw Asshat Craig's car and came to a full stop halfway across the street. My heart racing as my body froze in place.

Doug was at my side in a matter of seconds, scanning left and right while guiding me the rest of the way across the street. "Emily, are you okay? What happened?"

It couldn't be him, why would he be here?

I sucked in some much needed air and counted to ten. Or at least I tried, Doug wasn't patient enough to wait that long for an answer.

"Emily?"

"I'm okay." Doug's eyes followed mine, as I looked back over my shoulder. "I thought I saw Asshat Craig, sorry, Craig. But it couldn't be him." It'd be too much of a coincidence for him to be driving by Grannie's, five hours from where he lived, in the middle of a work day, just as I was crossing the street.

No way could it be him.

Doug put his hand on my back, looked left and right, then steered me towards the door. "Let's get you inside."

Meg was already there, and unfortunately she'd just witnessed everything. "Is everything okay?"

"Yeah, just freaked myself out." I tried to laugh it off, and failed when my voice squeaked.

"Let's get you a coffee and you can tell me all about it." She called out over my shoulder, "Doug?"

I looked back, Doug was standing near a high top facing the door, talking to someone on his phone. *Great, he's probably telling Jamie what happened.* Which only made sense since it was his job and Jamie was his boss. So why did it bother me so much?

Doug held up his free hand, making the peace sign, in answer to Meg's question, never taking his eyes off the door.

As Meg delivered two coffees to Doug—*two, not a peace sign*—I grabbed a booth and looked around the dining room. It hadn't changed much since we'd all hung out here in high school. The dark wood tables and brown leather bar stools at the high tops were the same, bright ceiling lights providing plenty of light, while the soft hanging chandelier lamps provided a rustic candle glow. The walls were decorated with the same pictures of old saloons, though I noticed a few new black and white photos of employees and a few from the Wyatt Foundation fundraisers. *I'll be able to attend this year.* The shelves along the walls were still crammed with old fashioned glass bottles, and dusty cowboy hats hung on pegs below them. For a second, I was transported back in time, when things were simpler. Safer.

It didn't last long because Meg sat down across from me and asked how I was holding up.

"I'm okay, just spooked myself." I'd already convinced myself it wasn't Asshat Craig.

"Okay. Let me know if there's anything I can do to help."

I didn't think there was, well except maybe not talking about it. "Thanks." I changed the subject. "How do you like working at SSI?"

Meg glowed while she told me how much she loved it, especially working with Jack. Then she asked me what I do, so I told her about designing websites and managing social media accounts for businesses.

"That must require a lot of creativity? How do you know what to post?"

"I don't manage content, what I do is behind the scenes. It's a mix of number crunching and trend watching. The creative part is in designing their sites."

"That's so cool."

Meg and I both looked at the door when the bell chimed and saw Jack walk in. *That explains the two coffees.* He nodded in our direction before sitting down with Doug. I looked at Meg with a raised eyebrow.

"Just in case," her answer was short and to the point.

I hate that this is my life right now.

"Jamie said you and your friend Ashley are joining us for the county fair?"

"Is that okay?"

"Of course, the more the merrier!" Her smile was contagious. "The guys have been a million times, but I've never been so I begged Jack to take me."

"It's a lot of fun, we used to go every year. Though I haven't been in a few years."

"Then I'm glad you can join us." She looked over her shoulder towards Jack, before whispering behind her hand, "He thinks I'm crazy cause I can't wait to feed the baby cows."

It felt good to laugh.

I was about to ask Meg about her favorite books, because Jack and Jamie had mentioned we shared a love of reading, but I was interrupted by Mary's voice cutting across the dining room.

"Jack. Doug. What a pleasant surprise." She walked over and hugged Jack. When she pulled back, he pointed to us. I wouldn't have thought it was possible for Mary's smile to get any bigger, but it did.

"Emily Taylor, aren't you a sight for sore eyes." She crossed the dining room and pulled me out of the booth to give me a hug. It'd been a long time since I'd felt the love expressed in one of her mama bear hugs, and I relished it. I loved my mom, without question, and her hugs were food for my soul. But it never hurt to have more than one woman give you that kind of heartfelt hug.

"It's good to see you too, Mrs. Sheppard."

"Please, it's Mary." I looked to Meg and she nodded.

"I'm sorry, I'm interfering with your girl time." She squeezed Meg's hand. "I'll leave you two to it."

Meg and I made eye contact, and it amazed me that I could tell we both had the same idea. I nodded.

Meg suggested, "Why don't you join us, if you're not too busy."

"Never too busy for family," Mary said as she scooted in beside Meg. "How are you Emily?"

I figured she probably knew all about what was going on, since her husband and sons were hired to protect me, so I didn't hide.

"Pretty good, but I'll be glad when this whole mess is over." I nodded in the general direction of Doug and Jack, who looked like two friends hanging out for a relaxing cup of afternoon coffee rather than two bodyguards poised to intercept an abusive ex-boyfriend.

"I can understand that. I don't know what happened, but I hope for your sake it's all resolved soon." Mary's reply shocked me. I'd assumed because Meg, and well, her whole family, knew that she would too. When I looked at Meg, she answered my unasked question with a smile. They really take their client confidentiality seriously.

"Thank you." I picked up my coffee. "I can't tell you how much I've missed your coffee Mrs. Shepp-Mary." I corrected myself because her expression told me I probably should.

"Three generations of Winchester women thank you." Mary had inherited the coffee shop from her grandmother. It would've have passed to her mother, but she died before Grannie. Before that, this place had been a run down saloon, which explained the décor.

Just then a woman with a Grannie's apron came around the counter and started wiping down tables. Mary called her over, "Beth, have you met Emily Taylor, Anne and Chris's daughter?"

She transferred the wet cloth to her left hand before wiping her right hand on her apron and reaching out to shake my hand. "I don't believe I have. But I've heard so much about you." My heart jumped to my throat. *Does everyone know what happened?* "You're the spitting image of your mother. She gushes about you so much, I feel as if I already know you."

"Thanks." I didn't realize my mom was still close with Mary, or friends with Beth. Beth stayed and talked to us for a few minutes before returning to work. Mary stayed a few minutes longer then she too returned to work.

Meg and I talked until her lunch hour was over. When she stood, she said, "I'm glad we did this. I can't wait to spend the day with you, and Ashley. She sounds like a hoot."

"Me too." And I meant it. "Ashley can be crazy but she has a heart of gold."

When we got to the door, Doug went out first and scanned, then nodded. Jack held the door for me and Meg, then followed behind us. The three of them escorted me to my car. Total overkill. My face must have given me away because Meg said, "Sorry, Jack doesn't want to leave me alone, just in case, so you get a full escort." I might have thought she was annoyed based on her words, but her face was all smiles when she looked at Jack.

"No worries. Thanks again, Meg."

Jack waited with Meg until Doug got in his truck, then waved to let me know I was free to go.

God it sucks that this is my life.

On the drive home, I couldn't stop thinking about the car I saw. The one I thought was Asshat Craig's. It had been in the back of my mind while I had coffee with Meg, but was easy enough to ignore while I had someone to distract me.

I told myself there was no way it was him. I didn't think he'd take a day off of work just to drive around Weatherford, hoping to see me. If it had been him, he would have said something, or at least honked at me to scare me. He wouldn't have seen me and kept going without trying to hurt me, verbally or physically.

I'd finally convinced myself I was just being paranoid as I parked. I grabbed the bag of muffins I'd picked up for my parents, and glanced across the street to see if Doug had parked yet. Of course he had. I felt stupid for taking comfort from seeing him there, when I'd been telling everyone I didn't think I needed protection.

After getting out of the car, I made sure my locks clicked before walking to the front door. I noticed something on the porch.

Flowers? Maybe, but the colors seemed off.

When I got closer, I could tell they were flowers and the reason the color looked off was because they were dead. My breath caught in my throat as I looked over my shoulder, expecting to see Craig. He wasn't there. Taking a deep breath, I looked around to see if someone was watching, waiting to see my reaction, but the only person I could see was Doug. I thought about calling him, but didn't want to over-react twice in one day.

I'm sure it's just the neighborhood kids playing a prank. The last thing I needed was for the SSI guys to think of me as the girl who cried wolf.

I picked up the bouquet of dead summer flowers and carried them inside, hoping Doug hadn't noticed me, or if he had, didn't think it was worth his attention.

He noticed. When I got inside, I had a text from Doug asking if everything was alright. Not wanting to make a big deal out of what was most likely a prank, I told him everything was fine.

There was no way I saw Craig near Grannie's today.

There was no way he thought to buy flowers and let them die.

There was no way he drove five hours just to leave them for me to find on my parent's porch without making contact.

Right?

My hands were shaking, and my breath came in ragged spurts as I put the prank flowers in a garbage bag, then took them out to the trash bin in the garage. I didn't want anyone to find them.

Because it was just a prank.

Nothing to worry about.

If I say it enough, I'll believe it.

Chapter 18

Emily

A few days later, everyone met at my house for our day at the fair. After introductions and a few small pleasantries, Jamie explained the game plan. I knew this wasn't a date, but hearing him discuss protocols and game plans hammered it home. Technically it was Jamie's watch so he was the only one who couldn't drink, but they all agreed it'd be better, safer, if they all stayed sober. Before leaving, Jamie made us all promise to stay together as a group.

Ashley and I rode with Jamie. Jack, Meg, and AJ followed us. Chris and Vicky were meeting us there later, after dropping Zoe off at Vicky's parents.

Ashley practically drooled all over herself during introductions because she thought AJ was seriously hot. I'd be too embarrassed to be act like that, but Ashley was fearless and unapologetically herself, and AJ didn't seem to mind the attention.

I wish I was half as confident as Ashley. Then maybe I wouldn't have gotten myself into such a shitty relationship.

Ashley and I sat in the back seat, not that we had to, but she said she wanted to. She said it'd be more fun for us, plus it'd be easier for us to talk. When asked, Jamie chuckled and said there was no point in arguing.

When Ashley asked Jamie if AJ was seeing anyone, I blushed. God only knew why, she wasn't asking for me.

"Why, you interested?" Jamie teased.

"I might be. I mean, everyone's got a date except me, and him, so it seems like a good idea to partner up."

Damn it! I told Ashley last night this wasn't a date.

She told me I sounded disappointed.

Am I? Maybe a little. And is it that obvious? I didn't want to be attracted to Jamie. He'd never be attracted to me, and I didn't want to get hurt when he told me so. He'd try to let me down gently, but I still didn't want to go through all that. Besides, it'd probably cause problems between him and Chris and I'd never be able to forgive myself if that happened.

She hadn't mean to embarrass me, but she had. At some point, she'd decided Jamie and I should get together and wouldn't give up until she helped Cupid pierce our hearts with his arrows. She'd always said she didn't believe in love or happily ever after, but I'd always suspected it was a lie she used as a shield to protect her heart, because now, more than ever, I was sure Ashley was a romantic at heart.

I hope Jamie doesn't think that I think this is a date. Because I don't. It wasn't, we were was just a group of friends hanging out for the day.

Jamie glanced at me over his shoulder and grinned before answering. I tried to act casual and smile back, but I'm pretty sure I looked like a total freak with my red cheeks and over eager smile.

"As far as I know, he's single. But he's also working so don't distract him." He made eye contact with Ashley in the mirror. "Too much."

"Aye aye, Captain." She saluted him.

"Never made Captain." He laughed.

At the gate, Jamie insisted on covering our entrance fees, despite my protests. Ashley was no help and shamelessly took Jamie's side when I tried to argue. She was still pretending this was a date, so of course she thought he should be paying for me. She considered it a 'BFF Bonus' when he offered to pay for her too. Not that she couldn't afford the five dollar fee, because she totally could, but if she argued about paying her own way, I'd keep arguing about paying mine, and my clever best friend wasn't going to let that happen.

I held my breath and looked around as we waited for Jack, Meg, and AJ inside the entrance, half expecting to see Craig. Which was ridiculous. I hadn't heard anything from him since that day at the apartment, not one single text. Nothing else had happened since I found the prank flowers, which is what I called them anytime I thought about them to remind myself they weren't a message from Craig. There was no way he'd know I was here, besides he hated this kind of thing so it was unlikely we'd accidentally bump into each other. He was probably sitting around and getting drunk with his friends.

I felt Jamie's hand on my shoulder, warm and comforting, a split second before he said, "Relax Em, I won't let him hurt you." *Shit, I need to work on hiding my emotions better.* I didn't like how everyone always seemed to know what I was thinking or feeling.

I took a deep breath and nodded. When I turned around to thank him, words failed me as I met his gaze. His smile was confident, reassuring, and his eyes sparkled in the morning sun. *God he's gorgeous.* I was overly aware of the warmth of his hand as he slid it from my shoulder to my elbow.

A little kid screamed nearby, breaking my trance.

Ashley leaned over and whispered in my ear, "Not a date my ass."

I felt the heat rush to my cheeks as I elbowed her, and told her through gritted teeth to shut up.

Jack held Meg's hand as they walked towards us. AJ walked on the other side of Meg; she looked so small between them. Small and well protected. When they reached us, AJ walked around and stood on the other side of Ashely, putting us between himself and Jamie. I thought it was to be near Ashley, who was openly ogling him, but then I saw him and Jamie make eye contact. AJ nodded, sharing something unsaid between them. If I had to guess he was letting Jamie know he was ready.

"Where to, ladies?" Jack asked us as he opened a map of the fairgrounds. He looked at Meg and pointed at the map. "The cows are on the back side." Then he explained to the rest of us, "Meg is super excited to see them."

I remember her saying she wanted to feed the baby cows.

He winked at her. "She's been talking about them all morning."

He was teasing her, but judging by the huge smile on her face she didn't mind. They looked so comfortable and relaxed together. *I hope I can have that someday.*

"I can't help it. I love how cute and derpy they are."

"And tasty with cheese and bacon." AJ laughed at his own joke. "Am I right?"

Everyone agreed, including Meg.

It made sense for us to make a big circle, we'd see half the fair on our way towards the back, and the cows, then see the other half on our way out, so that's what we did.

We wandered around looking at the craft booths, us girls oohing and aahing at the displays and the guys looking mostly bored. I bought my mom a cute red, white, and blue wreath made of ribbons for her front door, which Jamie insisted on carrying for me. Chris and Vicky met up with us shortly after that, and we played a few games. I didn't win anything. When Meg didn't win anything either, she told Jack he needed to win her a huge stuffed teddy bear. He tried to convince her she didn't need one, but she was having none of it.

"I know I don't need one, Charming." Meg could have won an Oscar with her I'm so sad expression, including a full pout, big wide eyes, and hands in prayer. "But I want one."

Confused, I looked at Jamie for an answer. He whispered, "Charming is Meg's nickname for Jack."

Jack laughed and shook his head. "You know I could just buy you a big teddy bear. It'd save me time, and money."

"It's not the same thing." Ashley and Meg answered at the same time. Meg smiled at Ashley then looked back at Jack in triumph. She'd won, and by the look on Jack's face he knew it. If there'd been any doubt about how Meg and Ashley would get along, it was erased when they stood in solidarity against Jack.

Ashley grabbed AJ's arm, looked up at him with her big brown eyes and fluttered her eyelashes. "Don't you agree?" I knew her well enough to know that if he agreed she'd ask him to win one for her. I couldn't help but laugh, because from the look on his face, he suspected as much.

"Oh, hell no, I'm not getting in the middle of this." He shook his head and held his hands out, a mock expression of terror on his face.

Something about my expression must have given Jamie the impression I wanted a teddy bear because he leaned down and quietly asked me if I wanted him to win one for me as Jack walked up to the stall, muttering, "The things I do for love."

I shook my head no. While I sort of liked the idea of Jamie winning a prize for me, I didn't want to deal with Ashley teasing me. Or Chris getting mad because Jamie was being unprofessional.

I wasn't surprised when Jack popped several of the smallest balloons and won Meg a medium size teddy bear after only a few rounds. But he'd have to win a few more times to upgrade the bear to a huge size.

Meg laughed as she pulled him away before he could pay for the next game. "I love you, Jack." She hugged the cute, purple bowtie-wearing teddy bear, before pushing up to her toes and kissing him on the cheek. "It's perfect."

I didn't intend to be a creeper and stare at them, but they were so damn cute. I blushed when Jack caught me, but he didn't seem to care, he just smiled, put his arms around Meg and kissed the top of her head. "I love you too Princess. Want to try your hand at popping balloons?"

She shook her head no and pointed at the next booth, giggling. "I want to shoot the ducks."

After Chris won a small pink teddy bear for Zoe, we moved over to the duck shooting game. Meg stepped up and paid as Ashley challenged me to a shoot out, then we convinced Vicky to join us. It was good for her to get out and have some adult fun, she spent most of her days home with Zoe. Jack was standing behind Meg, cheering, and Chris was encouraging Vicky. Ashley looked back at AJ and told him he needed to cheer for her since she was all alone.

Damn, Meg isn't the only one gunning for an Oscar today. Ashley was laying it on thick, and AJ was eating it up.

He gave her a big smile, clapped his hands together, and said, "You got this!"

When Jamie stepped up behind me and said he'd be my cheerleader, the butterflies in my stomach went into overdrive.

We lined up behind the BB guns marked one through four, Meg, Ashley, me, and Vicky. Strangers took the last two spots. None of us won, but we had too much fun to care. The guys bought us all huge pretzels as consolation prizes. They were soft and gooey and covered in large salt crystals, and were way better than some cheap, tiny toy prize. I shared my pretzel with Jamie who took small pieces, one at a time, rather than just splitting it. It almost felt intimate to be sharing my pretzel with him; it was the same way Chris and Vicky were sharing theirs. Meg was pulling pieces off and feeding them to Jack so he wouldn't get salt on her teddy bear, which he was still carrying for her. AJ bought two pretzels, saying he was too hungry to share. Ashley didn't seem phased by it and made a joke about him keeping up his energy levels.

After finishing our pretzels, we wandered around looking at exhibits and various goodies for sale. They had everything: toys, homemade crafts, jewelry, fruits and vegetables and potted plants. I almost choked on my spit when I heard Ashley read a sign in front of a plant display, "Succulent means juicy."

The words themselves weren't that funny, but how she said them as she blinked and fluttered her eyelashes was hysterical.

We made our way to the barn, and after Meg got her fill of feeding and petting the cows, we played with the baby goats. They were stupidly energetic, and beyond adorable, jumping around in their Fourth of July themed pajamas. Chris shared a moment with Vicky as they gushed about wanting to bring Zoe to the fair when she was old enough.

I intruded on their moment when I insisted, "I better get an invite when your bring her."

We spent the rest afternoon walking around and talking. Before long before Chris said it was time for him and Vicky to go. They'd had fun, but wanted to get home to Zoe. The rest of us decided we were ready to call it a day too, so we walked out with them. We'd originally planned on staying to watch the fireworks but we'd had enough of the loud, chaotic environment and decided to watch the Weatherford show instead.

When we passed the Carousel on our way to the gate, Ashley and I decided we needed to ride for old-time's-sake. And we somehow convinced everyone to ride with us. Even Chris and Vicky. Ashley and I rode side-by-side horses and laughed the entire time.

We said goodbye to Chris and Vicky at the gate. Then Ashley suggested we go out for some real food since we had time to kill before the fireworks. Everyone agreed. I for one, wanted some real food after eating fair food all day.

Ashley asked if she could ride with AJ as she was opening the back door and climbing in. She turned and raised one eyebrow while grinning at me.

Damn her, she wanted me and Jamie to have some time alone even though I'd reminded her a thousand times this wasn't a date. Yes, he'd stayed closer to me than was necessary, and on more than one occasion he'd put his hand on my lower back as we walked through the crowd, but he was just being protective.

Doug did the same thing when I panicked in the middle of the road.

I mean, I liked it and it felt kind of personal, but I couldn't read too much into it. *This isn't a date.* Though he did insist on paying for me a lot, which Ashley had noticed, and pointed out.

Jack didn't answer Ashley, but Meg did, with a big shit-eating grin on her face, "Of course you can ride with us."

She sounded a little too eager and I had a sneaky suspicion she and Ashley were in cahoots.

Jack looked at Jamie, and shrugged. "See you at dinner."

I was quiet during the ride, too busy trying, and failing, not to think about much I enjoyed spending today with Jamie, and reminding myself today wasn't a date. It was stupid to even think about it. He'd never want someone as broken as me. *I'm his client. Plus he's my brother's best friend.* So I couldn't even think about liking him.

I hadn't meant to ignore Jamie, and felt bad when I realized he'd been asking me a question.

"I'm sorry Jamie, I spaced out for a second."

"I asked if you're okay? You seem sad."

"I'm fine." Then knowing that most men think when a woman says she's fine it means she is not in fact fine, I corrected myself, "Just thinking about what a great time I had today. Thank you for everything Jamie, really, it was the best day I've had in a long time."

"I'm glad you had fun."

I could look at his warm, sweet smile all day.

Chapter 19

Jamie

Emily's cheeks were an adorable shade of pink when she climbed into my SUV, and it wasn't from the sun. She was embarrassed because Ashley and Meg had been none too subtle when they arranged for us to ride back to Weatherford alone. If it hadn't been for the fact that they'd only met each other today, I might have thought they'd planned it all along. While they'd gotten along all day, I wouldn't have thought they knew each other well enough to start scheming together. *I've been wrong before.*

Emily apologized while I started the engine. "Sorry about Ashley. She's always been a bit crazy."

"No need to apologize, she's been shamelessly flirting with AJ all day, and I would've been more surprised if she hadn't asked to ride back with them." I knew that wasn't what she meant, but it was part of the reason Ashley rode back with them, and I wanted Emily to feel more comfortable, not less.

Several times throughout the day, I'd caught myself watching Emily, I couldn't help it, she was relaxed, laughing, and playful. *Relaxed looks good on her.* And I loved the way her pale blue eyes sparkled when she smiled. And she'd smiled a lot today. I was glad it had worked out for us to go together, and since Jack, AJ, and I shared Emily duty, we got to have fun too. I had to admit, it felt good knowing I was one of the reasons she was smiling so much.

I might have crossed the professional line by offering to pay for everything, but her smile had been so rewarding the first time that I kept doing it. Besides, she wasn't just a client, she was also a friend. And I'd let her pay for a few thing, when she'd argued and stood her ground. So, it wasn't like I was treating this like a date. Because I wasn't. But I'd definitely crossed the line when I'd placed my hand on her lower back, an escorting technique we use during protective detail which in itself it wasn't crossing the line, but doing it when there was no immediate threat, and then letting my hand linger, enjoying the feel of her warm back against the palm of my hand. Well, that crossed the line. A lot.

Unfortunately my actions hadn't gone unnoticed, though no one said anything. Well, no one except Meg and Ashley, who'd put their heads together and giggled.

I shouldn't have underestimated them. Thinking back, they'd been scheming most of the day. I wanted to be mad, but couldn't—I'd clearly brought it on myself by using the universal male signal for 'she's mine' any chance I got. I could probably explain my actions by saying I was concerned in a crowded area, especially since she thought she saw Craig earlier this week, but I didn't think they'd buy it, not for one second.

There were a few times Emily and I had locked eyes and each time I'd felt butterflies dance in my stomach and my breath catch in my throat. I'd also found myself tongue tied on more than one occasion while I watched her playing games or laughing at an inside joke with Ashley.

Before long I was wishing this had been a date.

But it wasn't. It can't be. Not today, not ever.

I shouldn't, couldn't, think about Emily like that. Not only would Chris kill me if he thought I was attracted to her, but I couldn't afford to get distracted. I couldn't risk Craig getting the drop on me because I was too busy thinking about how beautiful Emily was or how much I liked the sound of her laugh. Or how every touch of her skin sent shivers down my spine.

I'd found reasons to put my hand on her back, or touch her shoulder, or graze her hand with mine. Repeatedly throughout the day. I couldn't help myself. A quick touch on the arm, disguised as getting her attention. My palm on her lower back, disguised guiding her. I might have been able to stop myself if she hadn't been doing the same kinds of things. Holding onto my arm when she laughed, leaning closer to me when we talked.

Her touch felt personal, intimate, and I hadn't wanted her to stop.

But I can't get distracted. Knowing I couldn't live through failing someone again, I vowed I'd do whatever it took to keep her safe. Even if it meant keeping my distance.

I'd have to explain my unprofessional behavior to Chris, if he'd noticed. It wouldn't be easy, because my head was a fucking mess right now. And even if he'd be okay with Emily and I dating under normal circumstances, this was anything but normal and he'd be worried about me getting distracted and placing Emily in danger.

Which was a valid concern, and one I shared.

I won't let it happen again. I can't.

As if that wasn't reason enough, Emily was still recovering from emotional trauma, and Chris wouldn't want her jumping into another relationship so quickly. He might trust me with her life, but he'd struggle to trust me with her heart. Plus I was still dealing with my own loss. *What a fucking mess.*

I vowed not to touch Emily again, unless absolutely necessary.

When we got to the restaurant, I told AJ he was officially off duty for the night. He promptly ordered a beer and focused all his attention on charming Ashley.

"Why the sudden change of heart?" Ashley teased him. "I've been flirting all day and you've barely noticed." She tried to pout, but smiled instead.

"I was working so I had to behave." He cocked his head towards me and Jack, as if blaming us. "But you have my full attention now." He winked, turning Ashley to putty in his hands. She didn't stand a chance; AJ was quite charming when he wanted to be.

At first Emily seemed embarrassed by Ashley's open flirtations, but it didn't last long. She was soon laughing and shaking her head at Ashley's brazenness, even going so far as to tease her about being a lost cause. I sat back and watched the shenanigans unfold but didn't get involved.

The girls all ordered white wine while AJ and Jack ordered beer. I abstained since I was still on duty until Emily was home safe and sound. Then Sammie, one of our part-time security guys, technically our only security gal, would take over for the overnight shift.

After the initial high of flirting with AJ wore off, Ashley joined the conversation Emily and Meg were having about a book series they were reading. They were on different books in the series so Meg was being extra careful not to spoil anything.

Ashley chimed in, "I love that show." And practically drooled as she said, "Jamie is so fucking hot." She turned towards me, laughing. "The Scottish Highlander male lead in the show not you." She pointed her beer at me. "Not that you're not hot."

I shook my head in mock exasperation, she really was incorrigible. I glanced at Emily, and noticed a hint of pink in her cheeks.

I chuckled. "Believe me, I know I'm no James Fraser"

Ashley's eyes rounded. "Wait, you watch Outlander?"

It was Meg's turn to laugh.

"No, but Meg does so I've seen bits and pieces." Unlike Jack, I had yet to watch an entire episode. He'd initially started watching it to spend time with Meg, but now he watches it because he likes it. They'd tried talking me into watching it with them, but I hadn't given in, yet.

"He refuses to watch it with us," Meg added, like she'd read my mind. "I bet he'd watch it with you if you asked him," she directed her comment to Emily, a huge grin on her face.

I shot her a look, hoping she'd pick up on the 'please don't' in my pleading expression.

She smiled back at me, all sweetness and innocence.

Fuck. I knew that look; like a dog with a bone, she wasn't letting it go. I'd have to grin and bear it as she spent the night trying to hook me and Emily up. Ashley started to say something but luckily our server came and delivered our food; stopping her, or anyone else, from pushing the subject.

I was secretly thrilled when Meg invited Emily and Ashley to the BBQ we were having the following day. Something I'd thought about doing a hundred times today but kept telling myself I shouldn't. After crossing the line too many times, I hadn't wanted to look like I was hitting on her.

We were hosting a BBQ for the SSI staff and their families. It was totally casual, just hanging out in our backyard and stuffing ourselves with barbequed meats. Ma had invited Beth and Chase too, so Ashley and Emily wouldn't be the only non-SSI people coming.

Thank you, Meg. She could invite them without anyone questioning her motives. Well except me, I was most definitely questioning her motives. As an added bonus, if Emily was at our place, dad wouldn't have to work. He'd volunteered to cover the afternoon shift so everyone else could attend the BBQ.

"Doug's bringing a second grill, he says he needs it for his "world famous" smoked ribs, apparently they need to be slow cooked— just so." Meg rolled her eyes. She was still getting used to how seriously we men were about our grilled meat.

Our grill would be used for lunch, burgers, hotdogs, and chicken.

"Sounds fun," Ashley wasted no time answering. "We don't have any plans, right Em?"

"No. It'll be fun." Then she asked, "What can we bring?"

"Just yourselves, we've got everything covered," Meg answered with a flourish of her hands.

Jack added, "We'll have a fuck ton of beer, but you're on your own if you want something specific."

After dinner, Emily went to the lady's room. I turned in my chair so I had a clear line of sight to the doorway, and most of the hall, on the side of the bar. I heard Ashley mumble something about overkill just as I noticed two guys, who'd been loud and obnoxious the entire time we'd been there, get up and block Emily as she exited the hall. She put her head down, rounding her shoulders to make herself small as she tried to walk past them. They didn't let her.

I could hear them taunting her as I got out of my chair, and stalked over. They were drunk, but that was no excuse for rude, aggressive behavior.

One of them said, "You should come home–"

I stepped between him and Emily and cut him off. "Is there a problem?" I asked through gritted teeth as I held up my left hand, in a defensive position. My primal brain wanted

187

nothing more than to bust this guys nose, but my logic brain knew 'he's being an asshole to the woman who's mine to protect' wasn't a good enough reason to start swinging.

Come on dude, take a swing. Give me a reason.

I kept my left hand up, in the universal position of defensive posturing, and left my right hand relaxed near my side. It was "relaxing" near my gun, but I wouldn't draw unless I absolutely had to. As much as I wanted to punch this guy, I didn't want to have to shoot him.

"Who the fuck are you?" he sneered as he batted my hand away and stepped closer, pulling his right fist back to throw a punch.

Thank you.

I shifted my stance and watched his hand come forward. Then, just before he made contact, I grabbed his wrist and twisted his arm behind his back. I brought my hand back and formed a fist, but stopped short of swinging when I heard Emily gasp.

"You owe the lady an apology." I growled through gritted teeth. It'd taken every ounce of effort I could muster to not break the fucker's nose. I wasn't normally a violent guy, but this guy deserved it for threatening Emily.

I saw his friend moving to interfere in my peripheral vision a half second before AJ, using nothing except his six-foot-one frame and an intimidating posture, made him think better of it. He put his hands up and backed away muttering, "Sorry man just having some fun." Smart choice, AJ wasn't just big, he was a black belt in Brazilian Ju Jitsu, and an all around badass. That dude wouldn't have lasted two seconds.

Hell, I rarely ever last more than a few seconds in the ring with AJ.

"What the fuck man! Let me go before I call the cops."

I almost laughed; he had no idea. Too bad I wasn't still on the force. I wasn't going to lie, but the fear on Emily's face was enough for me to decide a little white lie wouldn't hurt anyone. I got close to his ear and said, "I am the cops. Now apologize."

"Oh shit." I felt him stiffen, then he turned towards me. "Sorry, man."

I applied a little more pressure to his arm. "Not to me, to her," I gave the order in my deepest, meanest cop voice.

He mumbled, "I'm sorry."

I wasn't convinced but I didn't want to create an even bigger scene so I asked AJ, who was making sure no one else tried to interfere, "Can you take Snow back to the table?"

Snow White was the code name we'd given Emily. Meg had suggested we use princess names for female clients after she started working for SSI. We'd given her the code name Cinderella, and she thought it'd be a positive, fun way to ID our other female clients during tough times in their lives. She claimed every girl dreamed of being a princess.

Unfortunately, most of them were damsels in distress when they came to us.

"On it." He walked around me and guided Emily back towards the table.

For the first time since they'd cornered her, I could see her face. Her expression was a mix of fear and surprise. I got the fear. But surprise? Did she think I wouldn't protect her just because these guys weren't Craig?

I counted to ten, then pushed him towards the bar. "Sit down and stare at the bar. Don't even think about looking up. Have I made myself clear?"

"Yeah man. I got it." Luckily for him, he did exactly what I'd told him to do.

When I looked over at the table, Jack tilted his head toward the door which I took to mean he'd settled the bill and we were free to leave. I nodded, then counted to ten after they walked out, never taking my eyes off the two assholes staring at the bar.

"Count to fifty before you even think of lifting your eyes off that bar top. Both of you." I waited for them to start counting before backing my way to the door. I stopped to smooth things over with the manager before leaving, but he said Jack had explained everything, and we were good. He asked if he should kick the two guys out, but not wanting to risk another confrontation in the parking lot I asked him not to. He agreed, then warned me that he'd be cutting them off so they'd probably leave on their own.

Everyone was waiting at my SUV. Ashley and Meg were comforting Emily, who was putting on a brave face, while Jack and AJ stood watch.

"Ashley, you should probably ride back with us."

"I'm not a total idiot, James." Ashley sounded offended that I felt the need to say it. "Later big guy." She blew AJ a kiss, opened the back door to my SUV. "Come on Em, let's drink some beer while we watch the fireworks with your hero."

Once they were in, I closed the door behind them and walked around to the driver's side. Tthe sound of Emily laughing through the open door surprised me. I didn't know what I'd expected to hear, maybe crying or Ashley comforting Emily, but it wasn't riotous laughter. I'd clearly underestimated her.

She's a hell of a lot stronger than she realizes.

I turned in my seat, smiled and asked, "What's so funny?"

"I was just saying, I bet that guy pissed himself when you shoved his arm behind his back," Ashley choked out.

"He kind of looked like maybe he did," Emily added. She turned to look at me, her eyes glossy with tears from laughter. Something she saw made her stop laughing.

Does she think I'm upset with her?

But Ashley kept going, "And you made him sit at the bar in his pee pants!"

Emily probably misinterpreted my surprise as anger. I had to think quick, so she wouldn't think I was mad, or that it wasn't okay to be laughing after such a crazy situation.

Fuck, I can't think of anything. What the fuck, Sheppard? *Say something. Anything.*

"It probably puddled in his shoes." I shivered for added comedic effect. I didn't think it was particularly funny, but Emily and Ashley did. They both stared at me for the space of a heartbeat then fell into each others arms as they burst out laughing. Ashley was cackling and Emily laughed so hard she snorted. It was the cutest sound ever.

I smiled as I turned in my seat and started the car. *She'll be okay.* My shoulders relaxed as relief washed over me. I'd talk to her before I left for the night and make sure she was good, but I had no reason to think those guys would cost her any sleep. Unless she and Ashley stayed up all night laughing at them.

On the drive home, Ashley told us AJ had stopped the manager from interfering. She practically swooned when she told Emily how much she appreciated his hot alpha male body. I could see her fanning her face with her hand in the rear view mirror.

I heard Emily ask Ashley if she thought they'd hook up.

"Maybe, if he's lucky. But maybe not tonight, thanks to Mr. I-peed-myself-after-being-called-out-for-being-a-total-douche-canoe."

I almost choked on my spit as I tried to hold back my laugh. Ashley had a colorful, entertaining way of nicknaming men she didn't like.

"There's still time, he's coming with us to the fireworks." Emily urged her friend on, then asked me, "Jamie, we can still go see the fireworks, can't we?"

"Of course." It hadn't occurred to me to cancel our plans unless she asked me to.

Emily looked at Ashley, raised her eyebrows, pursed her lips, and made kissing noises.

"Maybe. If he's lucky." Ashley grinned like a kid who just got away with stealing a cookie. AJ was in for one hell of a night.

"If *he's* lucky?" Emily turned around in her seat and stared at her best friend. "Like you wouldn't be just as lucky."

I watched Ashley's reaction in the rearview mirror as she shrugged with a devilish grin and a gleam in her eyes.

"Any man would consider himself lucky just to have the chance to be with me." She used both hands and circled around, indicating her whole body.

I almost choked on my spit, again. Fucking Ashley, I was wrong thinking she hadn't changed. She had. She was more confident, and gave even fewer fucks, than when we were in high school. And it worked for her. And truth be told, she wasn't wrong, any man who didn't consider himself lucky to have her, even if only for one night, needed to have his head examined. She was beautiful, intelligent, passionate, and a bit of a wild child.

"God I've missed you." Emily reached over and grabbed her friends hand. "I'm sorry I've been MIA for so long."

"I missed you too. Luckily, we've got all weekend to make up for lost time and a sexy chauffeur so we can start our party early. So, let's have him take us to a liquor store so we can grab some beer for the fireworks."

"Chauffeur, huh?" I asked.

Emily looked at me, with her hands in prayer position and her head tilted slightly to the right. "Please Jamie?"

How could I say no to those big, beautiful, blue eyes? Neither of them would be driving, thanks to me, their chauffeur, so I agreed.

"Under one condition. No drunken shenanigans." It was a silly condition, one I knew they'd agree to then not follow through with, but I had to at least attempt to sound like I wasn't giving in just because I couldn't say no to Emily.

They both agreed enthusiastically. Too enthusiastically. They put their heads together and whisper giggled.

I rolled my eyes as I grinned; it was going to be a long night. *There's no where else I'd rather be.*

I called Jack and told him we were taking a small detour to the liquor store. He didn't even bother trying to hold back his laughter when he overheard the girls, who were whispering at the top of their lungs, "We solemnly swear we will commit no drunken shenanigans." Before bursting into a fit of giggles.

Following them around the beer aisles of the local liquor store was more than any man should ever have to suffer. Ashley wanted something crafty and fun. Emily wanted something light and refreshing. After twenty minutes of listening to them arguing over which beer was the best I wanted a shot of whiskey.

"Just get both," I finally told them.

"Brilliant idea, James." Ashley gave me two thumbs up and took off to grab her craft beer while Emily grabbed a six pack of something light.

I winked at Emily and said, "If I was truly brilliant I would have suggested it fifteen minutes ago."

She blushed and a smiled, making the twenty minutes of torture worth every second.

Chapter 20

Jamie

The park was crowded, but we eventually found an open space big enough for all of us. It was further away than the girls wanted to be, so they all hammed it up, acting like it was the end of the world. It amazed me how in sync they were after only one day together. I was glad they got along, and a little worried about how much trouble they'd cause if they put their heads together. *Shenanigans.*

Ashley pulled out a beer and offered one to Meg. "We went shopping. Want one?"

"No thanks, I'm not a fan."

"I wish I'd known; I would've gotten you something," Emily apologized.

I handed Meg a single serving plastic bottle of sweet white wine. Knowing Meg didn't like beer, and not wanting her to feel left out, I'd grabbed it from a cooler near the registers. She didn't drink much, so I figured one bottle would be enough.

"Thanks Jamie. You're the best!" She hugged me and then looked at Emily. "Isn't he the best?"

"Meg," Jack drew out the e in her name.

"What? It's just a question." She looked at him and turned on her best innocent act.

I squinted my eyes as I watched them, trying to figure out what was going on.

Ashley interrupted before I could. "Anyone else want a beer?" She might have asked all of us but was looking directly at AJ.

"Boss man?" AJ was asking if I wanted him to stay on the clock after what happened at the pub.

Which I appreciated, but we didn't need him. "You're good. Thanks." Even if we did, I wasn't worried. AJ after a beer or two could still out match most sober guys.

"No. Thank you." He reached for the beer Ashley was offering him. "And thank you pretty lady." He gave her a bow and opened the can.

"Jack, you don't happen to have a blanket in your truck do you?" I hadn't thought to pack one since we had planned on being at the fairgrounds and wouldn't have needed one. I had an emergency blanket with my first aid/trauma kit but it wouldn't provide any comfort.

"I might, let me check." He returned a few minutes later. "I have one but we won't all fit, so the girls will have to sit on the grass."

"Hahaha! Funny, Charming!" Meg's ridiculous fake laugh was so over-the-top we couldn't even laugh, at least not for the first two seconds.

The girls immediately plopped down and started giggling after Jack and I spread out the blanket. Jack, AJ, and I shared a look—we were in for an entertaining night.

Meg sat on the left, and leaned against Jack. Ashley sat in the middle, with AJ on the grass behind her, close enough to touch her but not actually doing it. Yet. Emily sat on the right. I was to her right and back just a bit. We'd created a protective wall around our girls.

Our girls?

Sure Meg was Jack's girl, no question there. And Ashley was AJ's, at least for today. But Emily wasn't mine, and I had no right even thinking it. I shook my head to clear it and focused on the conversation.

When they played the National Anthem before the start of the show everyone stood up and sung along—cheering and waving their hats as the singer held the high note at the end.

The fireworks did not disappoint. They were bright and colorful, and noisy. Every once in a while, one of girls would jump after a particularly loud boom, and we'd all laugh. Jack promised Meg he wouldn't let the big bad fireworks hurt her, she slapped his leg and told him he better not. *They're perfect for each other.* AJ had moved closer to Ashley, his arm around her waist as she leaned into his chest, her hand on his leg.

Emily was hugging her knees with the beer-free hand, looking a little sad. I was sure she'd noticed the two couples, just as I had, and was probably feeling a little lonely, just like I was. I desperately wanted to wrap my arms around her and comfort her, but I couldn't bring myself to do it.

If I cross that line, I may not come back from it.

During the pause before the finale, AJ asked what everyone's favorite fireworks were, interrupting my thoughts. Meg spoke up first, saying she liked the ones that cascaded down after the initial burst of color. Ashley and Emily said they liked the big ones with multiple colors. We discussed the shapes, styles, and colors and why we liked them, in the end we all agreed that regardless of our favorite individual type of firework, the grand finale was always the best part.

I watched the tension leave Emily's shoulders while we talked.

A hush fell over our group, and the crowd, as the sky lit up with the first fireworks of the big, bright, booming finale. There was something decidedly Texan about it. We oohed and aahed along with everyone else as the loud booms rattled our ribcages and the smoke filled our lungs.

There was a moment of awe-struck silence between the last bang and the first sounds of the crowd cheering. After a few seconds, I stood and offered Emily a hand up. When she took my hand, I pulled a little too hard and caused her to lose her balance. She fell into me, both hands landing on my chest. My breath caught in my throat as I instinctively reached out to steady her, catching her by her waist.

Emily grunted and looked up at me before whispering, "Sorry." She didn't look away. Or move her hands.

I could smell the beer on her breath. If I bent down and kissed her I'd be able to taste it.

No. I can't.

I choked down the thought and said, "No need to apologize. I got you." I should've take my hands off her waist, but I froze in place, mesmerized as I watched the light from nearby sparklers dance in her pale blue eyes. Time felt like it stood still as we stared into each other's eyes, but it couldn't have been more than a few seconds. Though I doubted my ability to judge time.

Jack broke the spell when cleared his throat.

We were still standing on the blanket and he was waiting, with a stupid grin plastered all over his face, for us to move so he could pick it up.

Meg and Ashley were gaping at us with big I-told-you-so smiles. They thought Emily and I would hook up tonight, and judging by the knowing looks Jack and AJ were sharing, they thought so too.

But it can't happen.

I dropped my hands and stepped back. I knew they'd be disappointed when it didn't happen, but I couldn't hook up with Emily. Even if Chris was okay with it, she deserved someone who could love her without fear. Someone who wasn't afraid to take the risk. Someone better than me.

Chapter 21

Emily

I couldn't stop thinking about the moment I fell into Jamie, my hands landing in the middle of his warm, hard chest. Or how his strong, protective hands felt on my waist, steadying me as his gorgeous hazel eyes stared into mine. For one brief moment, the world stopped spinning. It felt like forever, though I'm guessing it was only a few seconds. Jack ruined the moment when he cleared his throat, loudly.

I felt the absence of Jamie's hands when he stepped back, but then he held a hand out to me. His eyes never leaving mine, the noise of people around us dulled to a slow, steady hum. I didn't need his help to step off the blanket, and I certainly didn't need to keep holding his hand after I'd taken the two steps needed to reach the grass. But I did it anyway. I couldn't help it. His stare was intoxicating. His touch comforting. This time, it was a child screaming nearby who broke the spell, and suddenly I was keenly aware of the silence of our small group.

Had they noticed? I brushed down my red, white, and blue t-shirt and looked around. If their grins were any indication, they'd seen it all, and were happy about it. I reminded myself this couldn't happen. Not only am I a mess, but he's my brother's best friend, and my bodyguard. *He's off limits twice over.*

Ashley had a shit-eating grin on her face the entire ride as Jamie drove us back to my parent's house. She'd clearly had a good night with AJ. Why didn't she go home with him?

Jamie kept glancing at me in the rearview mirror, an unreadable expression on his face, and a death grip on the steering wheel, like he was afraid he'd lose control. *Did I upset him? Did I cross the line?*

For a second, I'd thought I felt a connection when our eyes locked. Maybe I'd misread the situation, and he was just being helpful and polite. That was it. He was being nice, and I read too much into it. Now he's trying to figure out how to let me down gently, because there was no way Jamie was attracted to me. Why would he want to get involved with someone who let her ex-boyfriend hit her? Someone his company needed to protect?

Ashley got out without a fuss when Jamie asked to talk to me for a second. I twisted my thumb ring—knowing what was coming didn't make me any less nervous. Would he tell me he just wanted to be friends? Or that it wasn't me, it was him? Or some other cliché expression to let me down gently?

Or maybe he'd just tell me the truth, he needed someone smarter, stronger, like Isabelle had been.

"Emily, I…" He paused. "I just want to make sure you're okay."

"I'm fine Jamie, why wouldn't I be?" I wasn't, but I couldn't tell him why without embarrassing myself. Jamie was just doing his job, which included being helpful and nice, and I'd let myself forget that. I was mad at myself for thinking maybe he liked me, because despite how much I didn't want to, despite knowing it was a bad idea, I liked him. I could hear Ashley saying, "I told you so," in my head.

"Thanks for a fun day, Jamie." I was going to leave it at that, but couldn't. I'd acted out of line, and he deserved an apology. I gathered my courage as I sucked in a big gulp of air conditioned air. "Jamie, I-, I'm sorry if I crossed a line-"

He cut me off. "Don't. Please. You didn't." He looked like he wanted to say more, but he stared at his hands on the steering wheel instead. I waited. He was obviously trying to figure out what he wanted to say, and I wanted to hear it.

"Emily, I had a lot of fun today and I'm not sure how to handle this, us." He circled his hands to include both of us. "I'm not sure what I'm feeling right now." He didn't sound like his normal, confident self. "That's not true," His voice was barely above a whisper. He took a deep breath, ran his hand through his hair, and met my eyes again. "I like you, Emily."

My heart skipped a beat, then another. *He likes me.*

He reached over and held my hand. "And maybe under different circumstances…" He paused, his Adam's apple moving as he swallowed. "But for now, I don't think it's a good idea to be anything more than friends." I broke eye contact first but he lifted my chin until I was looking into his eyes again. "I don't know if I'm ready, and I think you deserve better than that."

"I understand." I didn't. "I'm not sure about all this either." I mimicked his hand motion. At least now we'd talked about it, and I knew where I stood.

He doesn't like me, he's just letting me down easy. He couldn't send his best friend's sister home in tears, could he?

"You should go." He looked out the window. "Ashley's waiting."

Did he just dismiss me? *Fine.* I didn't want to talk about it anymore anyway. All I wanted was to go inside, and drink the pain away with Ashley and forget how stupid I was for getting my hopes up.

"Good night Jamie. Thank you for a wonderful day." I tried to sound casual but my voice was more stiff, more formal, than I'd intended.

If Jamie picked up on the change in my tone, he didn't show it. "Good night Emily. I'll see you tomorrow."

Emily, not Em. He got out when I did, and waited. Halfway to the porch, I glanced over my shoulder. He was standing near his door, watching, making sure I got inside safely. *Because it's his job.*

I turned back when I heard Ashley say, "Come on, I need a drink."

Me too.

Chapter 22

Jamie

I'd been stuck in my head, trying to figure out how to talk to Emily about what had happened, so I wasn't very talkative on the ride home. But I needed to talk to her because I'd felt the pull between us when our eyes locked, and there was no denying the spark I felt every time I touched her. But we couldn't act on it.

Much to my surprise, Ashley didn't give me a hard time when I asked for a second to talk to Emily.

I still wasn't sure what I wanted to say, because my emotions were all over the place, making me feel like an awkward teenager. I wanted to put Emily at ease, but I couldn't even put myself at ease. It didn't matter, I couldn't leave without explaining why I was acting so strangely.

From the moment she fell into me, I knew it was stupid to keep denying my attraction to her. It felt good, right, to hold her in my arms. But it was a bad idea, possibly even a dangerous one, to get involved with her while she was also a client. And Emily wasn't just a client, she was my best friend's little sister. She was doubly forbidden so I couldn't pursue a relationship with her despite my attraction, at least not yet, and I needed her to understand that.

But when I looked into her eyes, I lost my nerve. She looked worried, and I couldn't bring myself to add more stress to her life.

Instead I asked how she was and immediately regretted it when she said fine, because no woman who said she was fine was ever actually fine.

I was being a total chicken-shit. I wanted to tell her our friends weren't wrong in thinking I was attracted to her, but that seemed like a lot to dump on her. She didn't need to be burdened with my feelings for her when I couldn't act on them. *Besides she's probably not ready.* If I said anything, things would end up being awkward between us and I didn't want that to happen.

But then she tried to apologize for acting out of line. And I couldn't let that happen.

So I manned up and explained how I felt, and why we couldn't be together. But judging from the expression on Emily's face, I'd fucked it all up.

Was I always this bad with women? Then I remembered I hadn't so much as flirted with anyone except Isabelle since my sophomore year of high school.

After Emily and Ashley were inside, I walked over and talked to Sammie, asking her to call me if she saw them leave the house, "Even if they're just hanging out in the yard."

"Copy that. Expecting trouble?" she asked. Samantha was one of our part-time security staff. Like the others, she was a local cop; we'd worked together for a couple of years before I left the department. She was a good cop, as tough as they come, and luckily for us she was single and used to working the night shift, so she picked up her fair share of our overnight jobs.

"Always. But that's not why I'm asking. They plan on drinking tonight and they tend to get a little." I paused, looking for the right word. "Adventurous when they're drunk."

She gave me a knowing nod. "Good times."

"Yeah. Thanks Sammie. Stay safe."

"Thanks boss man, you too."

I didn't want to leave, not because I didn't trust Sammie, because I did, but because I didn't like how I'd left things with Emily.

Chapter 23

Emily

Ashley didn't say anything until we got back to my bedroom, then she spat questions at me rapid fire. "What did he say? Did he ask you out for a proper date?"

"Ashl-"

"Did he want to kiss you? He looked like he wanted to kiss you. Did you want to kiss him? Because from what I saw, you looked like you wanted-."

"Ashley." I said forcefully, causing her to stop and stare at me.

"He's not interested. He gave me the "let's be friends" line."

"No way. We all saw you two have the perfect romantic moment. At least until Jack interrupted it. I thought Meg was going to kill him." She took a swig of the beer she'd just opened. "I like her, she's fun. And she's totally on Team Jemily. That's what I'm calling you when you finally hook up."

She wasn't listening, so I tried again, "Ashley, he's not interested. He was just being nice earlier. He's letting me down easy by saying he isn't ready. I'm sure he thinks I'm not worth the trouble." He hadn't used those words, but I was sure that was what he meant.

"Are you fucking kidding me right now? Em, you're totally worth it and he'd have to be an idiot not to see it. And I'm sorry, but even if he's not ready to admit it, he's into you. You can't fake that kind of chemistry. Not to mention what AJ said." She paused for dramatic effect.

I shouldn't want to know, but I did. "What'd he say?"

"He said Jamie's usually cool as a cucumber and it's not like him to lose his shit, like he did at the bar. That's got to mean something, right?"

It had been a bit much, and at first I'd been afraid. But it didn't last long, Jamie wasn't Craig and his response was done in a professional capacity to protect me. "I don't know, he's paid to protect me." Not wanting to cling to false hope, I shrugged it off. *But what if?*

She ignored me. "And you're clearly into him."

"Ugh, is it that obvious?" Everyone thought Jamie and I should get together, including me. I plopped down on my bed, feeling defeated.

Ashley sat down next to me and handed me her beer. I didn't think about it and took a sip, then almost spat it back out. I scrunched up my face as I handed it back to her. We agreed on a lot of things, but not our taste in beer.

"Sorry, I should've grabbed one of yours."

"That's okay, I probably shouldn't drink anymore." I wanted to get drunk and forget how the night ended, but was worried I'd end up crying over my shit-show of a life instead. I also didn't want to be hungover at the BBQ tomorrow.

"No, you need your beauty rest." She gave me a knowing look. "You'll have a chance to talk to him again tomorrow, and clear up this nonsense."

"Maybe, but I feel like I should give him some space. I don't want him to think I don't respect his feelings. Besides, I just left Craig. I'm not sure I'm ready to jump into a new relationship."

Ashley and I hadn't seen each other much over the last few years, but she still knew me too well to fall for my bullshit.

"Sweetie, Craig has nothing to do with this. And there's no rule about how long you have to wait before dating a great guy after leaving an asshat. I looked it up."

I laughed. Ashley had a way of making her point without it feeling like a lecture.

She was right, I shouldn't use Asshat Craig as an excuse. Jamie had made it clear earlier he didn't want to go out with me, but that didn't mean I had to sit home alone and wallow. There were plenty of fish in the sea. I just had to suit up and go swimming.

Ashley and I stayed up talking and laughing into the early morning hours. We talked about everything, including whether she wanted more than just a fling with AJ, which she didn't. They'd agreed a fling would be fun, but neither was looking for more. When I asked why she didn't go home with AJ tonight, she said she didn't want to ditch me.

Reconnecting with Ashley was the best choice I'd made in a long time, second only to leaving Asshat Craig.

I'd always thought one-night-stands and hook ups just happened, so it seemed weird to me they'd talked about it. But then again, I didn't have much experience. My only one-nighter was back in college and happened when I got drunk at a party.

When I reminded Ashley about that night, we had to bury our faces in our pillows to keep from waking up my parents with our laughter. I'd been trying to live life to the fullest after a breakup, and Ashley helped me pick up a guy at a party. It turned into a cluster-fuck of comedic proportions. Needless to say, my courageous stage was short-lived after that. But it was fun while it lasted.

We talked until we fell asleep, fully clothed, lying on top of my bed.

I woke up a little later and couldn't stop thinking about what she'd said about Jamie, and how he'd looked at me. Was she right? Was I right? Was he interested, or was he just being nice? I thought back to what he'd said earlier. He hadn't said he wasn't interested. In fact, he'd said he liked me but wasn't sure he was ready to date. Why had I assumed he was only being nice? That he didn't like me? Was I really that insecure?

The short answer was yes, because Craig had destroyed my self-esteem.

I started thinking about what it'd be like to go on a date with Jamie. I imagined him being the perfect gentleman, bringing me flowers and opening doors for me. He wouldn't give me judgmental looks if I ordered pasta.

I imagined Jamie was the kind of guy who would drop me off after a date, walk me to the door, then give me a hug and a gentle kiss. A kiss. It was stupid to think about kissing Jamie, but that didn't stop me from thinking about what his lips might feel like on mine.

His soft, full lips would gently brush mine, hesitant at first, then inviting. He'd let me decide if I wanted more and I'd part my lips just enough to let him know I did. He'd put his hand on my cheek, his strength obvious from how easily he controlled the pressure of his touch. Not too much, not too little. He'd tilt my head up towards him just a little as he parted his lips. Then he'd tease my upper lip with the tip of his tongue and I'd moan into his mouth as I returned his kiss, begging for more.

Holy shit. Just thinking about kissing him had me all worked up. I got up and went to the bathroom. If I'd been alone, I might have let the fantasy go a little longer. Maybe even all the way. I wasn't as adventurous as Ashley but I wasn't a prude either, and had satisfied myself a time or two.

But I wasn't alone. And it was too late, or maybe too early, for a cold shower. So I settled on rinsing my face in the coldest water the tap could provide.

Chapter 24

Jamie

I couldn't hang around but wasn't ready to go home yet, so I went to visit Isabelle instead. I needed to talk to someone, work through my feelings about Emily, and Isabelle was the safest option. She'd always been understanding and compassionate, and wouldn't judge me no matter how confused or stupid I sounded.

It felt weird at first, talking to my late wife about my feelings for another woman, but after a few minutes my words flowed as I settled into the one-sided conversation.

"I don't know if you remember Chris's little sister, Emily. Well, she's had a rough go of it recently and we're helping her out." I summed up why we were protecting her.

"The thing is, I'm attracted to her, and if she weren't a client and not Chris's sister, I'd consider asking her out. But she is, so it wouldn't be right. Right?" I fidgeted, picking at the grass as I talked to her in the moonlight. "I don't know what to do."

I didn't expect an answer, but I felt better getting it off my chest and out of my head.

I should probably talk to someone who can talk back.

When I stood up to leave, I heard Isabelle's voice in my head telling me everything would be okay, and reminding me that life was too short to be lonely and unhappy. Tears filled my eyes and this time I didn't bother holding them back—I was painfully aware of just how short life could be.

I kissed the tips of my fingers and laid them on her headstone. "I miss you."

I'd parked in the garage, and was walking down the hall when I overheard Meg ask, "Do you think Jamie will admit he likes Emily? I mean, did you see how he handled that guy at the bar?"

I stopped and listened.

"Yeah, that was a bit over the top, especially for him," Jack answered. That tone meant I'd hear about it later. "The manager was none too pleased, I had to talk him down from calling the local LEOs. He thought Jamie was a bit too rough for a cop."

They weren't wrong, I'd over-reacted. Seeing those guys corner Emily had triggered my primal protective instincts. At least I hadn't punched him.

"Ashley picked up on it too," Meg said. "I didn't say anything to you because you were busy, but she asked me if he's always like that."

Shit, does Ashley think I'm like Craig?

"What'd you tell her?" Jack asked Meg. I could hear his defensiveness from my position in the hall. *Thank you, Jack.*

"What do you think I told her?" Meg sounded offended. "I told her he's only like that when he's protecting people he cares about." She didn't say when he's working, she said when he's protecting people he cares about.

Was I that obvious?

"Sorry, I didn't mean for it to come out like that." I could imagine Jack looking apologetic.

"Forgiven." There was a pause before she spoke again. "I think she likes him too, but she seems nervous, like she's not sure it's okay to like him."

AJ added, "Ashley said Emily likes him but Asshat Craig fucked her up pretty bad, wrecked her confidence."

Great, it wasn't enough that Jack and Meg were discussing my non-relationship with Emily, but so were AJ and Ashley.

AJ continued, "She's rooting for them to get together. She said, and I quote, "Em deserves a hot guy who'll protect her and treat her like the queen she is." Then she reminded me that while she wants that for herself someday too, she's not ready to give up her single-girl lifestyle just yet."

Meg laughed. "Do you want more?"

"Nah." I could hear the humor in his voice.

Thank God, they're done talking about me and Emily. I was about to step around the corner but stopped dead when I heard Meg say, "A hundred bucks says they hook up tomorrow."

Well fuck! I waited to see what Jack and AJ would say.

"I never take a bet I'm guaranteed to lose." Jack laughed.

"He knows better than to bet against me, I'm a stud." AJ sounded proud as a peacock.

It wasn't about us. Thank God.

"And humble," Meg added, "but I was talking about Jamie and Emily. I expected you to hook up with Ashley tonight."

Shit. Meg was still talking about us. I debated walking away but couldn't make my feet to move. I wasn't proud of myself for eavesdropping but I couldn't stop myself.

"Nah, she didn't want to bail on Emily." Meg made that sound girls make when they think someone is being sweet, it sounds something like "aw" but is usually longer and at a pitch that makes dogs whimper.

"Should we try to encourage them?" Meg asked.

"No, we need to let them figure things out on their own. They both have some stuff to work through. And let's not forget she's his best friend's little sister."

Thank you, Jack! Now maybe they'd leave us alone.

"Chris knows Jamie's a great guy and he has to know Emily would be lucky to date him," Meg argued.

I was grateful to them for defending me, and annoyed they wouldn't stop talking about it. *My head's all over the fucking place.*

"You're right, but big brother's tend to get irrationally protective about their little sisters. Though I do think he'd come around eventually," Jack answered. After I pause, he added, "But we have to let them figure it out for themselves. So no playing Cupid, okay?"

I could have heard a pin drop in the ensuing silence.

"Meg?" Jack asked.

"Fine. I won't play Cupid. Happy?" I could imagine her pouting.

"Blissfully."

I didn't need, or want, to hear anymore. Knowing I couldn't pretend I hadn't overheard their conversation if I joined them, I slunk down the hallway and went to bed.

So much has changed in the last two weeks.

I ran towards the car, my heart pounding, my lungs gasping for air. I heard the gunshot cut through the eerie silence like a crack of thunder. Then another. My heart stopped. My feet didn't. Blood splattered the windows. After what felt like an eternity, I reached the car. My gun drawn as I reached for the driver's side door handle. I was too late. Dave was leaning against the steering wheel, blood, and flesh oozing from the hole in the back of his head. Please God. I looked over and saw Isabelle slumped against the passenger side window, lifeless. I ran to the other side and ripped the door open. Please, dear God, let her be alive. My stomach heaved as the metallic smell of fresh blood, her blood, overwhelmed me. I pulled Isabelle from the car and fell to my knees, clutching her still body to my chest, sobbing. She didn't have a pulse. "No No No!" I looked to the sky and released my heartbreak in a blood-curdling scream.

I jerked awake, haunted by the memory of Isabelle's death. I picked up my phone: three-twenty-two.

At least I hadn't woken anyone up by screaming. I walked over to my dresser. I didn't need light to see Isabelle's smiling face in our wedding picture—it'd been seared into my memory long ago.

"I'm so sorry," I whispered as I wiped away the tears rolling down my cheeks. Knowing I wouldn't be able to fall back asleep, I took my laptop to the kitchen table and updated my notes for Emily's file.

Chapter 25

Emily

The next afternoon, Ashley drove us to Jamie's for the BBQ. The SSI person shadowing me followed us and I'm sure it annoyed him when we stopped at the grocery store to get snacks, and then the liquor store to get beer and wine. They said we only had to bring what we wanted to drink but that didn't feel right to either of us, so we bought three dozen red, white, and blue decorated cupcakes, and enough beer and wine for a small army.

Ashley couldn't make up her mind so she grabbed a variety, saying she wanted options, "It's not like beer goes bad."

I couldn't argue with her logic.

On the drive over, Ashley reminded me not to let my history with Asshat Craig cloud my judgment about Jamie. I thought she was crazy when she told me to pretend he hadn't said anything last night, and start today fresh. But after thinking about it, I realized she was right. Even if Jamie wasn't interested in dating, we were still friends, and I didn't want to feel awkward around him. I decided I'd approach today as a friend, with no expectations.

Then Jamie answered the door, looking sexy as sin in his dark blue cargo shorts and a fitted gray t-shirt. A wide smile spread across his face when he saw me.

This is going to be a lot harder than I thought. Last night's fantasy flashed before my eyes, causing me to blush. *Way to stay cool.* I forced myself to stop thinking about what it'd feel like to kiss him, but my heart continued to beat a little faster. Wanting to hide the embarrassment written all over my face, I studied the cupcakes I was holding as if my life depended on my ability to memorize every feature.

Jamie took the cupcakes. "How many people do you think will be here?" His tone was light. "Hey Jack, come take these so I can release Eric."

Jack took one look at the stack of cupcakes and laughed. "That's a lot of fucking cupcakes."

"Come on in. AJ's helping Doug with his smoker. They'll be here in thirty or so," Jack said as he led us to the kitchen. Not that we needed a guide, we could see the kitchen from the doorway. Jamie had a spacious, open floor plan.

Ashley shrugged, like she didn't care, as she set the bag of wine bottles on the counter. "I'll go grab the beer."

"There's more?" Jack asked incredulously.

Just then Meg walked in and gave us each a hug, gushing about how happy she was we were there. "These things are usually alpha-male testosterone heavy." She rolled her eyes at

Jack, who'd lifted an eyebrow at her. "It'll be nice to have some girl power for a change."

"Did you just say alpha-male testosterone heavy like it's a bad thing?" Ashley asked, fanning her face. "Because that sounds like heaven to me."

Everyone laughed, then Meg told Ashley she only thought that way because she didn't have to deal with them all day, every day.

Jamie, who'd been low key staring at me since he came back in, laughed, then patted her on the head as he said, "You know you love us Meg, alpha-male testosterone and all." I expected her to argue, but all she did was swat his hand away and roll her eyes.

Ashley remembered she was supposed to get the beer. "Hey Em, come help me with the beer."

Jamie and Jack both spoke up. "I can grab it." They were cut from old school southern gentleman cloth. My mother would approve.

Whoa! No need to think like that.

"No, we got it. Girl power, right Meg?" Ashley showed off her biceps as she asked.

Jamie and Jack both turned and stared at Meg, waiting for her to answer—looking like cats ready to pounce. Based on their expressions, I had a feeling she let them do most of the heavy lifting.

Meg looked from Jack to Jamie then back to Jack, she obviously wanted to agree with Ashley, but her sheepish expression made it clear she knew they'd call her out if she did.

"Right. Except for lifting heavy things," Meg said.

"And reaching the top shelves," Jamie added.

"And killing spiders," Jack grinned.

"And open-"

Meg cut Jamie off. "We get it! I need a little help sometimes. No need to gloat or rub it in." She tried to sound upset but was laughing too hard to pull it off.

God I want what she has. Not only did she have a fun, loving relationship with Jack, but she had an easy going friendship with his brother. It was the kind of fairytale relationship every girl dreams about.

"We got it. Come on Chica."

I turned to Ashley after she closed the door. "What's up?" She wouldn't have turned down the guy's offer unless she wanted to talk privately.

"Just want to make sure you noticed how Jamie looked at you when we got here." She was grinning like the Cheshire Cat. "He may not be ready to say it, but he's definitely into you."

I smiled, not a nice normal smile but a goofy grin that ruined any hope I had of playing down my feelings. I looked at my pink flip-flops, hoping she hadn't noticed. She didn't say anything else as we each grabbed a case of beer from her trunk.

"Is it bad that I like him?" I asked as I put my case down on the trunk. "What if he's just being nice? Will people think it's too soon?" I didn't want Jamie, or anyone else, judging me for jumping from one relationship to the next.

"Emily, your last relationship was shit because your last boyfriend was an abusive asshat." She apologized when I cringed. She wasn't wrong I just didn't like hearing it put so bluntly. "You deserve to find someone who'll love you and treat you like the queen you are. You can't help the timing, and seriously, who cares what other people think if you're both happy?"

She was right. I shouldn't care about what other people thought, but I did. I always had. That'd always been one of the biggest differences between me and Ashley. I always worried about what other people thought, while she rarely ever did. It's why she could live a carefree, adventurous life and I, well, I couldn't. Truth be told, I was a bit jealous of her.

"I know you're nervous, but he's worth the risk. You know he's a great guy, always has been. It's not just an act to impress you. He has a great job, he's genuinely caring and protective, your friends and family already like him, he's-"

"I get it, he's great." I picked up my case of beer again. "But I'm not even sure he feels the same way so-"

"And hot. Like stupid sexy hot." She cut me off, completely ignoring my argument. "You can't tell me you don't want to ride that!" She laughed when I blushed all the way to my forehead. Never, not in a million years, would I have said something like that. *Even though I fantasized about it last night.* And she knew it, which was exactly why she said it.

"He is hot." There was no denying it.

"Maybe bat your eyes at him a little." She exaggerated batting her eyelashes at me as we walked. "To let him know you're interested. Guys love that shit."

"I'll look like a stupid cartoon if I try that." I'd never been good at flirting, especially the finer art of physical flirtation.

I couldn't get the cartoonish image of me batting my eyelashes at Jamie, all demure and innocent, and him gushing with big eyes and his heart beating outside his chest. When I thanked Ashley for the visual, we started laughing again. We were still laughing when we got to the door.

When Jamie opened it, the image came back stronger than ever and I laughed so hard I snorted. Which caused us to laugh even harder. Then Ashley got the hiccups. We were laughing so hard, we could barely stand up straight. Jamie grabbed the cases of beer from us, carrying one in each hand. "Do I even want to know why you're laughing so hard you're crying?"

I shook my head no, because there was no way I could answer yet. We finally stopped laughing enough to stand up and wipe the tears from our eyes as a truck pulled up. AJ and Doug. I looked at Ashley, and she looked at me. We batted our eyelashes at each other, and busted out laughing all over again.

"Do I want to know?" Jack was standing behind Jamie, smirking.

"Dude, I have no idea what's going on," Jamie said as he held the door open for us.

We hung on each others arms, trying not to laugh which only made us laugh more, as we walked to the island in the kitchen. I was sure everyone thought we were crazy.

Jack went out to help AJ and Doug bring the smoker, and their coolers, to the back yard. Luckily Jamie went out to help them after putting the beer on the counter, which gave Ashley and I time to recover.

We felt comfortable enough to tell Meg why we were laughing so hard as we helped pack coolers with ice, beer, and water. It'd lost some it's power, so we didn't lose control. Neither did Meg, which was good because if she had, we would have too.

"Are you going to do it?" Meg asked after we stopped laughing.

"Do what?"

"Bat your eyelashes at him? Let him know you're interested."

Oh my God, she's serious. "I don't know. I'm not sure it's a good idea." They both looked at me like I was crazy. To get them off my back I added, "If I flirt, it'll have to be something a little less cartoonish." I didn't think I could ever bat my eyelashes again without losing it.

"Good." She gave me a warm smile. "I think you should."

I was half hoping she'd say Jamie likes you too, but she didn't. Maybe she didn't know, or she knew and didn't want to betray his confidence. This was all so confusing; Jamie told me he's interested but not ready, so we should just be friends, and I assumed he was just being nice. But Meg seemed sweet, so I doubted she'd encourage me if she thought Jamie wasn't interested. Ashley was completely convinced he was interested.

I nodded but didn't know what to say, though I was comforted by her encouragement since it felt like a nod of approval. As flattering as it was, I was still unsure about the whole situation. Luckily, I was saved from having to respond by the arrival of the SSI guys.

Doug and AJ gave Meg hugs before greeting us. I noticed their guns when their shirts lifted a little and remembered something Jack had said earlier about all the alpha males making their house the safest place in Texas. Then I wondered if it was because I was here, or if it was normal for them to wear their guns everywhere. Probably normal, just about everyone in Texas had a gun so it'd make sense for guys who did security for a living to always wear theirs. I'd ask Jamie later if they were working. *I hope not.* I didn't want to feel guilty if they got stuck working because I was here.

AJ said hi to me without taking his eyes off Ashley. She was looking extra sexy in her tight jean shorts and a low-cut, white tank top with rhinestone fireworks decorating the front. How she managed to look casual and sexy at the same time was beyond me. I was in jean shorts, and a royal blue tank top with cute red and white flowers. I looked casual for sure but wasn't even close to looking sexy. Then again, I wasn't trying to.

Doug introduced himself, "Hi Emily, nice to meet you personally."

I shook his hand. "Hi Doug. Nice to meet you, too."

Then he introduced himself to Ashley, who turned to Jamie and asked, "Is everyone who works for you hot? I mean, I'm not complaining, just curious." She was still shaking Doug's hand.

Doug shook his head in disbelief, then pulled his hand away from hers.

Jamie mimicked Doug, but didn't answer.

Jack smoothed his hair back and stood taller as he answered, "It's our number one priority at Sheppard & Sons Investigations to provide top-notch security eye candy." He sounded like a radio announcer acting out one of those old fashioned ads, causing everyone to bust out laughing.

Meg rolled her eyes so hard I could have sworn I heard them hit the back of her head. "Good lord, I need a drink. Anyone else?"

Everyone raised their hands. We worked together to carry the coolers, food, and picnic supplies out to the backyard, where they'd set up canopies over two picnic tables. The grill and smoker were set up a few yards away. They'd also set up folding chairs around a fire pit which was piled high with wood. We'd have one hell of a bonfire later. I relaxed as Ashley and I helped Meg set the tables while the guys started grilling.

"Are you expecting a lot of people?" I asked as I put plastic utensils in the cute Fourth of July themed holder.

"Yes and no, people will be coming and going all day. Most of the SSI guys plan to stop by at some point. John and Mary are coming over later this afternoon and Jamie said your brother might stop by. So, there might be a lot of people, just not all at once."

I didn't realize Jamie had invited Chris. Though I shouldn't be surprised, they were best friends.

After we'd set the table, finished prepping the food, and the guys finished fawning over Doug's smoker, they started grilling. Jamie and Jack started the chicken first, since it'd take longer.

I paused, looking around to make sure the guys weren't within hearing distance before whispering, "I was thinking about maybe flirting with Jamie, but maybe this isn't the right time or place-" I cut myself off. Did I really want to go through with it? Hadn't I just decided I was okay staying in the friend-zone?

"Here." Meg pushed a plate of burgers into my hands. "Take this over to Jamie, and start flirting."

"Oh, I couldn't." I tried to protest, but she turned me towards the grill and gave me a gentle push.

"Of course you can, just follow Ashley's lead." We looked over to where Ashley was standing next to AJ, tracing the lines of his tribal tattoo, and gushing over his biceps.

"Well, maybe be a little more subtle than that." We chuckled like old friends sharing an inside joke. As I carried the plate of burgers to Jamie, I wondered if he had any tattoos. I couldn't see any, but he had a lot of skin I couldn't see.

When I handed the plate of burgers to Jamie, his fingers brushed against mine sending shivers down my spine. I looked up and gave him what I hoped was a flirtatious smile. My nerves had me worrying I might look like a deranged freak or something. I released the breath I'd been holding when he smiled back, his hazel eyes sparkling in the sunshine.

"Thanks."

I didn't want to leave, so I asked, "Need any help?"

"Nah." My heart dropped.

Then he winked. "But you can keep me company while I man the grill."

Once again, I assumed the worst. And was wrong.

Relieved, I answered around my smile, "I can do that." We talked about random stuff, nothing too serious, which was nice. I'd expected things to be awkward between us today, but was glad they weren't.

I hadn't eaten anything since a yogurt at breakfast, and almost died when the heavenly smell of grilling meat made my stomach growl. I didn't even get to finish thinking, *I hope no one heard that,* when Jamie said, "The burgers are almost done. Can you grab the cheese?"

He asked the crowd, "Who wants cheese?"

There was a chorus of "Me" and "I do" as everyone answered.

Jamie melted the cheese, then plated the chicken and burgers before carrying them to the tables where everyone was claiming their seats. It shouldn't surprise me that everyone made sure there was a space for me to sit next to Jamie, there or at a far end which would have been rude. I had a feeling we'd be pushed together a lot today. Everyone, including me if I was being completely honest with myself, wanted us to happen.

"I'm so hungry I could eat a cow!" Meg joked as she reached for a pan of baked macaroni and cheese.

"Is that bacon in the mac and cheese?" I asked as my mouth started to water.

Meg nodded as Jack said, "It's Meg's specialty." He practically glowed with pride. "It's become a staple in our house."

"It was my grandmother's recipe. It's super easy to make, and has always been one of my favorites."

"It looks delicious."

Then I heard Craig's voice in my mind, "*You should stick with a salad and a burger with no bun so you don't get any fatter.*" I closed my eyes and told the voice to shut up. *Great, now I'm worried I'll look like a pig in front of everyone.* I looked around, Meg and Ashley weren't being shy about loading up their plates. No one here would judge me or call me fat for eating some pasta. *Fuck you, Craig.* I helped myself to a big scoop of the mac and cheese, a burger with all the fixings, well except onions. I couldn't hide my smile when I noticed Jamie didn't put onions on his either. Then I chastised myself, it probably had nothing to do with me. *For all I know he doesn't like onions.*

I'm pretty sure I moaned a little as I ate. Not only did it all taste so good, but it felt good to enjoy a fun, judgment-free meal with friends.

We were finishing up with lunch when John and Mary arrived. There were hugs and handshakes all around. Jamie introduced Ashley to his parents.

When they joined us at the table, John helped himself to a burger and a big serving of Meg's mac and cheese before sitting beside me.

"Have you tried this yet Emily? It's amazing," he asked around a mouthful.

"I did Mr. Sheppard, and you're right, it was so good I'm pretty sure I was drooling." I blushed. *Did I say that out loud, to Jamie's dad?*

"I wouldn't blame you. It's drool worthy. And please, call me John." He called down to Jack, "Son, pass me a beer will ya?"

"Any preference? We have lots to choose from," Jack asked as he lifted the cooler lid.

"Surprise me."

"Mom?" Jack asked before closing the cooler.

"I'm good, I'll pour myself some wine." Mary was sitting next to Meg and they were whispering excitedly while glancing at Jamie. Meg's guilty smile told me all I needed to know, they were talking about me and Jamie.

I put my hands in my lap, and looked down at my plate as my mind started racing. If they were talking about us, then Mary probably knew I liked Jamie. Did that mean she thinks Jamie likes me? Did she want us to get together, or was she worried about her son being with someone like me? Is she worried I might bring trouble because of Craig? Does she even know about Craig? I knew there was client confidentiality, and stuff like that, but did it count if it was the owner's wife, or mother?

I heard Craig's voice telling me I was stupid, ugly, and fat. I clenched my teeth in an effort to shut him up. My hands started shaking. *This is all too much.* I was barely out of my old relationship and here I was worried about what Jamie's mother thought of me. I was thinking like someone who was worried about meeting her boyfriend's parents for the first time, like we were already dating. Which we weren't.

I felt a warm hand on my shoulder. "Em, are you okay?" Jamie's voice was thick with concern as he whispered in my ear.

Shit, I must look pathetic. I felt the heat in my cheeks as I nodded but didn't look up.

"My mom brought brownies and cookies, want to come help me carry them out?"

Oh my God, I could hug him right now. He'd just offered me a chance to get away from all the prying eyes.

"Yes please." *That was a stupid response.* Nothing like making it obvious I wanted to run away and hide. Luckily, no one except Jamie and John heard me. I tried to hide my embarrassment by looking at my feet, because everyone was watching us as we walked away, even though they tried to look like they weren't.

I followed Jamie inside, not sure how I was going to respond if he asked me if I was okay again. Should I say 'nothing,' or tell him the truth. *Can I do that without being embarrassed? Or making it weird between us?*

Jamie stopped in the kitchen and faced me. "Are you sure you're okay? Did someone upset you?" He looked, and sounded, worried.

"No. I'm not upset. I'm just, it's…" I tried to collect my thoughts and failed. Then started rambling, "I saw your mom and Meg whispering, all animated and eager, and then Meg gave me this huge grin like she knew some big secret and I know it's stupid but I kinda freaked out because Meg knows

I like you." I stopped short and snapped my eyes up to look at him.

Holy shit, I just blurted out that I like him.

When he didn't say anything I tried to apologize, "Oh my God, I'm so sorry Jamie-"

"Em-"

"I didn't mean to-"

"Emily." Jamie raised his voice, I stopped talking and looked back up at him. My first instinct was to be afraid, but it only took a second to realize he wasn't mad. He had the cutest smile on his face. "I like you too."

He tucked a strand of hair behind my ear.

"But you said-"

"I know. I lied." He paused. "To myself, and to you. I'm sorry."

"Really?" *God, I sound like a pre-teen. Get your shit together.*

"Yes, really." He reached out and gently grabbed my hands, then pulled me closer. "I have a long list of reasons why I shouldn't ask you out, but right now all I can think about is how nice it'd be to get you alone so we can talk."

"I'd like that." I was pretty sure I'd just agreed to go out on a date with Jamie. Of all the scenarios I had running through my mind when we came inside, this wasn't even close to being on the list.

He pulled me in for a hug. "Me too." His arms felt warm and strong as he wrapped them around me. I wanted to stay there, warm and safe, for a lot longer than the few seconds the hug lasted.

He pulled away. "It's kind of weird, isn't it? We've known each other most of our lives, but we don't really know each other. Not as adults. I want to get to know the adult version of you, Emily." He paused. "Does that make sense?"

"Yeah, because it feels the same for me." *A date!*

We were quiet for a moment. "Jamie, can we keep this between us for now? I'm not sure I can deal with." I looked outside. "All that right now."

"Of course." He chuckled. "They can be a bit much."

I nodded, grateful he understood.

"We'll have to talk to Chris sooner rather than later. He'll kill me if he finds out from anyone else."

I laughed. It seemed insane that Chris would go all protective big brother against his best friend, who he hired to protect me. But whatever, guys were dumb that way.

"I guess, but not yet."

"Come here." He pulled me into a hug, and it felt… different, more intimate, more meaningful. Maybe it was the way he placed his hands on my lower back, or the way he applied a bit more pressure than he had before. I couldn't put my finger on it, but this hug felt like more. I rested my head on his chest, wrapped my arms tighter around him, and sighed.

"We'll figure this out together, okay?" He pressed his cheek to my head, and my heart melted. I went from I don't know, to my heart melting in less time than it took to cook a burger medium rare.

"Okay."

Chapter 26

Jamie

I can't believe I asked Emily out on a date.

The SSI company BBQ was a full-day event with food and games, plus a bonfire and s'mores after sunset. It was the perfect opportunity for me to talk to Emily as friends, with no pressure, and get to know her better. I wasn't sure either of us was ready to take our relationship to the next level, but I figured it couldn't hurt to talk, test the waters, and if nothing else we'd strengthen our friendship.

But then Emily got uncomfortable at lunch and I'd asked her to help me inside so I could check on her. While she was word vomiting, must be a female thing because Meg did it too, she let it slip that she liked me.

That was all it took for my defenses to crumble.

I grinned like a goofball, then asked her out in a round about way instead of directly, like a gentleman. In my defense, I hadn't planned on asking her out at all, at least not today. The plan was to wait until things had settled, and then plan something nice. I totally fucked up that plan.

How did I get from I can't because I'm not ready, and she's my best friend's sister, to asking her out so quickly? Maybe it was the relaxed atmosphere, maybe is was the vulnerability in her eyes when she confessed. It didn't matter. Whatever caused it, I'd given up the fight.

I couldn't help but notice the expectant faces when we walked out together, carrying trays of baked goodies. I tried to convince myself they were all eager for my mom's cookies and brownies, but I couldn't.

They were bound to notice we were both more relaxed, and my-kid-in-a-candy-store grin. I'd never been good at policing my facial expressions outside of work. As a cop I'd had to, and you'd think it'd carry over into my personal life too, but no.

We didn't say anything, and no one asked. They didn't have to, their knowing glances said it all. It probably didn't help that we sat a little closer and smiled a little more than we had before our trip inside.

Chris and Vicky came over about four-thirty, just missing my mom and dad, who, not wanting to miss out on Doug's famous smoked ribs, said they'd be back after taking care of a few things. After Chris introduced Vicky to anyone she didn't know, they grabbed a drink and sate down.

Emily was nervous, and it showed. She stared at the ground anytime she wasn't busy organizing or cleaning something. She wasn't acting like herself and Chris was bound to notice.

This isn't how I want him to find out about us.

As if on cue, Chris asked, "Is everything okay? Did we interrupt something?"

"No man, it's all good." I hated keeping this from Chris, but now wasn't the time or place to talk to him. I'd talk to Emily later, and we'd figure out a good time to do it together.

Chris and Vicky couldn't stay long because they were taking advantage of a Zoe-free day and going to see a movie. Who could blame them? I wouldn't want to spend my baby-free time with a group of people either.

Emily and I walked them to their car, hugged them goodbye, and sent them on their way. I refused to let the nagging guilt take up residence in my mind. We'd talk to him later, before our first date, because there was no way in hell I'd sneak around behind his back.

Emily and I both relaxed after Chris left. Probably a little too much because it wasn't long before I saw Ashley and Meg corner Emily, looking like expectant puppies waiting on a treat.

I barely had time to wonder if she'd tell them before AJ and Jack cornered me. Doug joined us a few minutes later. I could only assume Ashley put AJ up to this, and Meg probably encouraged Jack to help him. It was starting to feel more like a high school party instead of a business outing.

Doug crossed his arms but didn't say anything as he watched Jack and AJ interrogate me, a grin on his face. I'd told Emily I wouldn't tell anyone yet, but I wasn't sure I could keep our secret without lying, so I feigned ignorance and did my best to avoid answering their questions.

Then I heard the giggles, and looked over at the girls, who were laughing and hugging. When I made eye contact with Emily, she shrugged and nodded. She'd told them. Which meant it was okay for me to tell the guys. When I begged them not to make a big deal out of it, they refused to make any promises.

Jack slapped my shoulder and congratulated me. "I'm happy for you, big brother." He looked over his shoulder at the girls. "Meg is clearly thrilled. Don't be surprised if she tackles you with a hug later."

I laughed, knowing he was right. Which was fine by me, I never minded getting a hug from Meg.

After a few rounds of congratulations and more back slapping, we sat down around the unlit fire pit. Not long after, the girls joined us. Emily sat in the chair next to me, giving me the sweetish, shyest smile I'd ever seen.

And my heart melted.

Turns out, it wasn't so bad having everyone know about us. I doubted the guys would tease us too much, they liked Emily and wouldn't want to make her uncomfortable. Of course, that didn't mean they wouldn't tease me when she wasn't around. They didn't give two fucks about making me feel uncomfortable. *The price of admission to the brotherhood.*

As I stood up to grab a round of drinks, Meg ran over and tackled me in a bear hug. Good thing I saw her coming, so I could brace myself. All the congratulations and excitement seemed overkill for a simple date. I had to ask, "It's just a date, why are you so excited?"

"Because you look so happy."

"She's right," Jack agreed. I'd say he agreed to make Meg happy, but I knew he meant it. "I'll help you with the drinks."

I had a feeling we'd be revisiting the talk we'd had earlier this morning, when I told him I was thinking about asking Emily out but wanted to know what he thought about the potential conflict of interest if we started dating. When I asked if it'd been difficult to stay professional when Meg was in danger, he his raised an eyebrow. He was kind enough to not ask me if I was blind, or stupid, or both. Because it'd been damn near impossible for him to keep his cool when Meg was in trouble.

Instead, he said he trusted me to remain professional unless she was in immediate danger. "Then you'll lose it, like I did. It's part of who we are. You won't be able to distance yourself any more than I could. In fact, it may be harder for you because of what happened to Isabelle. But trust me, we'll bench your ass if we think you can't keep your head on straight."

Seven months ago, I'd said the same thing to him. Today, I replied the same way he had, "You'll try."

Then we laughed.

Jack was right, my history with Isabelle could make this job a hell of a lot harder for me. And while they might try, they wouldn't be able to bench me anymore than we'd been able to bench Jack. We'd managed to help him hold his shit together, but I don't think Death himself could have prevented Jack from going after Meg. And he wouldn't be able to keep me from doing the same for Emily.

Jack snapped my attention back to the present when he clapped me on the shoulder.

"You know, if anything happens, we'll have your back. And hers. Just like you had mine and Meg's." Jack paused, giving it time to sink in. "I know your worried, but she's worth the risk. You haven't so much as looked at a woman since Isabelle died, let alone shown interest. This is a big deal."

"Thanks. I needed to hear that."

"Anytime, big brother." He gave me a hug. "Now let's get moving, our women are thirsty."

Our women. My smile stretched from ear to ear.

Conversation ebbed and flowed as we hung out, waiting for the ribs to finish smoking. The rich sweet smell of BBQ sauce hung thick in the air, making us all hungry even though we'd stuffed our faces at lunch.

After a while, we teamed up and played bags, which quickly turned into a game of dodgeball when Doug and I faced off against Jack and AJ. The girls had been watching but scattered once bags started flying. I couldn't blame them for not wanting to get caught in the line of fire. We'd all be sporting some pretty ugly bruises tomorrow, the consequence of not moving fast enough. We were going at it hard when Ma's voice cut through the chaos.

"James Richard and Jackson Edward, what do you think you're doing?"

Oh fuck! She'd used our middle names.

We all spun around and stood at attention, dropping any bags we were holding. Unfortunately, AJ had already let one fly, and I didn't know it, until it hit my arm.

"Fuck." His eyes opened wide as saucers as he realized he'd just sworn in from of my mom. "Sorry."

Mom looked annoyed, but ignored him. Dad looked amused, and shockingly didn't say anything. I didn't understand why she was upset until I noticed a bag on the ground a couple of inches to her left. *Shit, it must have just missed her.*

"Sorry Mrs. Sheppard," AJ and Doug said at the same time Jack and I said, "Sorry Ma."

"Game's over boys." Dad chimed in. "Unless you can play like civilized adults."

I heard AJ grumble, "Where's the fun in that?"

"What was that, Janerek?" His grin lessened the threat in his question.

"Nothing, sir." AJ was only willing to push my dad, his boss, so far. Even if he didn't seem upset. Funny, he never worried about that with me or Jack—his other bosses.

I'd been so focused on not getting yelled at that I hadn't noticed Beth or her five-year-old son, Chase, until I heard him giggling. He loved it when dad got all authoritarian with us. I think it's because we all stand at attention like the obedient soldiers we are whenever he used that tone.

"Beth, Chase, glad you could make it." I walked over and hugged Beth before picking up Chase and swinging him around. "You're getting so big. I won't be strong enough to lift you if you keep growing."

He hugged me back, giggling, then asked, "Where's Auntie Meg?" He was squirming to look around me, so I put him down and pointed him in the right direction. He ran towards her, squealing.

Meg had met Beth, one of my mom's closest friends, when she started working at Grannie's, mom's coffee shop, and they'd became fast friends. One night, Beth needed a babysitter on short notice and Meg had volunteered. She and Chase had been 'bestest friends', as he liked to say, ever since. Meg adored him as much as he adored her.

Jack grabbed Chase and lifted him up just before he barreled into Meg. "Whoa there, little buddy, let's not knock Auntie Meg over, okay?"

"Okay." He sounded impatient. "Put me down."

Beth yelled, "Chase! Manners."

"Please?"

"As you wish." Jack winked at Meg as he placed Chase on his feet.

Meg went to one knee so she could hug him. "Hey Chase. What's up?"

"I got a new coloring book and dinosaurs…" Chase talked up a storm, going a mile a minute. Meg listened patiently, indulging him until he got bored. *She'll be a great mom someday.*

Beth made the rounds, greeting, or meeting, everyone. Then, as we watched Meg help Chase cheat at bags against Jack, I happened to look at Beth. She wasn't watching Chase. She was staring across the game. At Doug. *Really?* I looked at Doug to see if he'd noticed, but he was busy checking the ribs.

Chapter 27

Emily

I couldn't stop thinking back to Jamie putting his hand on my lower back as he introduced me to Beth's son, Chase. He hadn't left it there long, just long enough for me to miss it after he moved it.

And for his parents to notice. Neither said anything, but Mary's eyes sparkled with joy.

Doug announced the ribs are done as he carried over a tray heaping with slabs of barbequed meat. My mouth watered as the sweet smell wafted over to us. Everyone commented on how good they looked and smelled as we took our seats. Doug set the tray down, then bowed his head in appreciation as he soaked up our rowdy applause. AJ carried over a second tray and placed it on the other end of the table before sitting down next to Ashley.

Once again, there was enough food to feed a small army. We heaped our plates with ribs, cornbread, potato salad, and corn on the cob. I savored every bite, and anytime I heard Craig's voice scolding me, I looked at everyone laughing and stuffing their faces, and reminded myself that he was wrong. It didn't matter if I indulged, or even over-indulged, on a good meal. No one here would judge me, and my value as a person wasn't tied to my waist size. It was the perfect meal. Somewhere between my first and second piece of corn bread—I had to have two because Beth had made regular and jalapeño and it would have been rude not to try both—my anxiety about me and Jamie dating started to fade away. The steady flow of wine might have helped, but mostly it was the warm, welcoming atmosphere.

Jamie's phone interrupted my thoughts. He answered, "Hey Eric, you're just in time, come around the back and grab some food."

We all scooted to make room for the two part-time SSI workers who'd just arrived. Jamie introduced me and Ashley to Sammie and Eric, which felt a little weird, since they'd been sitting outside my house, shadowing me, but also made perfect sense because we hadn't actually met yet. It was nice to officially meet the people who sat outside my house day after day, keeping me safe.

After dinner, we played more bags, and this time everyone behaved. Chase insisted on teaming up with Meg. When I told Jamie I thought Chase had a crush on her, he agreed, saying, "Jack likes to tease Chase about trying stealing his girl."

Ashley and AJ challenged me and Jamie to a game. I tried to decline, because I legit sucked at most games that required hand-eye coordination, but they wouldn't let me. We lost, despite Jamie's high point count. Jamie handled AJ's trash-talk like a champ. I was too, until fear swept through me. Would Jamie be upset that we lost? Craig hated to lose at anything, and would get angry, especially if he thought it was my fault. And Jamie and I definitely lost because of me.

Jamie must have sensed my worry because he held my hand and said, "We'll get 'em next time."

My shoulders dropped about two inches as the tension drained from them. He didn't care that we lost. He joked about how bad I was as we walked away, whispering that he couldn't wait to give me private lessons. I blushed, praying those private lessons would include physical contact.

Chase wanted to play against his mom, so Beth asked John to be her partner. At one point I thought I saw Doug watching Beth, no, not watching, staring. But I dismissed it, somehow I couldn't image stoic Doug having a thing for happy-go-lucky Beth.

I challenged Ashley and AJ to a rematch with some wine-induced smack-talk. Ashley promptly told me I talked a big game for someone who had to rely on her partner to score all the points. Jamie laughed and told her he'd happily help me kick their asses and let me take all the credit. *He's so sweet.*

We won, by one point.

I jumped up and down and gave Jamie a big hug. "Thank God we won. I wouldn't have been able to show my face if we lost after all my smack-talk."

"We?" he asked, his arms around me, laughing. "Who's this we you're speaking of?"

I'd only scored two points. "But, I thought we were a team?" I asked with a fake pout.

"We are."

Everyone was having a blast, talking, playing, and drinking. As the sun set, Doug lit the bonfire and eventually everyone made their way over to sit and relax.

Chase had the energy of a puppy, running around talking to everyone and eating up all the attention heaped on him. Beth and Mary laughed as they blamed the three cupcakes he'd eaten.

Beth said, "He rarely gets a lot of sweets, but today's a special occasion."

"He'll sleep great once the sugar high wears off," Mary added. She should know, she'd raised three rowdy energetic boys.

Ashley and AJ were no longer being subtle as he played with her hair while she sat on his lap. Jamie noticed too, and offered to drive me home later so Ashley didn't have to worry about it. I didn't want to ruin the moment, so I didn't tell him I had Ashley's keys because she planned on making AJ drive her home after their night together.

The guys bonded over stories about high school and sports, while we girls got to know each other better. It felt a little weird talking to Mary as an adult, since I'd spent most of my life looking up to her as Mrs. Sheppard. But it was nice. Eventually, the two conversations converged and turned to more adult topics like careers, military service, family, and business.

Every once in a while, my mind would wonder back to the kitchen, where I'd agreed to go on a date, with Jamie Sheppard. Never in a million years would I have thought I'd be going on a date with my high school crush. Somewhere between high school and now he'd gone from being cute to being the kind of guy I read about in romance novels. I felt my cheeks flush and hoped no one would notice.

As the evening wore on, people started saying their goodbyes and going home. Mary gave me a hug when she and John said goodbye, which caught me off guard, but in a good way. When Doug offered to carry a sleepy Chase to Beth's car for her, she gladly accepted. Eric and Sammie thanked Jamie for the invite, then reminded me not to take it personally if they didn't say hi to me while they were working. I thanked them and promised them I wouldn't.

There were only six of us left as the fire was slowing burning itself out. Meg was now sitting in Jack's lap, her head resting on his shoulder, and Ashley and AJ had moved to the other side of the fire so they could make out. I didn't know if they realized we could still see them, or if they even cared.

When Jack yelled across the fire, "Get a room."

AJ replied, "On it, boss."

Jack and Meg. AJ and Ashley. *Jamie and me?*

My nerves got the best of me, again, so I told Jamie I had to use the ladies' room and went inside. Once safely behind the locked bathroom door, I let my tears fall as I took care of business. Then I rinsed my face in cold water and told myself to take it one day at a time. Just because Ashley was hooking up with AJ, and Jack and Meg were engaged, didn't mean Jamie and I had to pretend we were a couple, or hook up, or any of the other possibilities I had running through my head.

Yes, we were sitting close to one another. And we'd hugged each other, a lot, during the games. But we hadn't gone on our date, so we weren't a couple, yet.

Jamie was waiting in the hallway when I walked out of the bathroom. "Are you okay?"

Damn, was it that obvious? "Yeah." I nodded without conviction.

"Em." He took a step towards me. "You don't have to pretend with me."

I looked into his eyes and forgot why I was nervous. *He's so sweet.*

And sexy. I wanted to kiss him. Right now.

"I know." And I meant it. I slowly closed the distance between us as if under a spell. All I could think about was kissing him. I broke eye contact to look at his lips. My breath caught in my throat when one side of his mouth lifted in a grin.

Am I going to do this? Can I take one more step, wrap my arms around his neck, and kiss him?

I could. When I pressed my palms against Jamie's chest, I felt it rise just before he exhaled my name. His rough voice sent shivers down my spine.

I raised up on my toes, so our lips were even, and slid my hands up his chest and around his neck. I could feel his warm breath on my face and his hands on my waist.

"Kiss me." I said a second before I pulled him closer. Our lips close enough to touch.

I kissed him.

Jamie gripped my waist tighter before sliding his hands around my back and pulling my chest into his. I tilted my head and parted my lips to deepen the kiss. He moaned as his tongue danced with mine, making my head swim. I'd never felt so sexy in my life.

Jamie turned me and pushed me against the wall, his hand grabbing my ass, his kiss demanding. I gripped his neck, begging for more.

Then he was gone. The pressure of his hands. The warmth of his lips.

"Fuck. This is a mistake."

My heart shattered. A mistake? With fresh tears blurring my vision, I pushed past him, grabbed my purse off the counter, and ran out the front door.

I ignored him when he called out, "Emily, wait."

I'm a mistake. I unlocked Ashley's car, hopped in, and fumbled with the keys. My tears were flowing freely, making it hard to see. But not so hard that I couldn't see Jamie as he ran across the street.

As soon as the engine turned over, I yanked the car into drive and pulled away. I didn't want to hear anything else he had to say. The word mistake echoed like a pinball through my mind as I drove home, the road blurred by my tears.

God, I'd been so stupid. I tried to be more assertive, more carefree, more like Ashley. And it had totally backfired. *Jamie thinks kissing me was a mistake.*

He'd been so nice all day. So charming.

Craig was charming too, in the beginning.

When I turned onto our street, I looked for the SSI car but didn't see it. *Right.* I was with SSI all day, so the person assigned to shadow me for the night wouldn't start until I came home. Which I'd just done rather abruptly. I could only assume Jamie called whoever was scheduled after I left.

I pulled into my parents driveway, shoved the car into park, and shut it off before getting out, slamming the car door and storming to the porch. I looked over my shoulder as I fumbled with my keys, suddenly feeling exposed. There was no one here to protect me if Craig showed up.

Chapter 28

Jamie

"What the fuck just happened?" Ashley's angry voice cut through the chaos in my mind as I walked back into the house.

What the fuck, indeed.

One second I was kissing Emily, the next she was running out the door. Except that's not exactly what happened. I was holding her against the wall, kissing her, claiming her. When I grabbed her ass and pulled her into me, something in my brain clicked—Emily deserved better than being groped in the hallway. I doubt she'd expected me to act like a horny college frat boy when she initiated the kiss.

I'd pulled away, jerked away really. I meant to tell her what I was thinking, how I felt, that she deserved to be treated with respect, wooed, loved properly.

But what came out? This is a mistake. I didn't have time to correct myself before Emily's eyes rounded in shock and filled with tears, then she pushed past me and ran out the door. I'd called out, unable to make my stupid feet move to follow her, but she ignored me. My feet finally obeyed my head when she slammed the door, and I ran after her calling her name. But I was too late, she was already in the car, and had sped away the instant the engine revved to life.

I fucked up, big time.

"Shit." I needed to get Dean to the Taylor's house. I pulled out my phone and called him. When Ashley started demanding answers, I put up my hand to quiet her and turned around so I didn't have to see her glaring at me. I could only put out one fire at a time.

"Dean, it's Jamie, Emily just left, can you get to the Taylor's ASAP?" I was afraid if I followed her, I'd make things worse. But I wouldn't leave her without protection.

I pocketed my phone and turned back to Ashley. And AJ. *Great, an audience.*

"What the fuck happened, Jamie? Why did Emily race out of here?" Ashley crossed her hands over her chest and shot daggers out her eyes at me.

"I was kissing her. But it was all wrong." Ashley raised an eyebrow. "Not kissing her, the circumstances." I looked over her shoulder to see Jack and Meg walking in. Their concern evident in their body language, and etched on their faces.

I didn't want to talk about this, at least not with them, so I did what I do best and started problem solving. I was about to tell Ashley she needed to go support Emily, but she beat me to it.

"AJ, can you take me home?" Her voice was laced with anger as she glared at me.

"Sure thing." He gave me a sympathetic look before turning to Jack and Meg. "I'll come back and help clean up after I drop Ashley off."

"No worries, we got it," Jack answered.

Ashley grabbed AJ's hand and dragged him towards the front door. "Let's go."

After they left Meg asked me what happened. I gave them the abbreviated version, highlighting my stupidity. Then asked what I should do.

I can't believe I'm asking Meg for relationship advice. Then again, she went through something like this with Jack, so maybe she was the perfect person to help me get through to Emily.

Meg suggested I give her time, let her calm down, because right now she was acting on raw emotion.

It wasn't what I wanted to hear, so I ignored her.

Chapter 29

Emily

I pulled out my phone to text Ashley that I'd come home, and tell her she should stay and enjoy herself. I saw no point in ruining both our nights.

But as soon as I touched the screen to unlock it, it lit up with alerts.

Sixteen texts, all from Craig. *Fuck.* I started trembling all over. I took a deep breath and unlocked my phone.

Great, there were five voice messages too.

Shit. I sat on the couch, opened the texts and scrolled to the first one.

It was time stamped at five-seventeen.

I miss you baby.

I know you miss me too.

What are you doing today?

I bet you're sitting home alone and regret leaving me.

Why aren't you answering me?

Where are you?
Who are you with?
Why aren't you answering your phone?
You need to answer me.
I'm worried about you.
What the fuck Emily.
You can't just ignore me.
You bitch answer your phone!
You're with some guy aren't you?
You better pick up when I call you.
You bitch. You'll pay for this.

My breath was coming in short, ragged spurts as I finished reading his texts. The time-stamped on the last one was nine-forty-two.

With shaking fingers I opened my voicemail app and hit play on the earliest message.

Craig had tried to sound sweet, concerned, but I could hear the anger behind it. He didn't try as hard in the second message, and by the fourth he'd given up the pretense. In the fifth, his hateful, angry words were slurred so badly I could barely understand him. After a few seconds, I heard a thud and dead air until my phone cut the message off. My hand shook as I pulled the phone away from my ear.

I can't fucking believe this. The day had started out so well, great in fact. But now I had one guy tell me I was a mistake after kissing me, and another threatening to tie me up, drag me home, and teach me a lesson.

Fear, anger, and disappointment fought for priority in my mind as I wiped at the tears rolling down my cheeks.

I told myself it sounded like Craig had passed out so I had nothing to worry about. He was way too drunk to drive. The cops were always out in full force on holiday weekends, especially ones that involved a lot of drinking, so he'd never get to Weatherford without getting pulled over. *Assuming he's in Houston.*

I got up, looked out the window, and sighed in relief when I saw a familiar car parked out front. SSI was here. *That was fast.* I sucked in a deep breath and felt some of the tension leave my shoulders as I exhaled. If Craig somehow got here, they'd see him and stop him. I tried convincing myself there was nothing to worry about, but it didn't work.

I saw Ashley get out of a truck, which I assumed was AJ's, then let herself in with the key I'd given her yesterday.

"Emily? Are you okay?" She closed the distance and pulled me into a hug.

How does she know? Did Jamie tell her?

I decided to talk to Ashley before messaging Jamie. I couldn't handle talking to him after what had happened, and the last thing I wanted right now was run to him crying about Craig.

I shook my head but didn't answer. It was pretty obvious I wasn't okay. *Which problem do I tell her about first?*

"What happened with Jamie?" Ashley asked, saving me the trouble of having to decide. She sat next to me and put her arm around me.

Could this night get any worse? Guilt washed over me because I'd cock-blocked my best friend. Or whatever the female equivalent was. It wasn't my biggest concern, but it was the easiest, least painful one, to think about.

"I kissed Jamie, and–" I sniffled. "And he said kissing me was a mistake."

"What the fuck?" My head snapped up when I heard Chris's angry voice from the doorway.

Shit, I didn't hear him come in. My night had officially gotten worse. I was already upset about Jamie, worried about Craig, and feeling guilty for ruining Ashley's night, the last thing I needed was to add my brother's self-righteous anger to my list of problems.

My phone buzzed, alerting me to a text message. I held my breath as I picked it up, scared it might be Craig again.

But it was Jamie. Ashley read the text over my shoulder, "Jamie's here."

Before I could say anything, or even process that Jamie was outside, Chris said, "I'll handle this." Then he stalked out the door looking like he wanted to kill his best friend. The sound of the door when he slammed it made me jump.

Vicky sat next to me and rubbed my back as I buried my face in my hands and cried.

This is all too much.

Chapter 30

Jamie

I parked on the street in front of the Taylor's house and texted Emily from my SUV. Then I waited.

She didn't text back, but I saw the door swing open, so I got out of my car and started up the driveway.

It was Chris, not Emily, and he was closing the distance fast as he marched towards me.

Fuck, he knows. I stopped in the middle of the driveway, put my hand out to signal to Dean to stay put.

Chris's body language, and the look of murderous rage in his eyes, made it clear I was about to get punched.

"You asshole!" He pulled his right arm back and closed his fist. I could have easily blocked his punch, but I braced myself for the hit instead, knowing I deserved it.

I rubbed my jaw as he stepped back, shaking his hand in pain. "I'm paying you to protect my sister, not kiss her."

I growled. "Watch it." I'd let him punch me for being a stupid idiot as much as he wanted, but I wouldn't let him insult Emily. "You don't know what happened."

"What I do know is that when I came to pick up my daughter after a lovely evening with my wife, I found my baby sister crying." He poked me in the chest. "Because of you." He stepped back and crossed his arms over his chest. "You need to leave." He nodded towards my truck. "Now."

"Please, give me two minutes to explain." I repeated, "Please?"

After glaring at me through squinted eyes for what felt like an eternity, he barked, "Two minutes."

"We were kissing," I said, ignoring the fury in his eyes. "And I realized I was out of line. Emily deserves better–"

"Damn straight she does."

That stung, but I ignored it and continued, "I'd asked her out on a date earlier, and she said yes. We were going to talk to you first, I swear." I paused and took a deep breath. "But then I kissed her." Technically she'd kissed me, and it was crazy sexy, but I didn't think he'd want to hear that. "And when I realized how inappropriate it was, I said: Fuck, this is a mistake." I ran my hand through my hair. "Except I didn't mean kissing her, or dating her, I meant the circumstances."

Chris's expression had slowly changed from murderous to pissed off as I explained.

This wasn't how I'd wanted to have this conversation with him, but I didn't have much of a choice, so I confessed.

"I like her Chris. She's the first woman I've considered dating since Isabelle." It wasn't an exaggeration, I hadn't even looked twice at a woman. And he knew it. "I didn't plan on this. Hell, the last thing I expected when I took this job was to be attracted to her. But I am. She's an amazing woman." He nodded. "And if she's willing to listen to me, I'd like to apologize and beg her to forgive me." I paused, giving him a moment to process it all. His face relaxed into a slightly less miffed expression, so I pushed forward. "I'd like to take her out, do things the right way. With your permission, of course, but first I have to apologize."

I held my breath while I waited out the awkward silence as Chris took forever and a day to make up his mind. Despite having known him most of my life, I wasn't sure what he'd decide.

After a few more seconds, he said, "You need to fix this. And if you ever make my baby sister cry again, I'll kill you."

"Noted." I held out my hand and waited for him to shake it.

"I'm only giving you a chance because I know you, and I trust your intentions, despite how pissed off I am right now."

"Thank you." That meant a lot. "Listen, I know it's a big ask, but any chance you can convince her to talk to me tonight?"

Chris shook his head in disbelief, then said, "I'll ask, but I won't force the issue." His back was to the house so he couldn't see Ashley staring out the window, turning back towards the room every so often.

I assumed she was reporting what she was seeing to Emily and the look on her face gave me hope.

"Wait here."

I nodded, folded my hands in front of my waist, and mentally prepared myself for a long wait. After a few minutes, Chris opened the door and waved me in.

The first thing I noticed when I stepped inside was how badly Emily's hands were trembling. There was no way that was because of me. I might have hurt her, and even pissed her off, but I hadn't scared her.

Every other thought fled my mind as concern drove me across the room in a few long strides. I got on my knees and took her hands in mine. Ignoring everyone else in the room, I asked, "Emily, what happened?"

She shook her head as tears started to well up in her puffy, red-rimmed eyes.

"Emily, please. I'm sorry I hurt you, but I don't think that's what this is about." I wiped away a tear, then gently lifted her chin so she had to meet my eyes.

She sniffled, then glanced at Chris, Vicky, and Ashley before whispering, "Craig texted and called me."

I ground my teeth and forced myself not to clench my fist around Emily's delicate hand. It wouldn't help the situation if I let my anger show.

"What? When?" Chris asked, sounding both shocked and angry.

I looked at Vicky, begging her without words to let me sit next to Emily; thankfully she understood, got up, and stood near Chris. I sat down, put a comforting arm around Emily, and felt her shoulders relax under the weight of my arm. I pulled out my phone and quickly texted Dean to let him know Craig had made phone contact.

Emily answered her brother's questions while Ashley interjected her support for Emily, and her anger at Asshat Craig.

"Emily, can I see the texts and listen to the voicemails?" I needed to know what he'd said, and gauge if he was an immediate threat. She nodded and handed me her phone with the text app open. It wasn't hard to see the anger escalating in his texts. When I handed it back to her, so she could pull up the voicemails, she asked if she should play them on speaker.

I said no; not only did she not need to hear them again, but no one else needed to hear them either.

My blood boiled as I listened to the voicemails, and it took every ounce of training I'd ever had to keep my face neutral and my hands relaxed. I wanted to kill the bastard for threatening Emily.

After I finished, I thought Emily was probably right, the thump at the end of the last call was more than likely him passing out, but I wasn't taking any chances.

Without thinking about how it sounded, I said, "Emily, I think you should stay with me tonight." Emily looked shocked, and Chris grumbled, so I quickly corrected myself. "Not with me, but at the house. You and Ashley can have my room. I'll sleep on the couch."

I didn't like the vacant look in her eyes as she nodded her head, like she didn't think she had a choice. Because she did. I might not like it, and I'd stay up all night watching the house if she said no, but I'd respect her answer.

She can't read your mind. "Emily, it's up to you. And I'll respect your decision." I said, at the same time Chris asked if it was really necessary.

Emily asked, "What about my parents?"

I answered Emily first, "Dean's parked outside, he'll watch out for them."

I looked at Chris. "I'd feel better if Emily is somewhere Craig doesn't know about, at least for tonight. We'll report the restraining order violation first thing tomorrow morning and re-evaluate the situation when we have more information."

Emily looked at Ashley. "Is it okay?"

"We'll do whatever you want." Then she looked at me. "It might be fun to have a slumber party at the hot bodyguard's house."

Emily's laugh was hollow, but I saw her shoulders relax a little more.

I rubbed Emily's back, comforting her. "Everything's going to be okay. I won't let him hurt you."

Maybe it was overkill to be treating the situation like the threat was imminent, but we didn't know Craig's state of mind, or where he was. For all we knew, he was already in, or on his way to, Weatherford and I wasn't willing to take that risk.

Chris wanted to stay but had to take Vicky and Zoe home, so I reassured him we had everything under control and told him I'd text him when we got back to my place. We shared a surreal moment when he shook my hand, and thanked me.

"What a fucking night," he said, shaking his head.

I rubbed my jaw. "What a fucking night," I agreed before hugging Vicky and kissing my goddaughter on the forehead. Making eye contact with Chris, I said, "She's a lucky girl." Her dad might not be a warrior by trade, but he'd always be there to provide for and protect her.

"Thanks."

While I waited for Emily and Ashley to pack their bags, I called Jack to let him know what had happened. Then I called Dean and let him know Emily would be leaving with me, but I needed him to stay and finish his shift.

When Emily and Ashley came down, I messaged Dean to let him know we were on our way out. Before we left, I asked if she'd left a note for her parents so they wouldn't be worried.

"I did. Thanks."

Ashley held Emily's hand, offering what little comfort she could, on the quiet drive back to my place. I could see Emily's lip trembling as she held back tears.

Fucking bastard! My knuckles turned white as I clutched the steering wheel in a death grip, wishing it was Craig's neck. I wanted to strangle him for what he'd done, was still doing, to her.

Emily's mine to protect. I will not fail!

The smell of freshly brewed coffee greeted us the instant we entered the hall. I put their bags down near my bedroom door, and ushered them into the kitchen.

I wasn't surprised to see Meg with Jack when we walked into the kitchen. Like Jack, she'd want to help any way she could.

Jack greeted us, then said, "AJ's on his way." He looked at Emily, concern written all over his face. "Are you okay?"

She nodded, though it was clearly not true. "I'm sorry you had to get up."

"No worries, we always stay up late to celebrate the Fourth." I don't think I've ever loved my brother more than I did in that moment.

"I made some coffee, and boiled water if you'd rather have tea." Meg acted like making coffee and tea at eleven-thirty was perfectly normal.

"Thank you." Emily voice was still shaky but not as bad as it was. With any luck, we'd help her feel safe enough that she could relax and get some sleep tonight.

Emily and Ashley sat at the kitchen table with me and Jack. No one spoke as Meg brought over coffee, hot water and tea bags, some snacks, and tissues. "I'll be in the office if you need me."

"You're not staying?" Emily sounded like a scared child, and it broke my heart.

"I can if you'd like."

"I would." She looked down at her hands. "Please?"

"Of course," Meg said as she sat next to Jack.

As Emily told Jack what had happened, I watched her body language. Craig was a potential threat, but I needed to know if she believed he was an immediate one. She'd tell me more non-verbally than she might realize.

When Jack asked her if it'd be okay if he read the texts and listened to the voicemails, she unlocked her phone and handed it to him.

Based on Emily's body language as Jack listened to the messages, she fully expected Craig to make good on his threats, if not tonight, soon. Jack and I made eye contact and without words agreed a shadow wasn't enough anymore—Emily would have a bodyguard for the foreseeable future.

"Emily, if you're okay with it, I'd like Doug to copy the texts and voicemails from your phone for our records. It'll also allow us to provide a copy to the police when we report Craig in the morning." I hated the look of terror that flashed across her face. "This is the second time he's violated the restraining order, and we can't let it slide, especially since he's threatening you again."

Emily nodded her consent and understanding.

"Meg, can you email Doug and ask him to come in tomorrow morning?"

Jack looked down at his phone and stood up. "AJ's here."

Jack stayed with the girls while I filled AJ in on the details. He didn't hesitate to volunteer his services, "Any time I'm not on the clock, that is."

I slapped him on the back. "Thanks man. I appreciate it."

"Anything for family." It felt good knowing he had my back, and Emily's. Not that I ever doubted it, but it never hurt to be reminded when shit went south. "So what's the game plan beyond hunkering down at Chez Sheppard for the night?"

We sat down and talked strategy for about an hour before the girls started nodding off.

I quickly changed the sheets on my bed while Emily and Ashley used my ensuite bath to change. I made sure they had everything they needed before returning to the kitchen.

Meg had started a list of things we needed to do, and we added to it as the night went on. We did what we could by email, including letting everyone know we'd upgraded Emily's detail to full-time bodyguard and asking who wanted extra hours since we'd still be covering the Taylor's home. Luckily, Emily worked from home, so it wouldn't be difficult to provide the extra coverage. When I said as much, Jack was quick to remind me that I'd probably be volunteering for bodyguard duty twenty-four-seven." I wanted to argue, but what was the point, he was right. I'd be taking as many shifts as I could.

Before retiring, fully dressed, to the recliner, I emailed the SSI team with a detailed update of the situation, and the new game plan.

Chapter 31

Jamie

The recliner was great for napping, but not for getting a good night's rest, so I was up early. Careful not to wake AJ, who was sleeping on the couch, I wrote a quick note letting Meg and Jack know I'd gone shopping, and put it in front of the coffee maker before checking on Emily.

She and Ashley were still asleep in my king size bed.

Emily. In my bed. I quietly closed the door as I forced myself not to think about how natural she looked lying there in my bed, her hair spread out on my pillow, one leg sticking out of my sheets. Regret washed over me, I hadn't had a chance to apologize properly to Emily last night. *Hopefully I'll have a chance later today.*

At the store, I grabbed fresh baked pastries, a variety of yogurts, and pre-cut fruit, then headed home to brew some much needed coffee. I could hear voices when I walked into the hall from the garage. Jack, Meg, and AJ were standing at the island, drinking coffee—our list in front of them.

Emily and Ashley were the last to get up, and before joining us, Emily asked if she should strip the bed. I waved my hand and told her I'd do it later. *I wonder if the pillowcase will smell like her?* I shoved a piece of melon in my mouth to interrupt my thoughts.

After breakfast we met Doug at the office so he could download the texts and voicemails from Emily's phone, and make copies for the local PD. Ashley stayed at the office with Meg, AJ, and Doug while Jack and I escorted Emily to the Weatherford PD to report Craig's restraining order violation. Once that was done, we called Houston PD since that's where it was originally filed, and where Craig lived. We emailed them copies of the local police report, text messages and voicemails.

They issued a warrant for his arrest, and put out a BOLO between Houston and Weatherford but couldn't actively go looking for him yet. It wasn't ideal, but I understood. Today was the Fourth of July, and they'd been swamped all weekend, and would be again today, with the typical holiday bullshit every police department dealt with when people got drunk, plus the added fun of drunks playing with explosives. *I don't miss those days.*

Dad was waiting for us when we got back to the office. "How are you holding up, Emily?"

"I'm okay, Mr. Sheppard." Emily looked less scared than she had last night, but I could see her nervousness in the way she kept playing with her thumb ring.

Dad didn't know I'd asked her out, though he was observant enough to know I was attracted to her. Not that it mattered now, after what had happened last night, I needed to press pause on our relationship. Before it even begun. Keeping Emily safe had to be my number one priority.

I filled him in as we walked upstairs to the conference room. Meg stayed with Emily and Ashley in one of the upstairs meeting rooms. Because Craig knew SSI was protecting Emily, neither Jack nor I felt comfortable leaving the girls alone downstairs. We'd locked the door, but it could be breached. And while Meg was pretty handy with her gun, she wasn't a trained professional and shouldn't have to act as one. It was a harsh reality—one we were well acquainted with—that shooting someone, even in self defense, came with consequences: legal, emotional, professional, and social. We didn't want Meg to go through that again.

As a team we reviewed the logistics of adding extra coverage for Emily, and the Taylors, around our existing jobs.

Doug asked, "Has Emily reconsidered our offer to install cameras?"

"She's still against it, doesn't want to feel like she's living under a microscope." I wish we could insist, but it was up to her and her parents, and they were against it.

Once we had everything organized, we went back to our place for lunch. Luckily, we had a ton of food left over from the BBQ. Meg, Emily, and Ashley set out a buffet on the counter and everyone made themselves a plate.

Emily picked at her food but ate little, not surprising—nerves tended to either kill or enhance an appetite. *Now I know which it is for Emily.*

Ashley had to leave a couple of hours after lunch, she was reluctant to go but Emily insisted. "I'll be fine Ash. And I'll call you every day."

"Okay, but know that I'm only a phone call away if you want some company."

Emily hugged her. "Thanks."

"Love you girl." Ashley hugged her back.

"Love you too."

AJ said his goodbyes before walking Ashley to her car so they could say goodbye privately. Then he had to go to the Taylor's, he'd volunteered for the afternoon shift, joking that he'd rather earn holiday pay than be a fifth wheel with us all day. I didn't care why he was doing it; I was just glad we didn't have to ask someone to cancel their holiday plans. We understood how hard it was for cops on the holidays because we'd lived it—they rarely had them off, and valued the few they could spend with their families and friends. Dad and I worked more holidays than we had off when we were cops, and with Madi, Jack and Jaden serving in the military, let's just say our family was used to celebrating the holidays when schedules allowed. We hadn't a holiday dinner with all of us in the same room in over a decade.

"Emily, can we talk for a few minutes?" I wanted to clear the air between us.

"Yeah, sure." She looked nervous, so I put her at ease by taking her hand and leading her to the couch. We had an open floor plan so we wouldn't have complete privacy, but it was better, less distracting, than talking to her in my bedroom. Thankfully, Jack and Meg took the unspoken hint and went on the porch to look through wedding magazines.

"I'm sorry for what I said last night." She started to speak, but I wasn't done. "Please let me finish. I don't think you're a mistake. I don't think we're a mistake. And I sure as hell don't think kissing you was a mistake." Emily's eyes rounded as they glossed over.

"I thought I was being disrespectful by groping you against the wall. We haven't even gone on a date and I was ready to rip your clothes off and take your right then and there." I hadn't intended to be so blunt but I couldn't take it back, so I continued, "That's the part that was a mistake. Being disrespectful." I squeezed her hands. "But you deserve better than that."

I reached over and wiped away the single tear rolling down her cheek. "I'm not sorry I stopped, but I am sorry for hurting you with my careless words."

"I forgive you. Can you forgive me for over-reacting?" I didn't think she needed to apologize but it was easier to accept it and move on.

"Forgiven." I released her hands. I needed to stay professional. For now. No matter how difficult it might be.

"Thank you." Her soft smile turned my insides to mush.

It's been a long time since I've felt like this. We talked for over an hour before I heard her stomach rumble softly.

"Want to order a pizza and watch a movie?"

"You don't have to order pizza." She smiled shyly. "I'm not very hungry and don't mind having leftovers again." Her stomach growled louder.

She might not have minded, but I didn't want leftovers again. Guessing she wouldn't argue if I got Jack and Meg involved, I texted Jack asked him what they wanted on their pizza.

They were laughing as they walked into the kitchen. Jack asked, "Dude, did you just text me from the living room?"

I shrugged. "It was faster and easier."

"I want all the cheese." Of course she did, Meg always wanted extra cheese on her pizza. Sometimes she'd get pepperoni too, but mostly just cheese.

Jack said he didn't care, "As long as there's meat."

"Em, anything you don't like?"

"I'm good with all the cheese," she quoted Meg.

I ordered two pizzas, one supreme and one with extra cheese.

Emily asked Meg about the wedding plans while we ate. Meg practically glowed as she gave Emily all the details. Jack smiled, nodded, and agreed as needed.

"We're having a small ceremony here in the back yard. I want lots of fall colored flowers. Other than that, I'm not too picky. We're keeping it small and simple." Meg didn't know Jack had always wanted a big traditional wedding, but Meg didn't have any family, so Jack had embraced the idea of a smaller one. He said the size wasn't nearly as important as making sure his future wife felt comfortable at her own wedding. *Good man.* Meg was doing most of the planning, but Jack had a few non-negotiables: having the family pastor marry them, and having the food and open bar catered, so everyone could relax. Meg was happy to agree.

After eating, I told Emily to pick a movie, and thanks to Meg, we now had a female friendly selection of movies for Emily to choose from. She picked a romantic comedy, then fell asleep a few minutes after it started. I didn't last much longer.

I woke up when I heard Jack come into the living room to shut off the TV. Half asleep, I didn't realize Emily was leaning against me until it was too late, and I woke her up when I moved. She sat up with a start and gave a little yelp when she realized she wasn't in her bed.

"I'm so sorry, I didn't mean to fall asleep," she said around a yawn.

"No need to apologize. I fell asleep too."

She looked around the room, noticing it was dark outside. "It's late, I should go home."

I understood but was still disappointed. "Okay, I'll take you. Do you want me to stay while you talk to your parents?"

"If you don't mind."

"Of course not." I tucked a wayward hair behind her ear, then pulled my hand away and shoved it in my pocket.

It's going to take an ungodly amount of effort to keep myself from touching her.

Chapter 32

Emily

When Jamie dropped me off he told me he wanted to hold off on dating because he didn't want to lose focus.

"Why?" I wanted to sound confident but my voice betrayed me—giving away my confusing and hurt.

"I'm worried I might not be able to do my job if I'm distracted."

He thinks I'm a distraction? What the fuck? I felt my hurt shift to anger.

"It's fine. I get it-"

He cut me off, "Emily, you're not listening to me."

"I heard you Jamie. You don't want to get distracted. It's fine." Of course it wasn't fine. I was pissed off, and hurt. After all his talk at the BBQ, and his eloquent apology earlier, he dumped me before we had our first date. *Whatever, I should have known.*

"Emily, please, I–"

"Don't worry about it Jamie. I won't distract you anymore." I rushed out of the car and ran up the walkway.

I heard him call my name just before I slammed the door behind me, shutting him out.

All I wanted to do was eat a gallon of ice cream and cry. I felt like such an idiot. I'd gotten my hopes up when he'd apologized, so I was totally unprepared for this.

My mom called out from the kitchen, "Em is that you?"

"Yeah." I wiped the tears from my face.

"Dad and I are having ice cream, want some?"

"Love some! I'll be right in." I needed to tell them what happened, so they'd be prepared, but I didn't want to. Fucking Jamie, he was supposed to help me. Whatever, I didn't want his help anymore.

I could see the bags under my eyes when I looked in the mirror. Evidence of a sleepless night, and too many tears shed. *Fucking Craig. And fucking Jamie.*

I splashed cold water on my face. It wouldn't help me look less tired, but at least it washed the tears away.

I put on my best fake smile and walked into the kitchen. Dad was half watching a baseball game on TV as he and Mom talked.

"Cookies and Cream okay?" Mom asked as I walked towards the fridge. I had half a bottle of rosé that I intended to finish with my ice cream.

"Yeah, sounds good. Anyone want a glass of wine?" I didn't expect them to say yes, Dad was a beer guy and Mom had tea.

"No thanks." My dad said at the same time my mom asked, "With ice cream?"

"It's been a day. So yeah, with ice cream." I thought about saying 'so don't judge me' but it seemed rude.

Dad gave me his full attention and asked, "You want to talk about it?"

"What did Chris tell you?" *That came out snarky.* "I'm sorry Dad. I'm tired and stressed. Forgive me?" I gave him my best puppy dog eyes, the expression I reserved for those special occasions when I knew I was wrong.

"Of course." He patted my hand. "And to answer your question, all he told us was that Craig contacted you, and SSI is assigning a bodyguard for you anytime you leave the house, as a precaution."

That was the abbreviated version, but it was enough. They didn't know about what had happened with Jamie, nor did they need to. They adored Jamie and I didn't need them telling me I should be more patient. I'd had the patience of a saint with Craig, and look where that got me.

"That's about it. He violated the restraining order so Houston PD issued a warrant for his arrest. This should all be over in a few days."

My dad lifted his coffee. "Cheers to that." My mom raised her tea, which she always drank in her grandmother's delicate floral china. It felt comical clinking my wine glass to his coffee mug and her dainty tea cup, but I did it anyway.

"Cheers." I took a big sip and prayed I was right.

Chapter 33

Emily

Four days later and Craig still hadn't contacted me. All that worrying for nothing. All the added stress, for nothing. All the extra coverage Chris would have to pay for, for nothing. I felt like an over-reactive scaredy cat.

I hadn't heard from Jamie either. Except yesterday, when he came to the house to tell me officers had arrested Craig the day before, at work, and he'd posted bail that morning. When I mentioned wanting to block Craig's number, Jamie asked me not to. He said Craig might contact me before coming here, giving SSI time to prepare.

That was it, he didn't try talking to me about anything else. *I was right, he doesn't want to go out with me.*

After four days with out a peep, I was beginning to think Craig had finally given up. SSI helped me move and reported him when he violated the restraining order, so maybe he finally realized it was stupid to keep harassing me.

Is it finally over? I hoped so. I was done with him; he'd never touch me again. Sadly, it seemed I was done with Jamie too, though that wasn't by choice.

Later, Ashley called and said, "I'm coming over tomorrow." She insisted on take me out to Sunday brunch, and shopping, claiming I needed some cute new clothes, and something sexy for when Jamie got his head out of his ass and finally asked me out. She didn't believe for a second that Jamie didn't want to go out with me.

"Listen Em, it can't be easy worrying about protecting you when all he wants to do is kiss you. He's afraid he'll fuck up."

I can't believe she's defending him. "I don't think that's it. I think he realized I'm too messed up and have too much baggage. He changed his mind after he saw all those texts from Craig."

"You forget, I was there. I saw the look on his face. He was scared-"

"Of failing at his job."

"You don't really believe that, do you?"

"I don't know. He told Chris I was more than a job but now, now he's acting like I'm nothing more than a client he has to protect. He said I'm a distraction."

"You're acting like an idiot-"

Did she really just called me an idiot? "What?"

"You heard me. I love you Emily Taylor, but right now you're acting like an idiot. Think about it, he lost his wife to a stalker. He's not afraid of failing at his job. He's afraid of making a mistake and losing you. Like he lost Isabelle. Why can't you see that?"

"I…" Could she be right? I hadn't really given him a chance to explain. Had I twisted his words and freaked out over nothing? What would he have said if I hadn't run away?

"Listen, I know you're not an idiot, so please just think about what I said."

Maybe she had a point. Jamie had felt helpless when he lost Isabelle a few years ago. And maybe he was worried about me getting killed by Craig. *But wouldn't he want to be closer to me, if that's the reason?* I convinced myself it wasn't the same. Isabelle was the love of his life. I was his best friend's little sister who wasn't smart enough to leave the guy who beat her up. He wanted to do his job and protect me. And that was all.

When I didn't answer her right away she said, "We'll talk about it tomorrow, over mimosas."

I emailed Meg at SSI, so they'd know I was going out. I pounded the keys on my laptop as I apologized for not having enough details.

Why am I apologizing for having plans with a friend? I told her Ashley was picking me up around eight, then we were going out for breakfast and shopping. I hit the enter key harder than necessary to send the email. My frustration was unjustified, but I was sick and tired of having to report my every move like a kid who got grounded for missing curfew.

I want my life back. I knew it was for my safety, but I was convinced the threat had passed. Craig hadn't contacted me and I'd didn't think he would, so I thought it was crazy I still had a bodyguard. Craig's messages had scared me, so I'd felt better the first day or so knowing someone from SSI was nearby. But I didn't need them anymore. Surely if he was going to retaliate, he would have done it by now.

In her reply, Meg told me not to apologize for not having all the details, which took a little of the energy out of my anger. She asked if we wanted Eric to drive, suggesting it'd be easier for everyone. She added it might be fun if we thought of him as our chauffeur, adding we could have mimosas at breakfast or drinks at lunch without worrying about driving. Meg had no way of knowing Ashley and I had teased Jamie about being our chauffeur when we went to the fair last week. I cringed at the memory. What had started as an amazing weekend had ended in fear and heartache.

For the last week, every time I looked at the car outside I'd hoped to see Jamie. It didn't matter that Meg sent me a schedule so I always knew who was assigned to watch the house, and who was assigned to me if I went anywhere—I still hoped to see Jamie. At first I was surprised Jamie was never listed as my bodyguard, but then I remembered he thought I was a distraction, so it made perfect sense.

I wanted to decline—I didn't want a driver, or a bodyguard, and I didn't want to keep being reminded about Jamie and his need to keep a safe distance from me—but figured I should talk to Ashley first.

My text to Ashley was more about venting than asking her opinion. And once again, she sided against me.

Come on Em, it'll be fun to have a driver.

Seriously??

Seriously! We can call him Jeeves and act all posh and drink in the back seat.

I couldn't help but laugh, despite how annoyed I felt with her.

We can't drink in the car, it's not a limo.

Fine, but I like the idea of having mimosas with breakfast and starting the day off right.

She had a point. A mimosa or two might help me relax and take my mind off things for a few hours while we went shopping.

Okay, I'll tell Meg Eric can drive us around.

Yay!! *smiley face emoji*

The next morning, Eric parked in the driveway twenty minutes before Ashley's expected time. He waited in his car, then met us at the door when I texted him we were ready to leave.

Does he really need to escort us to his car and open the doors for us?

I forced myself to laugh when Ashley made a joke about there still being a few gentlemen left in the world, before climbing into the back seat. Eric didn't crack a smile. Something about his professional tone when he answered her with 'yes ma'am' made me anxious. His presence reminded me that Craig was still a threat. Or at least SSI thought so. Which was exactly what I didn't want to think about today.

Today was supposed to be a fun girl's day and I regretted not taking our own car. *At least then we could try to lose him.* I shook my head at my foolishness. Not only did I think we weren't clever enough to ditch a professional bodyguard, but I couldn't do that to my family, or SSI—they'd assume the worst if I succeeded. Not to mention, SSI would start a man hunt, and then everyone would be mad at me. And in the end I'd feel even worse, so it'd be a lot of chaos for nothing.

Ashley searched online and found a cute little café just outside Fort Worth. "They're famous for their breakfast mimosas," she said with glee as we looked at the menu during the drive. We'd be ready to order as soon as we sat down.

I tried to think of Eric as our chauffeur, not my bodyguard, like Ashley was, because she was having fun, and I wasn't. But I couldn't.

I need to relax.

Ashley texted me that Eric totally fit the SSI eye-candy bodyguard criteria. I rolled my eyes but didn't reply.

Eric was a good looking guy, but his harshness detracted from his looks. *Does he ever smile?* I tried to remember if I saw him smile at the BBQ, but I'd been so focused on Jamie I'd barely noticed anyone else.

At the café, we each ordered two different mimosas so we could try four flavors. The lavender blueberry was my favorite, but Ashley thought it was too sweet. Her favorite was called Sweet Heat, and had chili powder in it, but I thought it was too spicy. One of the great things about our friendship was how different our tastes were, because we always encouraged each other to try new things. Sometimes it was a hit, sometimes a miss, but we always had fun trying. Well, usually.

During breakfast I tried not to notice Eric sitting three tables down, pretending to read on his phone as he drank his coffee. But I did. I couldn't forget about him, or why he was there.

It wasn't any better at the mall. His presence was distracting and despite my best efforts, I couldn't stop thinking about him hovering nearby. Jamie wouldn't have hovered menacingly, he would have stayed close and offered to carry my bags.

Stop thinking about Jamie.

To the other shoppers Eric probably looked like he was browsing casually, but if anyone paid attention for more than a few seconds they might have thought he was a stalker, because he followed us where ever we went, lingered near us while we tried on clothes, and he never bought anything.

Ashley was none too quiet when she showed me a low-cut, form fitting dresses. "This'll look amazing on you, Jamie will go gaga if you wear this on your first date."

And of course I was worried Eric would overhear her and tell Jamie I was shopping for our no-longer-happening first date. *Does he know Jamie had asked me out? Does he care? What would Jamie think if he heard what Ashley was saying?* I made it a point to loudly remind Ashley that we weren't going on a date. Just in case.

"Yeah, yeah, says you. I say it'll happen eventually."

"I doubt it."

Eventually I found a cute dress and matching shoes that could work for a date, but not our date because we weren't going on one. I also found a cute pair of boots and some fun new tops. It was nice to buy myself new clothes and not worry about getting yelled at when I got home for wasting money, or trying to impress 'some guy' who only existed in Craig's head. As a fuck you to Craig, I splurged on some new leggings and sports tanks for running. I wanted to look cute now that I could run outside again. *I wonder if the SSI guys will run with me, like Jamie did, or if they'll drive slowly behind me.*

We'd stuffed ourselves at breakfast, so we skipped lunch. But we were hungry again by the time we finished shopping, so we decided to stop for an early dinner on the way home. We found an Irish pub with good reviews, and decided pub grub was exactly what we needed. It was a bit early for the dinner rush so we were told we could sit anywhere. They might not care, but Eric did. He pointed out a table for us, then sat down nearby, choosing a table that allowed him to see us and the door without having to turn around. He ordered a burger, a beer, and a water.

I wasn't supposed to be paying attention to him and wished I could pretend he wasn't there, but I couldn't. So, I noticed he ate his fries with ketchup, and drank his water, but not his beer. He would pick it up and lift it to his lips but he never actually drank it. I only knew because the glass stayed full. Again, something you'd only notice if you were paying attention for any length of time.

I felt a little better after our first round of beer, and even better after the shots of whiskey Ashley insisted on ordering to celebrate my new wardrobe.

"It's hardly a new wardrobe, just a few outfits," I argued, but didn't decline the shot.

"Then here's to you not cutting your bangs." We clinked our shot glasses and tossed back the amber liquid. It burned going down, causing us both to cough.

After I recovered I yelled at her, "We agreed to never mention that again!" But there was no bark to my bite.

She grinned and shrugged.

I'd done what many women do after finding out their boyfriend cheated—I got drunk and cut my bangs. Luckily, I hadn't cut them too short, but I did have to pay someone to fix them because they weren't even close to even.

"I still can't believe you thought it'd be a good idea."

"I know, I looked so awful."

"You really did." We both laughed, then ordered another round when the server came to check on us.

"Thanks, Ash." She didn't correct me. "I needed this."

Before long, Ashley turned the subject back to Jamie. She thought I was over-reacting and should talk to him.

"Emily, you're looking at it all wrong. You're not a distraction, his feelings for you are. We literally just talked about this. He's scared because of what happened to Isabelle."

It wasn't like Ashley to be the hopeless romantic type. Or for her to try so hard to convince me to be with a guy. *But I like him, and she knows it.* And I did run out on him without giving him a chance to finish. Maybe she's right, maybe I should give him a chance to explain.

"Okay, I'll call him after I get home. Happy?"

"Yes." She raised her glass, we clinked and finished our beers in one big swig.

I made sure to text my parents to let them know I was okay and having dinner with Ashley, and promised to text them our ETA when we left. I didn't bother messaging anyone from SSI, knowing Eric would keep them updated.

Ashley had to leave as soon as we got back to my place so we said our goodbyes in the driveway while she tossed her bags in her trunk. Eric stood nearby, watching. I'd be so glad when this is over.

I think I'll tell Jamie I don't need a bodyguard anymore. If Chris still insists on someone shadowing me, then fine, but I didn't want someone hovering over me every time I left the house. It was unnecessary, and obnoxious.

"Remember, you said you'll call Jamie."

"I remember." I couldn't hide my smile. I didn't want to get my hopes up too much, but I missed him and wanted to talk to him. And more than anything, I wanted Ashley to be right.

"Call me after you talk to him. I want to know how it goes."

"Promise. Later Ashley. Text me when you get home, okay?"

"Will do. Later."

I picked up my shopping bags, refusing Eric's help, and carried them to the door. I saw him getting in his car as I shut and locked the door behind me.

Chapter 34

Jamie

I started pacing when I read Eric's text: Snow and Flirty are at O'Neill's, having dinner and drinks. Will update when we leave.

Ashley had wanted her own code name after hearing Emily's. Meg had suggested using one of the seven dwarves, but none of the names suited her. When AJ suggested an eighth dwarf, Flirty, she'd jumped up and down, clapping with childlike joy. She'd probably love that we used their code names in messages. *Emily would hate it.*

"What the hell is she thinking?" I yelled at my phone.

He'd included a link to the O'Neill's website along with the address. I forced myself to calm down before punching out a my reply: Copy that.

"What happened?" Jack asked.

"Emily and Ashley are out drinking at a bar."

"Eric's with them, and driving, so what's the big deal?"

"It's not safe. What if Craig shows up? Bars are too chaotic to effectively protect someone." It wasn't true but that didn't stop me from wearing a path on the kitchen floor with my pacing.

"Will you please sit down?" Jack was sitting at the kitchen table, monitoring the video feed from a camera Doug had set up for a client who wanted to know if her husband was cheating. Catching cheating spouses was our least favorite part of the job, but it helped pay the bills.

I didn't respond, or stop pacing, as I thought about all the things that could go wrong. I was getting ready to text Eric and ask for an update, wondering if I had time to drive to the bar before they left.

"James!" Judging by his tone, and the use of my full name, he'd been trying to get my attention for a while. "Sit down. Tell me what's going on." He kicked a chair out to emphasize that it wasn't a request.

I sat but didn't say anything. I was still thinking I might drive to the bar, until Jack reached over and took my phone out of my hands. "Jamie, remember me telling you I'd let you know if you weren't handling this well?"

Shit. I nodded.

"You aren't handling this well. The chance of Craig randomly showing up at the bar they chose at random is next to zero."

"But–"

Jack cut me off. "No. No buts. Something's eating at you, but it's not Emily being in immediate danger." He continued to monitor his screen while talking to me.

"I don't think this thing with Craig is over but she won't talk to me. She barely said a word when I went over to tell her Craig had been arrested."

"And?" he prodded when my pause lasted too long.

What a pain in my ass. "And, she thinks I canceled our date because I don't want to take her out at all."

Jack knew all this, I'd talked to him after I got home that night. Meg was there too, and hadn't been afraid to tell me she thought I was an idiot for postponing our date.

"I tried telling her she was wrong, but she wouldn't listen. She slammed the door in my face, figuratively and literally." I'd been giving her space since then, even though I'd thought about calling her a hundred times a day.

"That was your first mistake. You can't tell a woman her feelings are wrong."

Of course he was right. I'd learned that lessen the hard way with Isabelle, but had clearly forgotten.

I'd tried to tell her she'd misunderstood me, not that her feelings were wrong. *Did I make the distinction clear?*

"Have you tried talking to her since then? Done anything to show her she misunderstood your intentions?"

No. "I've been giving her space. Though I went to the house to tell her in person about Craig's arrest, rather than just sending a text, hoping she'd talk to me." She hadn't.

Meg had been listening quietly as she skimmed a magazine in the living room, but put it down and joined us.

"I wanted to talk to her but she was so cold and formal, she practically pushed me out the door as soon as I finished delivering the news."

Meg asked, "Did you tell her you wanted to talk to her? Or did you just deliver the news like a cop?"

"What?" I asked, a little harsher than I'd intended. What kind of question was that?

"Don't take this the wrong way, but you can be very un-charming when you're doing your job. You come off as professional, impersonal. You can hardly blame her if she didn't realize you showing up in person was some grand romantic gesture." Meg waved her arms around dramatically.

I took a second to think about it. I had been professional when I delivered the news, but only because it was necessary. And I tried to make small talk, but hadn't told her I wanted to talk to her.

"So how do I get her to listen to me if she thinks I'm just doing my job every time I try to talk to her?"

"Buy her flowers," she said, her voice thick with judgement. The implied 'dumbass' was loud and clear.

"It worked for me," Jack said as he smiled at Meg.

"Okay, okay. I'll order a dozen pink roses and have them delivered tomorrow."

"That's not good enough. Eric will update you when she gets home, right?" I nodded, so she continued, "Give her a few minutes to get settled in, then show up with flowers in hand. Be her Prince Charming and sweep her off her feet." My soon to be sister-in-law was a hopeless romantic.

"Or you know, just tell her you were wrong to postpone the date, and apologize," Jack offered less romantic advice.

"Sure you could do that." Meg rolled her eyes at us. "But if you do, make sure you ask her out and set a date for your date. That way she knows you mean it."

"She has a point," Jack agreed with Meg.

"I'll think about it."

I couldn't stop thinking about Emily, and how badly I still wanted to take her out. But could I do my job and protect her if we started dating now? Because I couldn't, wouldn't, risk anything happening to her. I'd never forgive myself if I failed to protect her the way I'd failed Isabelle.

I don't think I can do it. I'd have time to make things right after Craig was out of the picture.

"Jamie, you okay?" Meg asked.

"I can't do it. I can't risk anything happening to her because I'm not focused."

"Jamie, I know you still think you're responsible for Isabelle's death but you aren't. And this situation isn't the same. She's protected, Jamie. We won't let anything happen to her." When I didn't say anything, Jack asked, "Want to know what I think?"

Hadn't he been telling me for a while now?

"I think you'd be less distracted if you were dating her. Right now you're distracted twenty-four-seven by the fact that you want to ask her out, but won't, and it's killing you to keep your distance when all you want is to be close."

Well fuck. That was a dose of reality I needed, but hadn't wanted, to hear. But he was right, this is different. Isabelle hadn't had any protection except the restraining order the school insisted she file. Emily had a bodyguard.

I wasn't sure I'd feel less distracted if we were dating, but trying to keep my distance and remain completely professional was distracting me to the brink of insanity.

"I don't know."

"Jamie," Meg said as she reached over and laid her hand over mine. "You both deserve to be happy. She was obviously hurt when you delayed your date, and you're obviously hurt that she shut you out after misunderstanding your intent. Don't you think you both deserve the chance to talk about this?"

She has a point. I'd been trying so hard to protect her that I'd ignored how much I'd hurt her. If nothing else, I had to talk to her and explain how much I hated having to postpone our date, and try to make her understand I was trying to do the right thing.

Chapter 35

Emily

The first thing I noticed after I closed the door was how quiet it was. Usually I'd hear the TV, or music playing on the radio in the kitchen.

I had a sinking feeling in my gut as I called out, "Mom, Dad?"

"About fucking time," Craig's voice dripped with hatred.

My dropped my bags and my hand flew to cover my scream as I froze in place.

"Shut up, you bitch. I know they got a guy watching the house; if he hears you I'll kill your fucking parents."

The hand covering my mouth trembled as I nodded.

"Good. Now get over here."

I tried, but when I noticed the gun in his hand my feet froze to the floor.

He's going to kill me. My whole body started shaking..

"NOW!" He pointed the gun in his right hand at the floor in front of him.

Somehow, I found the strength to move. When I stopped in front of him he back-handed me. I tasted blood. He grabbed my hair and yanked my head back. I tried not to make a noise, but I couldn't stop myself from wincing in pain.

"Not one fucking word, you stupid bitch. You got me arrested and fired from my job." Spit flew out of his mouth, reeking of alcohol. "And now you're gonna pay."

My cheek stung from the slap, and my eyes watered as he continued to pull a fist full of hair. He'd violated the restraining order so it was his own damn fault he got arrested, but he didn't see it that way. He didn't blame himself for breaking the law; he blamed me for reporting him.

He dragged me to the kitchen were both my parents were sitting at the table, terrified. My dad's left eye was swollen, and turning black and blue. My mom's eyes were red and swollen, tear tracks stained her cheeks. I could see an empty whiskey bottle and several beer bottles on the island.

"You didn't have to hit him." I tried to pull away but he yanked harder causing me to wince a I stumbled back.

"He shouldn't have insulted me."

I bit back my screams when he punched me, knowing he'd hurt my parents if he thought Dean might hear me. The metallic taste of blood filled my mouth. My dad stood up, then sat back down when Craig pointed the gun at him.

"You don't want me to have to shoot you in front of your wife and whore daughter, do you?"

I cringed as my father scowled. I prayed he would listen, and luckily he did. I could tell it was killing him to witness what was happening, but what could he do? Craig was holding a gun and threatening his family. My mother reached out and grabbed one of my father's hands as tears rolled down her cheeks.

"Craig, let's go in the living room and talk. You can tell me how stupid I am, and I'll crawl on my hands and knees and beg for your forgiveness." I watched him as he looked from them to me, considering it.

Hoping he still had one, I tried to appeal to his compassionate side, "They don't need to see that."

I saw the glint of madness in his eyes a second before he grinned and said, "Yes, they do. I want them to see you grovel."

He was too drunk, too angry, to feel even an ounce of compassion.

I got down on my knees, willing to do anything to keep Craig from hurting my parents. They didn't deserve any of this, and it'd kill them to watch, but they didn't have a choice.

Chapter 36

Jamie

Eric messaged me when he dropped the girls off just after seven-thirty. Dean's text arrived a few seconds later, confirming they'd arrived and Ashley had left.

I'd decided to take Meg's advice and talk to Emily tonight. I didn't want to wait any longer. After showering, I talked to Isabelle as I got dressed, and asked for her blessing. It was getting easier to talk to her about Emily. I knew Isabelle wouldn't want me to wallow in grief forever and I could imagine her telling me to take my head out of my ass and go tell Emily how I felt.

I stopped at a store and chose the best looking bouquet of pink roses available. Then because I felt like it wasn't enough I bought a dozen red roses, too. My SUV reeked of roses by the time I pulled into Emily's driveway a few minutes later. I'd texted Dean to let him know I was stopping by, and was counting on his discretion if, no when, he noticed the two dozen roses in my hand. Everyone knew I had a thing for Emily, but that didn't mean I wanted them knowing I'd shown up at her door with roses, like a love sick teenager in a rom com. I'd never hear the end of it.

It was about eight-thirty when I knocked on the door, ready to man up and fix my mistakes. No one answered so I rang the doorbell, thinking maybe they hadn't heard me knock. I saw lights on inside, but no one answered.

Is she ignoring me?

"Emily, I know you're home, please answer the door."

"I don't want to talk to you," she yelled through the closed door.

I gripped the roses hard enough to feel the thorns pierce my palm. I'd come all this way and she wouldn't even open the door, let alone talk to me. What the fuck? Frustration and disappointment fought for top billing.

Then I realized it wasn't anger I was hearing in her voice—warning bells went off in my head.

"Emily, is everything okay?" I needed to hear her voice again so I could verify my suspicion. She would tell me to fuck off if she was angry. But she wouldn't if she was afraid.

"I'm fine Jack, please just leave."

Did she just call me Jack? It took less than a second for me to realize it was a cry for help.

Fuck! Craig's here. The best thing I could do for her right now was to walk away. No, not the best, but the safest. Craig had to think I believed her, and that I wasn't a threat.

"Okay, sorry I bothered you." It took every ounce of strength and courage I had to turn and walk away. And even more to drive down the street so I was out of sight from the Taylor's house. I sent a group text to Jack, Dad, AJ, Doug, and Dean.

> 9-1-1 at Snow's Castle. Prep to go in hot. Dean – sit tight for now.

> Stand by for details.

I called Jack, told him what had happened, and what I suspected, and gave him the address of the vacant parking lot where I'd parked. While he organized the rest of the team, I called Dean and asked what he'd seen prior to Emily returning home. Fortunately for us, Dean was retired and wouldn't feel the need to call 9-1-1. Not that they could do anything. They wouldn't break down the doors and raid the house just because my gut said something was wrong. Her calling me Jack might be a neon sign flashing: help me; but they couldn't act on it.

We could. And we would.

Dean said he hadn't seen any movement in the house since Mrs. Taylor closed the curtains about an hour before Emily got home.

Shit, if he'd forced her to close the curtains, then he'd been in the Taylor's house for almost two hours. I could only imagine the hell he'd put them through. Was putting them all through. We didn't have any proof Craig was there, but every cell in my gut was screaming he was, and we didn't have a lot of time. *Please God, let us get in there in time.* I wouldn't be able to live with myself if he killed them.

I'd picked a secluded, tree-lined parking lot at the end of the street for our command center because we couldn't risk gearing up in the middle of the street. It'd be hard not to notice five guys putting on bullet proof vests and slinging rifles.

Jack was the first to arrive; he'd had Meg drive him so he could work on the way over. It might be a short distance from our house to here, but every second counted. My gear bag was on the open tailgate of my truck and I was putting on my vest when Jack hopped out.

"Anything new?" Jack reached into the back seat of Meg's car and grabbed his gear bag. He already had his vest and duty belt on. We all kept a duty belt ready to go, with extra magazines for our pistols and rifles, as well as a tourniquet in case the worst happened, so we were always ready to roll.

"Negative. Dean's got eyes on the house but hasn't seen any movement."

"Let me know what I can do to help," Meg offered. Just because she wasn't trained to gear up or breach doors, didn't mean she couldn't help.

"Thanks Meg." I turned my attention back to Jack. "ETA for the others?"

"Less than five."

"Good. Meg, can you drive around the block and look for Craig's car? We've had eyes on the front twenty-four-seven but none on the back. That's the only way he could have gotten in unnoticed."

"On it. Jack, you need anything else from the car?" He shook his head no. "I'll make a note of any cars parked on the streets around the block and report back."

"Thanks."

The others arrived while Meg was circling the block. I called Dean and put him on speaker phone so he'd be up-to-date with our plans. We formed two teams, one to breach the back door, the other the front. I'd go in the front with Jack, and Dad was taking the back with AJ. Doug and Dean would be on over-watch; Dean in his car, and Doug in the back yard. Just in case Craig managed to get by us.

He won't get past me.

My anger-fueled impatience was growing by the second. I wanted to be breaking down doors and shooting that fucker in the face. Dad and Jack reminded me I wouldn't do any good if I was too pissed off to stay focused. I grunted in reply and Dad, worried I'd go in guns blazing and fuck shit up, made a command decision and gave Jack the lead.

I wanted to argue but he was right, it would only take a second for shit to go south if my fear or anger took over. I had to trust Jack.

Meg came back, she hadn't found Craig's car but she saw two cars parked on the streets. She'd called Sammie and asked her to run the plates. One was registered to the address it was parked at, the other to Daniel Spencer, from Houston.

Craig must have borrowed someone's car, knowing we'd be looking for his. Fuck, he was smarter than we'd given him credit for. Which meant he was also more dangerous.

"Meg, did you tell Sammie what's happening?"

"Give me some credit." I should have known better. Sammie was on duty tonight and Meg knew if she'd told Sammie what was going on she couldn't, in good conscience, keep it from her commanding officer.

What we were doing wasn't exactly within the parameters of the law. If things ended badly, we'd be in big trouble, but I couldn't let myself think about it. For once, I didn't care about the rules, because the only thing that mattered was saving Emily and her parents.

With our strategy in place, we climbed into two trucks, drove to the house with our lights off, then took up our positions at the doors. We confirmed everyone was in place, then went radio silent.

We weren't knocking or waiting for an invitation.

We were going in hot and fast.

I heard the click signaling Dad and AJ were in position at the back door, and Jack's click confirming our ready position. We counted to three then kicked in both doors simultaneously.

Chapter 37

Emily

I instantly recognized Jamie's voice when he called out after knocking on the door. I made eye contact with my parents, begging them with my eyes not to give anything away.

Craig grabbed my hair and yanked me up. "Tell him you don't want to talk to him."

He pushed me into the living room, towards the door, making sure we couldn't be seen through gaps in the closed curtains.

I couldn't scream for help, not with a gun pointed at my head so I could only hope Jamie would hear the fear in my voice. I needed to think fast and let him know something was wrong, but I had to be subtle.

Craig doesn't know who's on the other side of the door. I called Jamie Jack, praying he'd figure out what I couldn't tell him.

Jamie apologized, and left.

Did he understand?

Craig waited until we heard the car drive away before dragging me back to the kitchen.

"Who was that, you fucking slut? Are you cheating on me?"

Something in me snapped. For some reason him accusing me of cheating on him was what sent me over the edge. How could I be cheating on someone I wasn't with, with someone I wasn't seeing?

"I can't cheat on you Craig, I fucking left you. Remember?" I regretted it the instant the words came out of my mouth.

He didn't bother answering, instead he punched me in the face hard enough to make my head spin. I lost my balance and almost fell over. Tears filling my eyes as blood dripped from my mouth. I heard a chair scrape against the floor and looked up to see my father step towards Craig.

"Dad, no!" Blood sprayed from my mouth as I screamed at him to stop. When my dad turned his head to look at me Craig swung the gun down. Time slowed down as I watched him slam the gun into my father's head. My mother screamed as my father crumpled to the floor in an unconscious heap. She got up to help him but Craig pointed the gun at her.

"Do not move."

My mother fell back onto her chair, never taking her eyes off my father as tears flowed down her face.

"See what you made me do?" Craig screamed at me.

"Please Craig, I'll do whatever you want." I got back down on my knees, knowing he liked it when I was submissive. "Please, just don't hurt my parents anymore."

"Don't tell me what to do!" he yelled, but then told my mother to check my father. She slowly got down on the floor and checked my father's pulse. Relief washed over me when I saw her nod.

"I'm not, I swear." I leaned forward so I was on my hands and knees, then crawled towards him. "See, I'm on my hands and knees, begging. Please, can we go in the living room?" I didn't dare look at my parents.

He looked back at me with hate filled eyes.

I won't survive this. My only hope was that he'd be satisfied with killing me and leave my parents alive.

"Stand up."

I looked at my mom as I stood, knowing he'd knock me back down. He'd done it before. I begged her not to interfere with my eyes.

Craig punched me in the gut. Hard. I doubled over in pain, coughing as my arms instinctively clutched my stomach. He hammered me between my shoulder blades, causing me to fall to my hands and knees. I looked at my mom through the tears in my eyes. I needed her to help my dad, not watch what was happening to me so I mouthed: I'm okay.

I was anything but okay, but I had to stay strong. He was going to make this as painful, and as humiliating, as he could, and I couldn't risk my mom interfering and getting hurt too. Craig kicked me in the head causing me to see stars as I fell onto my side.

When I didn't get up right away he kicked my leg. "Get up."

Struggling to stand, I blinked rapidly trying to bring the spinning room into focus.

"Beg." It was more growl than word as he sneered at me.

I choked on the metallic taste as I swallowed. "Please?" I didn't have to fake the pleading in my voice. "Please?" my voice squeaked.

"Please what?"

"Please forgive me for–"

I was cut off by the kitchen door shattering inward. My heart started racing and the air left my lungs as I collapsed to the floor and covered my head with my hands as chaos erupted.

I heard someone shout, "Drop the gun! Don't move–" Then a loud crack filled the room making my ears ring. I looked up at my mom, she was slouched over my dad's body.

No no no.

Chapter 38

Jamie

When I heart the gun shot echo through the house, I tried to run past Jack but he grabbed me. He would have held me back if we hadn't heard, "Tango down. Repeat Tango down."

I clicked my rifle to safe and ran into the kitchen.

The first thing I saw was Craig, lying in a pool of blood. AJ was standing over him, making sure he didn't move. The next thing I saw was Emily curled up in a ball on the floor, arms covering her head. I watched as she lifted her head and looked at her parents, who were also on the floor, her mom on top of her father. Dad checked their pulses and gave me a quick nod, letting me know they were alive.

I slung my rifle over my back so I could move more freely. "Emily?" When I reached down and touched her shoulder she pulled away from me, her eyes never leaving her parents.

I kneeled next to her and gently turned her face towards me. "Emily, it's okay, you're okay." It wasn't exactly a lie, but it wasn't quite the truth either. Bruises were already forming on her blood and tear stained face. Judging from the way she was clutching her mid-section, she probably had a few cracked or broken ribs. Not to mention the emotional scarring from going through a traumatic hostage situation. But she was alive. *Thank God.* And so were her parents. We'd deal with the rest later.

Emily looked dazed as she shouted at me, "MY MOM AND DAD?"

From the look on her face, and the fact that she was shouting, I assumed her ears were still ringing. Gun shots in a small space were hell on the ears.

"They'll be okay." I pointed at them, and my dad who was still helping them. She nodded then slowly looked around the room.

I scooted closer and started evaluating her injuries.

I asked the team, "Ambulance?"

Dean answered, "ETA three minutes."

I held Emily as I listened to Dad and Dean on the radio. Weatherford PD would be on scene in two; Dean would run interference, so they didn't come in guns blazing. The Taylors didn't need to experience that twice. Dad called Doug in to stay with Emily's parents, then went outside to help Dean.

"Where's Craig?" Emily asked with a shaking voice.

Craig had been shot in the chest and was bleeding heavily. I wasn't sure he'd make it. I more than half hoped he wouldn't—securing me a special place in hell.

She couldn't see him because Jack had dragged him behind the island. But she could see the pool of blood, and the bright red drag marks.

What little color there was drained from her face. "Did he shoot anyone?"

He hadn't. AJ had given us a summary of what happened: they breached, Craig raised his gun, dad shot him. I shook my head back and forth as I answered in case she was still struggling to hear.

Emily nodded and opened her mouth to answer but her eyes rolled back in her head as she started to sway.

"Emily?" panic laced my voice as she passed out.

I caught her before her head could hit the floor.

Her mom cried out.

My hand shook as I checked Emily's pulse. *Thank God.* I whispered into the comms as relief flooded my system, "She's okay. She's alive." I trusted Doug to tell her parents.

The sounds in the room faded to a dull hum as I held her and repeated, "I'm so sorry I failed you," over and over as tears welled up in my eyes. I felt Jack's hand on my shoulder a second before he reached over and removed my ear piece. Not that I cared if the team could hear me. I couldn't stop thinking about how helpless I felt as I cradled her in my arms and whispered in her ear, "I'm so sorry."

"Jamie," Jack's voice cut through my pain. "The paramedics are here."

I nodded as I pulled myself together and gently lowered Emily back to the floor. "Thanks." I stood up and stepped back, giving the paramedics room to work. There was nothing more I could do for her right now, so I wiped my face and squared my shoulders.

Putting aside my fear and guilt, I surveyed the room, focusing on what needed to be done so I didn't go crazy.

The paramedics were helping Emily and the Taylors. They didn't need me. AJ was standing near Craig, but not helping him.

Jack whispered, answering my silent question, "He didn't make it."

I nodded as relief washed over me. Not my normal reaction to hearing someone had died, even a bad guy, but I was relieved Craig could never hurt Emily again.

Dad was talking to the police officers, and had everything there under control.

More officers arrived, along with a forensic specialist, and the coroner. WPD wouldn't let me leave without giving my statement, so I couldn't ride with Emily, but Jack told me Meg was waiting to take me to the hospital, once I was cleared to leave.

We'd have to play nice with the local PD for a good long while. They'd be mad we stepped on their toes, and bruised their egos, when we took the law into our won hands and crashed into the Taylor's home, rescuing them rather than calling 9-1-1.

Fortunately, we had a good working relationship with them. *Hell, I served with most of the guys on the Weatherford force*. And given time, they'd understand that while there may not have been enough evidence for the PD to act, we'd made the right decision by going in. The Taylor's would agree. Dad and I would get a lecture, or two, and we'd have to kiss the Chief's ass until it eventually faded away. I didn't regret a thing.

Dad asked the scene commander to take my statement first, and she agreed. After I finished, I checked with Dad to make sure I was good to leave.

"We've got this, son, go to the hospital. I'll stop by as soon as we're done here."

"Thanks."

"Shit, we need to call Chris."

"I got it. Go." Jack gave me a gentle push. "Meg's waiting just west of the police parameter."

I took off my gear and locked it in the safe in the back of my SUV, then grabbed the roses from the front seat before jogging to Meg's car.

"Thanks," I said as I put on my seatbelt. It felt weird having Meg drive; hell I'd never even been in her car before. It was a gently used, navy blue compact. It wasn't my taste but it suited her, and was way better than the beat-up old SUV she was driving when she first came to Weatherford.

We didn't have any trouble finding out what room Emily was in when we got to the hospital. Which was good. I wanted, needed, to see her and didn't have the patience to argue with the nurses. I asked for her parent's room numbers too, I'd check on them after I made sure Emily was okay.

We had just finished talking to the nurse when Chris stormed in. "What the fuck happened, Sheppard?" he yelled as he crossed the room.

"Sir, you need to keep your voice down," a nurse scolded him.

Chris looked at the nurse, anger dripping out his pores. I thought for a minute he might keep yelling. But he didn't, he got right in my face instead and poked me in the chest as he growled, "You were supposed to prevent this."

"I know."

"You know?" His voice rose an octave. He was still pissed, but he sounded surprised too. Maybe he'd expected me to defend myself, but I couldn't. He was right. I had failed him, Emily, his entire family.

"I know. And I can't tell you how sorry I am." I felt tears well up, and didn't bother hiding them. I didn't have anything to prove to Chris. He'd been at my side for the best, and the worst, days of my life.

He sucked in a deep breath and released it slowly. "Jesus Jamie, what the hell happened?" he asked, sounding calmer.

"Can I fill you later?" I asked. "Right now I want to check on Emily."

He noticed the roses I was holding. "You stopped to buy flowers?"

His voice gave me the impression I might get punched again.

"No," I shook my head and tilted it to the hall. "Let's walk and talk." I didn't wait for an answer before I turned around and started walking. "I bought them earlier, before I stopped by the house to talk to Emily. I never had a chance to give them to her." I paused and took a deep breath, grateful I'd trusted my instincts and pushed a little harder when she told me she didn't want to talk to me. A cold chill ran down my back as I thought about what might have happened if I had walked away.

I stopped when we reached her door. "I'll fill you in later, but that's how I found out Craig was there." I looked at the door then at Chris, and against my deepest desires asked, "You want to go in first?"

"Yeah, I do." He turned and opened the door before turning back to me. "Thanks."

Chapter 39

Emily

I lifted my head when I heard a soft knock on my door, and said come in. My mom didn't say a word as she walked to my bed, leaned down, and pulled me into the fiercest gentle hug that only a mama bear can give.

"My baby girl. I'm so sorry," she cried onto my shoulder. I had no idea what she had to be sorry for. I was the one who brought Craig into their lives, I was the reason my dad had a concussion and I was in the hospital beaten black and blue.

I couldn't find my voice to say any of that, so I hugged her back and let a fresh wave of tears fall. When I finally found my voice I asked, "Are you okay? How's Dad?"

"I'm better now." She pulled back and patted my hand. "Dad'll be okay too, but they're keeping him overnight for observation as a precaution. How are you? Are you in any pain? I can have the nurse get you something."

"I'm okay. Nothing's broken and the bruises will heal. The doctor already gave me something for the pain." I didn't tell her I'd asked him for something that wouldn't put me to sleep, so it'd only taken the edge off. I didn't want anything stronger until after I'd seen her.

And hopefully Jamie.

I vaguely remembered him being there, but the details were fuzzy. I remembered the pool of blood on the kitchen floor, but not seeing Craig. Had Jamie told me he was dead?

"Mom, is Craig dead?"

She nodded. "I'm sorry honey, but he tried to shoot John." She squeezed my hand. "John had to defend himself."

"That's what I thought." I thought about it for a second. "I'm sorry he's dead, but not that Mr. Sheppard shot him. He wanted to kill me." I paused when she pulled back. "And he would have killed you and Dad, too."

On second thought, I'm not sorry he's dead. If he'd survived, I would've spent the rest of my life looking over my shoulder. Terrified.

"I'm not sorry."

My eyes opened so wide I thought they'd pop out of my head. "MOM!" I winced, yelling hurt my head and my bruised ribs.

"I'm sorry honey, but after what he did to you, to us, he deserved what he got."

It was good to see the color back in her cheeks. To see her fired up. She'd looked so scared and shocked in the kitchen that I'd been worried it'd be a good while before I saw the real her again.

"Thanks, Mom." I sniffed. "I'm sorry-"

"None of that." She handed me tissue just as someone knocked on the door.

"Come in."

Chris came in and practically ran to my bed. He glanced at my mom before bending down and squeezing me in a big brotherly hug that made my ribs hurt like hell.

"Be careful, Christopher."

"Right, sorry." He pulled away, his eyes searching my face. "Are you okay? How bad is it?"

"I'm okay, honestly. My ribs are bruised, my face is a mess, and I have a killer headache, but there's nothing that won't heal in a few days." Or maybe weeks.

Chris nodded as he searched my face.

I reached out and held his hand, "I'll be fine Chris, I promise."

Chris turned to Mom. "Are you okay?" he asked as he pulled her into a tight hug. "How's Dad?"

Mom teared up a little as she filled him in. Luckily, her only physical injuries were a few bruises on her face and wrists, but Dad hadn't fared as well. He had a concussion, and needed stitches for the gash in his forehead, plus several nasty bruises.

My brave, foolish father. He shouldn't have tried to stand up to Craig.

After Chris was convinced I was okay, he said he wanted to go visit Dad. Before leaving, he said, "Emily, Jamie's outside and wants to see you. Do you want to see him?"

I did but I was worried about him seeing me like this. Then I remembered he'd seen me looking even worse on the kitchen floor. I nodded. "Yeah, I do. Thanks."

Mom and Chris each hugged me before leaving.

Then I waited for Jamie.

Chapter 40

Jamie

Chris was only with Emily for ten minutes or so, but it felt more like ten hours as I wore a path in the tile floor outside her door. Meg put her hand on my arm, leaned up and whispered, "You're making everyone nervous."

I could only imagine how I looked to other people right now, pacing the floor like a man possessed, a mixture of fear, determination, and impatience written all over my face.

I couldn't help it, I needed to talk to Emily and make sure she was okay and every second I had to wait was torturous. I had to make things right, tell her how I felt, and beg her to forgive me. *This time she can't run away from me if there's a misunderstanding.*

I closed the distance to Emily's door when I saw it open. Chris had his arm around his mom's shoulders as he led her out. Mrs. Taylor still looked overwhelmed, but at least she wasn't in shock anymore.

"Mrs. Taylor, I'm so sorry." On impulse, I pulled out a pink rose and handed it to her.

"You have nothing to apologize for, Jamie. It was our fault, we left the backdoor unlocked."

They what? No, none of this was their fault.

"We never thought…" her voice cracked as she fought back tears.

"It's not your fault. Is it Jamie?" Chris asked.

I didn't need his prompting, the responsibility was mine and I wouldn't hide from it. "No, it isn't." I paused to gather the strength to tell her it was my failure for not posting someone at the back.

But Chris said, "Emily wants to see you."

And I forgot about everything else. "I'll check on you and Mr. Taylor in a few minutes, okay?"

"Take all the time you need with Emily." She patted me on the arm.

I heard Meg tell Chris as I walked to her door, "John will be here as soon." Her voice faded as I made eye contact with Emily from the doorway.

Now that she'd been cleaned up I could see the extent of her injuries. She was in bad shape; her left eye was so swollen she could barely open it and her left cheek was a nasty shade of purple. There were cuts on the left side of her swollen mouth. He'd hit her hard, and often. I clenched my teeth as any regret I might've had about Craig dying on scene vanished.

"Jamie?" Her voice, small and scared, broke me out of my trance.

"Emily, I'm so sorry." I closed the distance to the right side of her bed.

She shook her head. "Not your fault." She was lisping a little because of the swelling. And they'd probably given her a pain killer or muscle relaxant.

"If I had-"

She cut me off. "No. I didn't think he was a threat anymore. I'd even told my parents I didn't need protection anymore." She winced a little as she reached for a tissue. I grabbed the box and held it where she could easily reach it. She wiped her eyes, flinching when she put too much pressure on the bruised one. "I was wrong. I should have let you put a camera at the back door. I should have taken the threat seriously. If I had..." She closed her eyes.

It was killing me to hear her blaming herself. None of this was her fault. She didn't make him drink or get violent, and she couldn't have known the lengths he'd go to to get revenge.

"Emily, stop. Please. None of this is your fault, nor is it your parent's fault. The only person at fault is Craig." I looked at the IV in her arm and the bruises on her face. "And me, for not insisting on better coverage."

"It's not your fault either. You couldn't have known."

"But I did. I knew better than to leave the backdoor unguarded."

"Maybe, but you tried to tell me and I didn't listen."

I sighed. "Can we both stop blaming ourselves for a minute?" I was still holding the roses. "I want to apologize for-"

"I thought we weren't blaming ourselves." Her battered smirk let me know she was kidding.

I laughed. "That's not why I'm apologizing." I handed her the roses. "I came to the house earlier because I wanted to apologize for being a fool, and thinking I could stay better focused if we weren't dating."

She took the flowers and sniffed them. They must have tickled her nose because she sneezed, then cried out, "Oh, God, that hurt my whole body."

"Should I call the nurse?" I still didn't know how bad her internal injuries were.

"No. I'm okay now." She handed the roses back to me. "They're beautiful. Can you put them on the table for me?"

I did, then took her hands. "Emily, can you ever forgive me for being a stupid stubborn ass?"

Despite the swollen cut lip and the purple bruises, her smile lit up her face. "I already have. I was going to call after I got home from shopping with Ashley to tell you I was being stupid." She laughed, then clamped her jaw to bite back the pain. "I'm sorry too."

"Forgiven." I didn't think she needed to apologize, but it wouldn't get us anywhere to go around the 'it's not your fault loop' again. "What a pair we make, huh?" I kissed her hand. "Too stubborn for our own good?"

She laughed as she patted the edge of the bed. I sat down as gently as I could and asked her about her injuries; grateful when she told me they were mostly superficial. Though the doctor wanted to keep her overnight for observation, because of the kicks to her head.

I clenched my back teeth when an image of him hitting and kicking her flashed through my mind. Then I reminded myself; he's gone; it's over. And forced myself to relax. Emily's only other injury of note was her bruised ribs; which I knew from experience would bother her for a while.

Emily paled as she told me about her parents injuries, then said, "Mom's staying with Dad tonight, if the nurses let her." I made a mental note to talk to the head nurse and arrange for it to happen.

When she heard a light knock on the door, Emily called out, "Come in," .

Jack stepped inside the door and asked, "Hey Emily? How are you feeling?"

"Better. Thanks."

"Is everything okay?" I asked, knowing he wouldn't have come in without a damn good reason.

"You're not answering your messages."

I have more important things to do. I glared at him. "And?"

"There's an officer here to take Emily's statement." He turned to Emily. "You up for it?"

"You don't have to, we can tell them to come back." I didn't want her feeling pressured while she was still processing everything that had happened.

"No, I want to get it over with." She squeezed my hand, and asked, "Can you stay with me?"

Happily. Inappropriately, my heat thumped with joy because she asked me to stay. "Yeah, though they may ask me to stand off to the side."

"That's okay." She told Jack, "You can tell them I'm ready."

Her hands fluttered over her hair as she tried to tame it, then laughed. "I'm sure I look much better now that my hair is in place."

"You're beautiful." I kissed her hand again and stood up as Jack opened the door and let in two Weatherford officers. I knew them both, which made it easier for me to get permission to stay. They instructed me to stand at the foot of the bed, and keep my mouth shut. I knew the drill, I'd been in their position more often than I would've liked. One of the hardest parts of being a police officer was questioning someone after a traumatic experience, but it had to be done.

Emily put on a brave face and answered their questions like a champ. My heart filled with pride and respect. *She has no idea just how strong she is.*

As I walked the officers out, I asked if they knew when they'd release the house.

"We still don't have an answer."

Still? Dad or Jack must have asked. "Thanks. Stay safe out there." I shook their hands, then closed the door behind them.

Emily was asleep when I turned around. Not wanting her to wake up alone, I texted Chris and asked him to come sit with her so I could check on their parents. Two minutes later he knocked once before opening the door.

"You two okay?" he whispered when I met him near the door.

"Yeah, I think so." I paused then asked, "we good?"

"Yeah, I think so." He parroted with a sly grin.

The jury's still out. Chris would reserve judgement until he'd talked to Emily; as a brother, I completely understood.

Jack, Meg, AJ, and Doug were in the waiting room down the hall, so I stopped by and thanked them, then released them for the night. Not surprisingly they said they'd stick around for a while longer. Meg handed me a coffee and a vending machine sandwich. I hadn't even realized I was hungry until I heard my stomach growl at the sight of the cellophane wrapped food.

I scoffed down half the sandwich and chugged half the bitter coffee before going to see Mr. and Mrs. Taylor. There weren't enough words in my vocabulary to express how sorry I was, but I had to try.

I knocked on the door and heard a faint, "Come in."

My dad was talking quietly to Mrs. Taylor while Mr. Taylor slept. I wasn't expecting her to get up and give me a hug when I walked in, but that's exactly what she did.

"Oh Jamie, I can't thank you enough for saving us." I wasn't expecting that either, not after she'd been so reserved in the hallway earlier. I didn't deserve her gratitude, in fact, I was here to apologize. I looked at my dad, and he must have seen it in my eyes because he shook his head. So instead of apologizing I said, "You're welcome Mrs. Taylor."

She wiped a tear from her eye. "How many times must I ask you to call me Anne?"

I looked at my father, who smiled and shrugged. I was on my own. "Anne, how are you feeling? Is there anything I can get for you?"

"No, I'm just glad you're here. Did Emily talk to the officers? Is she okay?"

"She did, she is; she was sleeping when I left. Chris is with her."

"Good. Good." She patted my arm.

"How is Mr. Taylor? Emily mentioned he has a minor concussion, but is he okay other than that?" That was a stupid question, a concussion in a fifty-eight year old man was serious, no matter how "minor" it was.

"A few bruises and seven stitches in his forehead. It could have been a lot worse." She brought her hand to her mouth and exhaled sharply. I could see her fighting back her tears. "I thought the damn fool was going to get himself shot."

I pulled her into a hug. She might not have any physical injuries but she'd been held hostage, had her life threatened, and watched her husband and daughter get beat up—that'd leave an emotional scar. She'd need just as much time to heal from her emotional wounds as they'd need for their physical ones. *Maybe more.*

She pulled away. "Your dad was just telling me SSI is going to replace our doors as soon as the police are done collecting evidence. Can you please tell him that's not necessary?"

"No ma'am." I was going to suggest the same thing.

She gave me a scolding look. "You don't need to do that. You've already done so much for us."

The former cop in me wanted to say something like 'just doing our job ma'am' but I couldn't. This had always been more than just a job for me. *A lot more.*

"Mrs. Tay-Anne," I corrected myself when she gave me the mom look. "I'm sorry I couldn't prevent what happened tonight. I feel like I let all of you down."

"This isn't on you." My dad used his no-nonsense tone. Great, it wasn't enough that I was getting the mom-voice treatment from Mrs. Taylor, but I could sense an incoming lecture from my dad.

Please don't embarrass me in front of Emily's mom.

"I know you feel responsible because of your feelings for Emily, but this isn't on you. We work as a team, and we did everything we could given the circumstances. And while I don't feel good about what happened tonight, none of us are to blame."

"Yes, sir." The logical part of my brain knew he was right. We'd suggested things that might have prevented what happened tonight, but Emily had declined them all with a hard no. Not that we blamed her, or her parents, for not wanting to feel like she was living under a microscope. *I'm sure Chris is blaming himself too.*

But the only person to blame was Craig Hopper. *And he's gone now.*

"Are you sure I can't get you anything Mrs-Anne?"

"I'm good. I'm going to rest here a bit with Chris. I don't want him to be alone when he wakes up." Before I could respond, I was overcome with the visceral need to be at Emily's side, to be there when she woke up.

She saw me look at the door and said, "Go back to Emily." She sat beside her husband and held his hand.

I leaned down and gave her a peck on the cheek. "Thank you."

As my dad walked me to the door, I asked, "Any trouble with WPD?"

"Nothing I can't handle, son." I nodded, comforted with the knowledge we'd be able to repair any damage we'd done to our relationship with them. "And before you suggest it, I've already asked Meg to schedule a crime scene clean up company for tomorrow. And Dean and Eric are watching the house, front and back."

There might not be a threat to the Taylors anymore but crime scenes could attract all sorts of curious, and sometimes destructive, people. *And thanks to us, the Taylors no longer have functioning doors.*

"Thanks, Dad." He knew me too well. Not that it was hard, I was just like him.

And damn proud of it.

Dad had also convinced the nurses to allow me and Mrs. Taylor to stay the night. Which we did.

Emily and I spent the night talking a little and sleeping a lot.

I never thought I would feel this way about anyone ever again, but as I watched Emily drift off to sleep in the early morning hours I realized I could.

Chapter 41

Jamie

WPD released the house the next morning, and workers were onsite within the hour to install new doors while the clean up crew cleaned the kitchen. The new doors were steel-core, with dead bolts, which was an upgrade from the wood doors with handle locks they'd had forever. My dad didn't mess around. He also stayed there the entire time, making sure everything was done up to spec.

Mom cooked a huge casserole for Emily and her parents, and one for Chris and his family, saying they shouldn't have to worry about cooking for the next few days. I was blessed to be surrounded by so many loving, caring people and doubly blessed to call them family.

I took the day off so I could drive Emily and her parents to Chris's house. When I told Chris it was the least I could do for them, I neglected to mention that I needed to be with

Emily for my sanity. The plan was to hang out there until the house was ready, then I'd drive them all home.

While we waited, Emily and I set a date for our first date. Wising up and taking Meg's advice, I made it clear I'd take her out tonight if it was what she wanted, but I was just as happy to wait until she felt up to it. I wasn't going to make the same mistake twice. I might be a stubborn fool, but I wasn't a complete idiot.

When Emily asked if we could wait until her face didn't look like it had been used as a punching bag, I said yes, having fully expected that answer.

"If you want, I can come over tonight and we could watch a movie or something." Dad had offered to have someone from SSI outside the house, to give them a sense of comfort, but they'd declined saying we'd already done too much. If she said yes, I could offer the same comfort, while getting to spend the evening with Emily.

"I'd like that. Though I might fall asleep halfway through. I can't believe how tired I feel."

Thank God she said yes because I don't know what I would have done if she'd declined. *Parked outside the house all night.* My internal voice sounded a lot like Jack. "No worries; your body's working hard to heal."

Not long after that, Mrs. Taylor invited me to dinner, though she said she felt guilty for serving my mom's lasagna to an invited guest. I laughed and said, "Ma's lasagna is one of my favorite foods."

After dinner, Emily and I put on her favorite Disney movie and relaxed on the couch. I was the perfect gentleman and resisted the urge to put my arm around her.

Right up until she started to doze off and leaned into my side. Then the most natural thing in the world for me to do was to put my arm around her and hold her close so she'd know she was safe while she slept.

Chapter 42

Emily

Jamie and I were going on our first date tonight. The bruises Craig had given me two weeks ago had mostly faded, and my cracked ribs were a lot less painful.

My dad was recovering too. And while Mom's endless doting was driving him crazy, he didn't complain. Being an overbearing mother hen was her way of coping, and we loved her for it.

Ashley had taken a few days off after she'd heard what happened and stayed with us, which was a godsend. Mom thought because she hadn't been physically hurt everything should return to normal, but for the first few days she struggled being in the kitchen and kept looking at the door like she expected it to get kicked in any second.

Ashley's presence provided a sense of normalcy none of us knew we needed. She'd kept us company in the kitchen, chatting as she'd helped cook or clean. And now she was back to help me get ready for my date, saying she wouldn't miss it for the world. She was also slipping in, 'I told you so,' as often as she could.

I shook my head to clear it when I heard Ashley say, "Earth to Emily."

We had clothes spread out all over my bed as she attempted to help me find the perfect outfit. She was currently holding up a flowery summer dress. "What about this one?"

"Nah, too cute." We were having trouble finding the perfect happy medium between cute and flirty, and sexy. I wanted to look good for Jamie tonight, but not like I was trying too hard. I wondered if he was putting half as much thought into what he was wearing. "It's so much easier for guys."

"But not as much fun. They throw on a clean button-up shirt and pants and they're good to go." She rolled her eyes. "Bor-ring." She picked up the sexy red dress she'd brought for me to borrow. "But we get to wear the fun stuff that makes their heads explode." She held the dress to her body and shook it in time with her hips.

It was a gorgeous dress, but I didn't think I could pull it off. Besides, it was a little too much for the casual date we had planned. *I bet Ashley looks breathtaking when she wears it.* She had the body and the personality to pull it off. Me, not so much. Not that my body was bad. I was in decent shape, but I lacked the no-fucks-given attitude to wear it without feeling self conscious.

"Maybe for your second date." She winked at me.

I scanned the clothes strewn about the bed and saw it. The perfect dress. I picked up a long pale blue dress with spaghetti straps and a belted waist. It had small white flowers along the neck line and the hem. It was the perfect combination of fun and flirty with a hint of sexy.

"Perfect!!" Ashley beamed at me.

"I can't believe I'm nervous. We've talked every day." Seriously, it was stupid for me to be so nervous. Not only had we talked every day since that night in the hospital, but he'd visited me most days too. I had a sneaky feeling he came here instead of inviting me to his place for my parent's sake.

I no longer doubted Jamie's desire to see me. At least not most of the time. I only started to doubt it when I was alone and my demons would start talking. They always sounded like Craig.

But when Jamie was here, or I was talking to him, all I heard was his voice, reminding me of all the things I'd forgotten about myself.

I'd gone on the defensive a few times when he'd asked me what I was up to, but he wouldn't let it go unchallenged. He'd make sure I knew he wasn't checking up on me or judging me, often adding something like: I just want to make sure I'm not interrupting you.

"You're nervous because you're finally going out with your hot as fuck high school crush turned knight in shining armor."

"Ashley!" My mom said, her voice a mix of shock and humor.

Ashley and I shared a look, eyes opening wide, we hadn't heard her come in. Ashley winked at me as she apologized to my mom. They were almost as excited about my first date with Jamie as I was.

Almost.

The way things were going tonight, I half expected my father to give Jamie 'the talk' about respecting his little girl. Or for Chris to show up and threaten to punch him again if he did anything to hurt me. I laughed at how ridiculous they were. They'd known Jamie forever and he'd been nothing but polite, respectful, and caring the last two weeks, but dads were dads, and brothers were brothers, and mine were over-protective.

And I loved them for it.

Chapter 43

Jamie

"Dude, relax. You've known her most of your life and you've seen or talked to her every day for the last two weeks. You have nothing to worry about." Jack tried to calm me down as I paced.

But I wasn't worried about taking Emily out, despite this being my first first-date in fourteen years. It was because this wasn't just any first date, it was with Emily and I was already thinking about a future with her. A future that included me being terrified every day that I'd lose her.

I suspected Jack knew as much, but he didn't bring it up.

"You look great, Jamie, you're almost as handsome as my Prince Charming."

High praise coming from Meg.

"Thanks." I looked at my watch. "I should get going."

I stopped at the florist and picked up two bouquets of flowers. One was a dozen yellow roses with baby's breath, the other pink and purple tulips.

I'd given myself plenty of time to visit Isabelle before picking up Emily. "Tonight's the night. How do I look?" I asked as I placed the tulips in front of her headstone. I'd visited a lot in the last two weeks because talking to Isabelle helped me get past feeling like I was betraying her memory. Everyone told me I wasn't, but the only voice I needed to hear was hers. And while I didn't believe in ghosts, I'd swear I felt her presence whenever I talked to her.

After a few minutes of serene silence, I said goodbye and left for my date with Emily.

I wiped my sweaty palms on my pants after ringing the doorbell.

"Good evening, Mr. Taylor." He'd told me to call him Chris, and I'd been getting used to it, but this felt like a Mr. Taylor moment.

"Good evening, Jamie." He echoed my formality as he swung the door open. "Please, come in. Emily will be down in a minute."

"Thanks. How are you doing?" The only physical evidence of that night was the half-healed cut on his forehead.

"Can't complain."

I thought I was hiding my nerves well until he smiled and said, "Relax, Jamie. I don't bite."

I smiled as my shoulders relaxed. It was exactly what I'd needed to hear to stop acting like a stranger in the house I'd considered a second home my whole life. I was about to thank him, but I heard footsteps at the top of the stairs and instinctively turned towards the sound.

Time stopped as my heart beat out a rapid rhythm and my lungs forgot how to work.

Emily was gliding down the stairs in a simple low cut blue dress that clung to her curves.

I'll never think of her in pigtails and braces ever again. Her hair framed her face in soft curls and she'd put on a little makeup. Not that she needed it; she was perfect just the way she was.

"Breathe, son." Mr. Taylor said as he patted me on the back.

I nodded, sucked in some much needed air and took the three steps required for me to reach the bottom of the stairs. "You look…" I struggled to find the right word and settled for, "Amazing."

Ashley said, "Told you so."

At the same time Emily said, "Thank you."

I'd been so mesmerized by Emily that I hadn't even noticed Ashley, or Mrs. Taylor, on the stairs behind her.

I held out my hand and helped Emily down the last step, then handed her the bouquet. She held them to her nose and inhaled. "How'd you know they're my favorite?"

"A little birdie told me." I winked at her mom.

"Thank you." She handed them to her mom and asked, "Can you put these in water for me?"

I expected it to be awkward, being our first date and all, but we quickly settled into comfortable conversation as I drove to Dallas. I'd made reservations at an upscale restaurant recommended by a friend. We were about halfway there when I reached over and placed my hand over hers. I couldn't hold back my big stupid grin when she turned her hand over and laced her soft fingers with mine.

We arrived at the restaurant a little early, so we sat at the bar to wait. They had my favorite local craft beer on tap, so I planned on ordering one, but first I asked Emily what she wanted. Her voice was small and timid as she said she'd have whatever I was having.

I placed my hand over hers to stop her from playing with her thumb ring. "Em, order whatever you'd like." Then I added, "Please." I wanted to make sure she knew it was a request, not an order.

Whenever she slipped back into who she'd been with Craig, who he forced her to be, I'd remind myself to be patient while she learned to find her voice again. *I can wait, I've got all the time in the world.* And I meant it too—I'd wait for as long as it took. Though hopefully it wouldn't take too long because I'd had glimpses of the strong, feisty, silly Emily and I wanted more.

"Thank you." Her smile lit up the room. "I'll have a glass of sparkling rosé."

"You got it." I turned to the bartender. "A sparkling rosé for the lady, and an IPA for me."

After the bartender delivered our drinks, I lifted my pint glass. "To our first date."

"Cheers." She gently tapped her wineglass to mine.

Chapter 44

Emily

It was easy, being on a date with Jamie. Too easy. After years of being in an abusive relationship, Jamie felt too good to be true. But I knew better. Several times throughout the night, I had to remind myself that Jamie was just Jamie. He wasn't hiding a dark-side, or pretending to be charming to lure me in. I'd known him most of my life, and he'd always been a nice guy, a good guy.

And now he's my guy.

And a damn good-looking one, too. His steel gray dress shirt brought out the blue in his hazel eyes. *It's neat how his eyes seem to change color depending on the lighting or what he's wearing.* His black slacks showed off his sexy-as-sin ass and muscular legs.

"Jamie, can I ask you a question?"

"Of course."

I wasn't sure how to ask, because this was our first date, and I didn't want to spook him.

"Em? Is everything okay?"

"Yeah, it's just..."

Stop being such a coward. When I met his gaze, I saw the compassion and concern in his eyes. He put his hand on the table, palm up in invitation, so I put mine in his. "Is it just me, or does this not feel like a first date?" His knowing grin made my heart do a little dance in my chest. "I mean, first dates are supposed to be weird and awkward as two people get to know each other, right?"

He chuckled before answering, "I thought the same thing. But we've known each other most of our lives." He squeezed my hand. "So aside from wanting to make sure this is the best first date you've ever had, I'm not nervous anymore."

"Wait, anymore? You were nervous earlier?" I couldn't believe it. Why would Jamie be nervous?

He laughed. "You know this is literally only the second first date I've gone on? And the last one was fourteen years ago, when I was a sophomore in high school, so it barely counts."

"I didn't realize..." I trailed off as it hit me. Jamie hadn't dated a single person since Isabelle died. I wondered why, but didn't ask. All that mattered was that we were here now.

"It's okay. Really. I focused on work and building SSI, and while I had the occasional opportunity to date, it never felt right."

I didn't know what to say, too many things were buzzing around in my head, mostly the selfish joy at hearing I was the first person he'd considered dating since losing Isabelle.

"Sorry. That's kind of dark." He sipped his beer and changed the subject. "Were you nervous?"

"A little. Ashley said I was being silly. I quote, "Em, it's no biggie. You've spent more evenings together than apart in the last two weeks."

I didn't tell him I spent two hours finding the right dress, or how long I spent curling my hair so the curls hung just the way I wanted them to.

After we were seated, I ordered the shrimp scampi and a side salad, and Jamie ordered a filet, medium rare, with mashed potatoes and a side salad. He let me try his filet and I half regretted not ordering one; it was cooked to perfection and practically melted in mouth. I fed him a bite of my shrimp scampi, making sure the creamy garlic sauce fully coated the pasta. He closed his eyes and said we'd have to come back so he could order it.

After dinner, I enjoyed the warmth of his big, strong hand as he held mine while we walked hand in hand in one of Dallas's many parks.

It takes a lot of strength to be so gentle.

"Jamie?"

"Yeah."

"Can I ask you a question?"

"You just did." He laughed, then apologized when I raised my eyebrow.

"Why haven't you tried to kiss me?" It'd been bothering me for days.

We'd finally talked about what happened at the BBQ, when I kissed him in the hallway, and he'd assured me he hadn't stopped because he didn't want to kiss me. But he hadn't tried to kiss me, not once in the last two weeks, even though we'd had plenty of alone time.

"Believe me, it hasn't been easy. I've wanted to kiss you every second we've been together, but I needed to be the perfect southern gentleman."

"Why?" I hadn't wanted him to be a gentleman, perfect or otherwise. I wanted him to kiss me.

"Strict orders from your brother, and out of respect for your father." He grinned. "Besides, if Ma found out I'd been anything less, she'd kill me."

He stepped in front of me and held my gaze. "But the most important reason is because you deserve to be treated with respect."

Tears welled up in my eyes. *Well then, that answers that question.*

Jamie swept my hair off my face. "But if your question was an invitation, then I'll kiss you right here, right now, Emily Taylor." His hand on the back of my neck applied just enough pressure to encourage me to lean forward. I was still in control and could tell him no, but there was no way in hell I would because I'd been dreaming about kissing Jamie Sheppard most of my life, and right now I wanted him to kiss me more than I wanted my next breath.

Eight Weeks Later

Emily

Jamie held my hand in the crook of his arm as he walked me down the center aisle to my seat. "I'll be back in a little bit." He gave me a quick peck on the cheek then went back to seat my parents. He looked gorgeous in his new black suit, which showed off his deliciously muscled body. I didn't bother trying to hide how much I appreciated the fine work of his tailor, then blushed when I heard Mary say, "He looks good, doesn't he?" Good was an understatement—I was practically drooling.

Today was Jack and Meg's wedding day, and Jamie was an usher. They'd set up canopies, tables, and chairs in their backyard for the ceremony and reception. The backyard was decorated with colorful fall flowers, twinkle lights, lace, and ribbon. The design was perfect in its understated elegance.

Jack, with AJ as his best man, was standing under the arch with the Pastor. Jack looked happy, relaxed, and quite handsome in his suit. AJ looked good, too, so I snapped a quick picture and sent it to Ashley. She and AJ still hadn't hooked up despite their grandest efforts. Maybe it just wasn't meant to be. Of course, that didn't stop her from asking about him. *Maybe it'll happen tonight.*

Beth was Meg's maid of honor, and looked gorgeous in her long emerald-green dress. *I hope I look that good when I'm forty.* I remembered the day we'd all gone shopping for Beth's dress. Meg had invited me and my mom to go with them, and we'd made a full day of it, laughing and talking as we got to know each other better. I had a feeling they'd included me to welcome me to the family since Jamie and I were officially an item.

There were only about thirty chairs facing the platform where Jack and Meg would exchange the vows they'd written and become husband and wife. Meg had told me the wedding guest list was less than a third the size of the reception guest list. "We want an intimate ceremony, but a big party afterwards to celebrate." It suited them.

I was thrilled to be attending as Jamie's plus one despite having received my own invitation as Meg's friend. Turns out Meg and I have a lot in common, and we'd developed an easy, relaxed friendship soon after I started dating Jamie.

I'm dating Jamie. My high school crush. I smiled as girlish glee fill my heart. We were taking it slow, since we were both working through some issues, but things were going well. I felt comfortable with him in a way I'd never felt with anyone, and more importantly, I felt safe.

Out of habit, I kept expecting him to get angry with me for doing or saying the things that used to piss off Craig. But he never did. Though he did get upset sometimes because I kept asking him if he was upset with me. Which was a bit of a mind-fuck because I was literally creating the very thing I was afraid of.

But I'm learning.

And Jamie was still working through his feelings about dating after losing Isabelle. One night, he'd confessed that he felt like he wasn't honoring her memory by dating again. He said he knew better, logically, but sometimes, usually after a nightmare, he'd be overwhelmed with grief and guilt.

We'd both cried that night as we talked about it. It was a huge step in our relationship and we were closer because of it.

Jamie was patient with me. I was patient with him. Together, with the help of our families, we were both healing and moving on. And the best part was, we were doing it together. Slowly. But not so slowly that we hadn't slept together. I'd surprised him the night I told him I didn't want him to be the perfect gentleman anymore, and asked him to take me home with him for the night. I felt heat rise in my cheeks at the memory. *Oh God, I hope I'm not blushing.*

"Hey gorgeous, this seat taken?" I loved it when he called me cute nicknames.

"It is, actually. My handsome boyfriend will be back any minute." I knew my smile filled my entire face as I gazed up at him.

"His loss." He sat down. "My gain." Not breaking eye contact, he reached for my hand. "He shouldn't have left you unattended." He leaned in and kissed me gently on the lips.

And my heart melted.

"I love this man." *Please tell me I didn't say that out loud.* I pulled away, but couldn't look at Jamie, so I stared down at my cute black flats.

"Em, are you okay?"

I must not have, thank God. I knew I was in love with him, had been for a while, but I'd never said it out loud. The first time I realized it was when he walked into my hospital room with two dozen pink and red roses and confessed there were only twenty-three because he'd given one to my mom just before coming in to see me. Yeah, it was silly, but that was the moment I knew I was in love with him.

"Yeah, I, um, I just realized we probably shouldn't be kissing right now." Luckily, the music started so everyone stood and turned to watch Meg walk down the aisle.

She looked gorgeous in her simple white silk and lace dress. The sweetheart neckline framed the beautiful emerald necklace she was wearing. I'd noticed she wore it all the time and when I asked about it she said it was a gift from her late grandmother. Then she practically glowed as she held her engagement ring close to the necklace. "Jack designed my engagement ring to match it." *She's so lucky.* So was he.

Meg's long, auburn hair was pulled back in a soft braid accented with small white and green flowers. And she was positively glowing.

To everyone's surprise, Meg had asked Chase to walk her down the aisle. I thought it was a bold choice, asking a five-year-old to be her escort on her big day, but I'd misjudged the little guy. He was the picture of responsible control as he held her right hand in his left one, just above his shoulder. He was too short to offer her the usual bent arm, but neither of them cared. It was beyond adorable how proud he looked as he confidently walked Meg to the arch.

Jack radiated pride and love as he watched.

At the arch, Meg bent down and kissed Chase on the cheek, and to his credit he didn't wipe it off like he usually did. As she stood up and took her place, Jack reached down and shook Chase's hand.

"You better take good care of my Auntie Meg." Chase's voice carried as much authority as a five-year-old could muster. I heard the stifled laughter as everyone tried not to ruin the moment by laughing too loud.

Jack didn't miss a beat. "Yes, sir, I promise."

Chase gave him a nod and went to stand by his mom.

The ceremony was short and sweet. Jack and Meg recited their vows, bringing me to tears. I could tell by the sniffling all around me I wasn't the only one. I only looked away from the ceremony once, and that was to check on Jamie. He had tears in his eyes too, though he was trying to blink them away. I squeezed his hand to offer my silent support. When he squeezed back, I knew nothing else needed to be said or done. I was here for him, and he knew it.

Afterwards, wanting to take advantage of the natural lighting to capture the newlyweds and their family, the photographer took charge. Mary, thrilled to have all her children home at the same time (and looking like mature, responsible adults in their suits and dresses), asked the photographer to take a family portrait. The photographer was happy to make a few extra bucks and said she'd take the family photos after getting the shots she wanted of the bride and groom, and the wedding party.

Maybe someday I'll be in the family pictures. *Whoa. Where'd that come from?* Jamie and I had agreed to take it slow. And yes, I loved him, but I didn't know if he felt the same way about me.

It was way too soon to think about being in family photos!

I stood with my parents and watched the organized chaos. *They're a good-looking family.* Even Jaden, who managed to get leave for the weekend, was looking handsome in a rugged Marine kind of way. Watching Mary try to organize her grown-up children into picture perfect positions was a bit like watching someone herd cats. They were all voicing their opinions and playfully shoving each other around, until John spoke up.

"Listen to your mother."

And just like that, they fell in line.

It never ceased to amaze me how quickly they turned from fighting siblings to obedient soldiers when John gave an order. I guess being a Marine and cop helped him learn how to use his tone of voice, rather than the volume, to give effective commands.

The photographer captured some great photos.

And in at least a few of them, Jamie's smile was a little bigger because he was staring into my eyes when the camera flashed.

Ashley and I were sitting at our table chatting while Jamie & AJ went to the bar to get us drinks. "Your picture didn't do him justice. He looks amazing." She'd taken no time finding AJ and showing off the silky red dress that hugged her curves like it was painted on. The same red dress she'd tried to convince me to borrow for my first date with Jamie. Now that I'd seen it on her, I was grateful I'd refused. It wasn't my style, but she looked even more stunning in it than I'd imagined she would. AJ didn't stand a chance.

I was glad Ashley and I had rekindled our friendship, and that we'd become friends with Meg. *It's nice having girlfriends again.* And it was refreshing to hang out without worrying about getting yelled at. God it was wonderful dating a kind, trusting man, and living without fear.

After a delicious catered meal of steak, mashed potatoes, and salad, the DJ called the newlyweds to the dance floor for their first dance. After they finished with the traditional dances, they cut the small two tier ceremonial cake. They were serving guests cupcakes, frosted to look like the colorful fall flowers decorating the back yard, rather than a traditional wedding cake. Of course Chase was the first one to snag a cupcake, smearing frosting all over his face. Beth laughed as she wiped his face clean with a napkin.

Everyone was having a good time dancing to all the fun traditional wedding songs, or watching from the sidelines, like me and Jamie. I laughed as Chris and Vicky lit up the dance floor, enjoying a Zoe-free night out. *Good for them, they deserve it*. And luckily for me and Jamie, Chris had come to terms with us dating. Though every once in a while he still reminded Jamie that he better be good to me, or else.

When the music changed to a slow song, Jamie held out his hand and asked me to dance. At first, not used to public displays of affection, we kept a respectable distance between us.

I was looking around and saw Ashley and AJ laughing about something as they danced. But before I could finish wondering what they were laughing about, Jamie pulled me closer and wrapped his arms around me, holding me tight. I felt safe and comfortable in his embrace. *This is where I'm meant to be*. I just hoped he felt it, too.

I smiled, finally understanding Meg's joy. I knew in my soul I'd found my Prince Charming. Or was he my knight in shining armor? Could he both? *Yeah, he can be. He is.* I rested my head on his shoulder and sighed.

Jamie's hand slid up my back and settled between my shoulder blades, then I felt his lips near my ear as he whispered, "I love you too, Emily."

Acknowledgements

T hank you, Reader, for choosing to spend some time in my world. I hope you enjoyed it.

I want to thank my Proof Readers: Nina, Paige and Jocelyn. And my editor: Nina. Your feedback was invaluable in helping me polish my story. A big thanks to Maria Secoy, and the mentor team at All Write Well–this book wouldn't be in your hands if I hadn't found them!

I also want to thank my friends, who have surrounded me with love and support while listening to me chatter on endlessly about my characters and plot lines over many glasses of wine.

Thank you all!

Also by

<u>**Sheppard & Sons Investigations:**</u>

TAKEN: Jack and Meg's story
BEATEN: Jamie and Emily's story
MISSING: Doug and Beth's story
BETRAYED : AJ and Blake's story

Join the Resilient Hearts Sisterhood for exclusive behind-the-scenes action of SSI. RHS community members receive early updates, sneak peeks, and the chance to join our beloved characters in their exciting Weatherford adventures. As a gift for joining, you'll receive the SSI Origin story; the one tragic call that changed Jamie's life forever.

WebPage

About the Author

Eveline Rose fell in love with storytelling in a high school creative writing class. Eveline currently lives in the Chicago area with her cat, Prince, where she pours her heart and soul into her characters for your reading pleasure. She's a theatre geek who can swing a sword, and a self-defense instructor who can shoot the bullseye. Eveline spends her free time volunteering in her community, hanging out with her friends, and of course reading. One topic she can chat about for hours: Tudor history. Eveline's promise to you: every romantic suspense novel will include a strong protective male hero who will save the woman he loves, and every heroine will get her Happily Ever After. Eveline is a member of Chicago North Romance Writers Group.